THE *Rogue* YOU KNOW

SHANA GALEN

sourcebooks
casablanca

Published by Sourcebooks Casablanca, an imprint of Sourcebooks, Inc.
P.O. Box 4410, Naperville, Illinois 60567-4410
(630) 961-3900
Fax: (630) 961-2168
www.sourcebooks.com

Printed and bound in Canada.
MBP 10 9 8 7 6 5 4 3 2 1

For Emily Brabo and Amy Moss,
good friends and boot-camp buddies.

This is the story of how I died.

Don't close the book! This is actually a fun story, and if you want the truth, it isn't really my tale to tell. I feature prominently, of course, so you have more of me to look forward to. In all honesty, this is a novel about two women, but it's also two love stories. Naturally, one of the women falls in love with me. That's the romantic love story—well, one of them. It's also a book about the love between a mother and a daughter. I don't know much about that, so here's where I make a dashing exit. Before I go, one little hint: pay attention to the dog. She'll be important later.

One

"SIT UP STRAIGHT," THE DOWAGER COUNTESS OF Dane hissed at her daughter before turning back to their hostess and smiling stiffly as the marchioness prattled on about bonnet styles this season.

Lady Susanna straightened in her uncomfortable chair. She was wilting in the heat that all the ladies had already remarked upon as being unseasonably warm for June. Susanna fluttered her fan and tried to take an interest in the conversation, but she didn't care about hats. She didn't care about garden parties. She didn't care about finding a husband. If her mother ever heard Susanna admit husband hunting was not her favorite pursuit, she would lock Susanna in her room for days.

Susanna did not mind being locked in her room as much as her mother seemed to think. In her room, she could lose herself in her drawing. She could bring out her pencil or watercolors and sketch until her hand cramped. Sketching was infinitely preferable to spending hours embroidering in the drawing room, listening to her mother's lectures on decorum and etiquette.

Susanna did not need to be told how to behave. She had been raised to be a perfectly proper young lady. She was the daughter of an earl. She knew what was expected of her.

One: She must marry well.

Two: She must *at all times* exhibit good *ton*.

Three: She must be accomplished, beautiful, fashionable, and witty.

That third expectation was daunting indeed.

Susanna had spent two decades playing the perfect earl's daughter. She'd had little choice. If she rebelled, even minutely, her mother quickly put her back in her place. At the moment, Susanna wished her place were anywhere but here. She sympathized with her failed sketches, feeling as though it were *she* tossed in the hearth and browning in the fire. She burned slowly, torturously, gasping for her last breath.

Could no one see she was dying inside? Around her, ladies smiled and laughed and sipped tea. Susanna would not survive much longer.

And no one cared.

Ladies of the *ton* were far too concerned with themselves—what were they speaking of now? Haberdashery?—to notice she was smothering under the weight of the heat, the endless cups of tea, the tinny politeness of the ladies' laughs, and the interminable talk of bonnets. If she were to sketch her life, she would draw a single horizontal line extending into forever.

Susanna stifled the rising scream—afraid she might wail aloud for once, rather than shriek silently and endlessly. Before she could reconsider what she planned, she gained her feet. She wobbled, shaking with uncertainty and fear, but she must escape or go quietly mad.

Lady Dane cut her a look as pointed as a sharpened blade. "Do sit down, Susanna."

"E-excuse me," Susanna murmured.

"What are you doing?"

Susanna staggered under the weight of the stares from the half-dozen women in their circle. She had not thought it possible to feel any heavier, but the addition of the women's cool gazes on her made her back bow.

"Excuse me. I need to find—"

"Oh, do cease mumbling." Lady Dane sounded remarkably like a dog barking when she issued orders. "You know I hate it when you mumble."

"I'm sorry. I need to—"

"Go ahead, my dear," their hostess said. "One of the footmen will show you the way."

Susanna's burst of freedom was short-lived. She'd no more than moved away from her chair when her mother rose to join her. Susanna choked back a small sob. There really was no escape.

"Could you not at least wait until we had finished our conversation?" Lady Dane complained, as though Susanna's physical needs were the most inconvenient thing in the world.

"I'm sorry, Mama."

"Why don't you stay, Dorothea?" the marchioness asked. "Surely Lady Susanna can find her way to the retiring room by herself."

Susanna's gaze locked on her mother's. Inside, she squirmed like one of the insects her brothers used to pin for their collections. Lady Dane would most certainly defy the marchioness. She would never let her disappointing daughter out of her sight.

Susanna had one glimmer of hope. Her brother's scandalous marriage a few weeks ago had noticeably thinned the pile of invitations the Danes received. The family was not shunned exactly, but they had spent more nights at home than the debutante daughter of an earl should.

Not that she minded.

Her mother patted Susanna on the arm, the stinging pinch delivered under cover of affection.

"Do not dawdle."

Susanna need not be cut free twice. She practically ran for the house.

"She is perfectly safe here." The marchioness's voice carried across the lawn. "I understand why you play the hawk. She must make a good match, and the sooner the better."

The sooner she escaped this garden party, the better. Every group of ladies she passed bestowed snakelike smiles before raising their fans and whispering. Sometimes the whispers weren't even whispered.

"Dane introduced a bill to establish a central police force! What next? *Gendarmes?*"

A few steps more.

"I heard her brother began a soup kitchen."

Almost there.

"St. Giles! Can you imagine?"

Susanna ducked into the cool darkness of the town house and flattened herself against the wall. She closed her eyes, swiping at the stinging tears. *Breathe, breathe.*

Free from the whispers-that-were-not-whispers and the stares and, best of all, her mother, she slouched in smug rebellion.

"May I be of assistance, my lady?"

Susanna's spine went rigid, and she opened her eyes. A footman bestowed a bemused smile on her. She imagined it was not every day a lady ran away from the marchioness's garden party and collapsed in relief.

"The ladies' retiring room. Could you direct me?"

"This way, Lady Susanna."

She followed him through well-appointed though cold, impersonal rooms until she reached a small room filled with plants, several chairs, two small hand mirrors on stands, a pitcher of fresh water and basin, and screens for privacy. Susanna stepped inside and closed the door. Finally alone. She straightened her white muslin gown with the blue sash at the high waist. Her hat sported matching ribbons. She might have removed it if it would not have been so much trouble to pin in place again. At the basin, she splashed water into the bowl and dabbed at her face. One look in the mirror showed that her cheeks were flushed and her brown eyes too bright. She had the typical coloring of a strawberry blond, and her pale skin reddened easily.

In the mirror, she spotted something move, and a woman in a large, elaborately plumed hat emerged from behind the screen. Susanna's heart sank.

She willed the woman to return to the party quickly and leave her to her solitude. The screens provided a convenient shield.

"You are Lady Susanna, are you not?"

There would be no hiding. The urge to crumple into a ball on the floor almost overwhelmed her, but she was the daughter of an earl. Susanna pushed her shoulders back.

"Yes, I am. I'm sorry. I don't believe we've met."

The woman patted her perfect coiffure, which was tucked neatly under her hat, and poured water from the ewer over her hands. "I am Lady Winthorpe."

"*Oh*."

The countess's face brightened with amusement. "I see you have heard of me. Do not worry. All of my children have married." She bent, baring her teeth in the mirror and examining them closely. "I cannot tell you what a relief it is not to have to push them at every titled man or woman in Town. I imagine your poor mother is at her wits' end."

Heat rushed into Susanna's face, and her cheeks reddened most unbecomingly. Dane's marriage was indeed scandalous, and because it was, no one mentioned it to her.

"I…" Her tongue lay thick and clumsy in her mouth.

"What came over the earl?" the countess asked, patting the yellow and white plumes of her hat, which matched her gown. "Why would he make such a poor match?"

The countess turned to stare directly at Susanna.

"Lady Elizabeth is the daughter of the Marquess of Lyndon." She'd said it so often it had become a chant.

The countess flicked open her fan and wafted it. Painted on the fan was an image of a peacock with its feathers spread. "*Lady* Elizabeth was raised in a rookery as a thief. Even being the daughter of a marquess cannot redeem her."

She would not shrink. Susanna forced iron into her spine. "My brother loves her. That is enough for me."

"Love. How sweet."

The fan snapped closed, and the countess tapped Susanna's arm with it. "What does your mother think of this profession of love?"

"I—" Susanna had no idea. She'd never once heard her mother speak the word *love*, although she railed against her eldest son's mésalliance often enough.

"She was in love once. Did she ever tell you that?"

Susanna dared not open her mouth for fear she would only babble. Were they still speaking of the Dowager Countess of Dane? Surely, she had never been in love. Her mother did not know the meaning of the word. But perhaps Lady Winthorpe spoke of Susanna's late father. He had not exactly doted on his children either, especially not on her. But the countess might have mistaken the late earl's marriage for a love match.

"My father and mother—"

The countess waved the fan, narrowly missing Susanna's chin.

"I do not refer to your mother's marriage. She married him for the title and the money, I imagine. Your mother is no fool. But there were days, in our youth, when I thought she might choose another course." The woman's blue eyes had become so unfocused as to look gray. "Handsome young beaux. Picnics in Hyde Park. Nights at Vauxhall Gardens. Long, dark nights." She winked at Susanna, and Susanna flinched with shock.

The implication…or was it an insinuation…or an intimation…?

The countess was not to be believed.

"I don't know what you mean."

"No, I see that you don't. In any case, your mother made her choice." The woman's eyes, blue again, narrowed.

The countess stared at her so intently, Susanna actually took a step back.

The countess tapped her chin with the edge of the fan. "I wonder…"

Susanna held her breath, leaning forward to hear each and every syllable. All for naught. The woman didn't continue. The long silence, coupled with her curiosity, compelled Susanna to prompt Lady Winthorpe.

"You wonder?"

Voices rose and fell outside the door, and Susanna emitted a weak cry of protest. The door opened, revealing two young women speaking quietly to each other. One look at Susanna and their conversation ceased. The girls shared a look before they disappeared behind the screen and dissolved into giggles. Susanna toed the pale pink carpet with her slipper.

"Good day to you," the countess said, opening the door and stepping out into the music room.

Susanna stood rooted in place with the giggles behind her and questions swirling like dust motes in her mind. She should not pry further, but she was always doing as she ought. Her slipper dug into the rug, attacking the threads viciously. She caught the door before it could close all the way. The countess whirled when Susanna emerged behind her, and Susanna took advantage of the woman's surprise.

"I cannot help but ask, my lady. What do you wonder?"

"I think I had better not answer that." She spoke slowly, enunciating every word. Weighing each one against her tongue before speaking it. "Your mother would not thank me."

And there was that look again—the pitiful look one gave a pinned insect.

"But I see you, Lady Susanna, with that hair and that nose, and I do wonder." She sauntered across the music room. "Yes, I do."

Susanna touched her hair and her nose. What of them? Did the countess mean to deliberately confuse her?

Susanna crumpled onto the piano stool. She'd used every last ounce of bravery in the failed attempt to wheedle information. At this point, bravery hardly mattered. Chasing the countess was not an option, least of all because it would mean returning to the garden party.

Neither did she wish to return to the retiring room. She wandered to a harp and plucked at one of the strings, feeling the thick wires vibrate through her gloves. She'd always wanted to play the harp, but her mother had not allowed her to learn. Sitting with the instrument between her legs was unseemly. Susanna plucked another string, enjoying the light, airy sound of it.

What had the Countess of Winthorpe meant about her mother being in love? Had her mother fallen in love with a man before she met Susanna's father? A man her mother met at Hyde Park…no, not Hyde Park. Hyde Park was fashionable, the place to see and be seen. The sunny breezes of Hyde Park chased away any scandal.

But dark, sensuous Vauxhall Gardens...

Susanna had never been. Her mother would not permit it. Her brothers had undoubtedly visited, but Susanna did not possess their freedom.

She should ask her mother what Lady Winthorpe meant. Her mother's reaction might provide some clue. Of course, her mother might also tell her it was none of her concern, but Susanna was twenty now and would certainly marry in the next year. Lady Dane might relish the opportunity to share stories of her own days as a young debutante.

Susanna almost laughed aloud. Her mother relished nothing except ordering Susanna to sit still and stop slouching. Perhaps she might ask her new sister to take her. Marlowe had promised Susanna an adventure as the forfeit for losing a wager. Susanna would have dearly loved an adventure.

Her mother would never allow it, of course. Proper girls did not run away on adventures. Sometimes Susanna was so weary of acting properly.

The door of the music room swung open, and Lady Litton entered, shutting the door quickly behind her. She was a few years older than Susanna and had become betrothed after her first Season. She'd already given the viscount she'd married two healthy sons.

Susanna rose, and the viscountess, sensing the movement, spun around.

"Oh, it's you," she said with a dismissive wave. "Run back to your mama. She will be wanting you to laugh at her bon mots."

"My mother does not make bon mots." Clearly the woman did not know Lady Dane.

Even clearer was Susanna's mistake in speaking out. Lady Litton's dark eyebrows slashed together, and the ribbon of her pink lips thinned further.

"That was not my point."

No. Her point had been to encourage Susanna to run away. Undoubtedly, Lady Litton had a rendezvous with a friend or lover planned in this room. Though Susanna did not know who that could be, as this was a ladies' garden party. For a brief moment, Susanna wished she had simply run away.

But then something made her square her shoulders. Perhaps it was the thought of adventure. Perhaps she was still locked in her fantasy of Vauxhall, still imagining she could be someone else on those dark walks.

Someone brave and interesting and desirable.

"Why don't *you* run back to your mama?" Susanna said, surprising herself when the words from her thoughts came out of her mouth. "I am using this room at present."

"Then use another." Lady Litton advanced, her parasol held before her like a weapon.

Susanna's legs threatened to bolt for the exit, but she stood firm, even though she shook inside.

"*You* use another."

Lady Litton's eyes widened. Then she smiled, a very snide sort of smile. "Oh, I see. Your new sister has been influencing you. Tell me, Lady Susanna, what is next? Will you pick pockets and raise your skirts for every man in a dark alley?"

Susanna's arm rose without her permission, and her hand made loud contact with Lady Litton's cheek. A flower of red bloomed on the viscountess's pale skin, and with a look of shocked horror in her eyes, she raised her hand to the offending mark.

Susanna thought the look must have mirrored her own. What had she done?

What if her mother found out?

She opened her mouth to apologize, but Lady Litton shrieked before Susanna had a chance.

"You little bitch! Now look what you've done!"

As Susanna stared in silent amazement, a tear slid down Lady Litton's cheek.

"If you want the room, then take it." The viscountess stomped away in a flurry of skirts and flounces, her hand still on her abused skin.

Susanna stared after her until the door slammed, then looked down at her hand, still stinging with the force of the slap.

Perhaps she was not as much of a coward as she'd thought.

And perhaps now was the perfect time for that adventure.

❧

Gideon stood in the Golden Gallery in the dome of St. Paul's Cathedral. All of London sprawled before him. The sun set on the River Thames, clogged with ships of all sizes and shapes. The forest of masts jutted from the foul, murky water like dead tree branches in winter. Just beyond, the soot-blackened buildings of London were crammed together as though huddled in fear. The day was hot and the streets teeming with short-tempered people jostling their way through the throngs. Peddlers pushed carts, children chased dogs, and horses pulled rattlers. The noise on the streets deafened him at times.

High above it all, blissful silence reigned. The wind whooshed in his ears and ruffled his hair.

"I could get used to a view like this," Gideon said, spreading his arms like a king surveying his kingdom. He breathed deeply for effect, as the air up here wasn't much cleaner than that on the streets. "Smell that fresh air. The wind in my hair. This is the life."

But even in the heavens, he found only temporary escape from the world below.

Beezle stood just behind him, his gaze as dark as the dirt under his fingernails.

"You do the trick, and you can have any life you want," Beezle said quietly. With Satin dead, Beezle was the new arch rogue of the Covent Garden Cubs. Gideon had tried to distance himself from the gang since then, but old habits were hard to break. That, and Beezle was none too willing to allow one of his best rooks to walk away.

Reluctantly, Gideon abandoned the indigo-and-orange skies of London. "I pinch the necklace, and I never have to see your ugly mug again?"

"And here I thought it was the blunt you were after. A hundred yellow boys will make you rich as a gentry cove."

"The necklace is worth ten times that."

"The necklace is mine, and I choose to let you in on the game. Do we row in the same boat, Gideon?"

He didn't want to row in Beezle's boat. Hell, he didn't want to be in the same ocean as the arch rogue, but this was his chance. The blunt from this job would allow him to walk away from rooking. He could be his own man, start over in a new place, with a new name. Be whomever he wanted.

He'd never make it out of London without first lining his pockets. It took guineas to start over, and that's where Beezle came in.

Gideon rocked back on his heels, imitating the swells who had all the money and time in the world.

Beezle waited. His expression remained hooded, but Gideon would have bet a shilling—if he'd had one—the arch rogue chafed at being made to wait. They were of a similar height—he and Beezle—and both had dark hair. That was where the similarities ended. Beezle had a narrow, birdlike face perpetually twisted into a malevolent expression. Gideon liked to think of himself as a rum duke. He bore no one ill will and was generally good-natured.

Gideon held out a hand, offering it to the devil.

Beezle's icy fingers wrapped around his flesh, and Gideon's belly clenched in revulsion.

"Let's do the trick," Gideon said.

After that it was a simple matter to make their way to Mother Cummings's house at Six George Street. Mother Cummings rented rooms for as little as a shilling, but it was a bawdy house as well as a front for fencing goods. The molls' game was to lure a man into bed—the more foxed the better—then purloin his property and make a run for it. Then everyone in the house would claim never to have heard of the moll who'd filched the goods. At the first opportunity, Mother Cummings was sure to fence it. If anyone was likely to have cargo of real value in St. Giles, it was Mother Cummings.

Mother Cummings had dozens of hidey-holes for the goods she acquired. Gideon had either seen or heard of most of them since he'd fenced cargo through Mother Cummings a hundred times or more before he'd joined the Covent Garden Cubs. Gideon's job was to find where the necklace was hidden, filch it, and hand it over to Beezle. Beezle would fence it himself and give Gideon a hundred guineas.

A hundred yellow boys was more money than Gideon could even imagine, but he didn't want to start thinking about the blunt before he did the job. He would be a thief in a house full of thieves. He couldn't afford distractions.

Of one mind, Beezle and Gideon paused outside a gin shop on George Street, just across from Number Six. No one paid them any attention as they took careful note of the comings and goings at Mother Cummings's. A steady stream of men filed in and out. Gideon would be all but invisible in the public rooms.

"You coming in?" Gideon asked after a quarter of an hour passed.

Beezle's small eyes never left the door across George Street. "I'll wait here for the drop."

Gideon had been counting on that. He gave a casual shrug. "Suit yourself."

He started away, but Beezle gripped his shoulder with hard, bony fingers. "Don't even think about double-crossing me, Gideon. Racer and Stub are keeping watch in the back. Get the necklace. Give it to me. If you even think about keeping it, I'll smash you myself."

Gideon spread his arms in mock indignation. "Take the necklace for myself? Would I do that?"

Beezle dug his fingers painfully into Gideon's shoulder.

Gideon covered his heart with a hand. "You don't trust me. That hurts, Beezle." He tapped his chest. "Right here."

Beezle's grip slackened, but his expression remained deadly. Gideon missed Satin. The old arch rogue was quick to cuff the cubs, but he was also quick with a grin. Gideon had usually been able to make him laugh.

"Get the necklace," Beezle said.

"Work, work, work." Gideon rotated his shoulder, shrugging off Beezle's hand. "Be right back."

"You'd better be."

The interior of Mother Cummings's house was as Gideon remembered. The well-worn stairs led to the drawing room where molls plied men with gin, then coaxed them to nearby bedrooms. The rooms for rent were on the second floor, and the ground floor was for dining and business. Mother Cummings was rarely in residence after two in the afternoon, so if a rook wanted to fence something, he learned to come in the morning.

It was a long time until morning, so Gideon should have plenty of time to search.

A large woman with a red face and bruised knuckles pointed upstairs. "All the rooms are rented, but go upstairs and find a rum blowen to entertain you."

Mother Cummings was no fool. She had a guard on the first floor. Gideon had counted on at least one sentry. Upstairs, he made a pass through the drawing room, peeling the molls off when they tried to persuade him to sit or drink. Finally, he slipped back out and headed past the closed bedroom doors until he reached the servants' stairs. He shut the door behind him and started down them, only to topple over a young mort sitting on one of the steps with a bottle of Blue Ruin.

She looked up at him with bleary, red eyes. "Shh. Don't tell."

"It's our secret." Gideon pressed a finger to his lips. He moved around her and cracked the door on the first floor, peering out. The entry was just a few feet away, where the guard woman growled at a young man. Mother Cummings's library—if a room with no books could be called such—was across from him. That library was the most likely hidey-hole for the necklace.

Gideon slid across the corridor and lifted the library door latch.

The door didn't open.

He cursed under his breath and, with a quick glance at the guard, retrieved a dub from his coat pocket. With slow, steady movements born from years of practice, he slid the tool into the lock and maneuvered it about until he felt it snap into place. His gaze never wavered from the guard. If she saw him now, he was stone dead.

A group of coves came in, but they were looking up the stairs, thinking about what lay ahead. They had no reason to note a man standing near a door by the servants' stairs.

He twisted his wrist, hearing the lock click. The sound was deafening in his ears, but the guard dog didn't turn. Withdrawing the dub, Gideon slipped it back into his coat, turned the handle, and slithered into the dark library.

Gideon felt his way toward a window and tossed several gowns draped over it onto the floor, allowing more light inside. He was met by a dozen haphazard piles of random treasures. Silk handkerchiefs lay on top of a table beside slabs of cheese and bacon. Brass knobs and shutters shared space with a mound of ladies' petticoats, hats, and shoes. In the corner, a duck quacked. Stacked beside the creature's cage were pails and coal scuttles. Gideon scanned the larger items, noting a tall chest in one corner. He crossed to it quickly, opening drawers and feeling inside for the contents—lead, glass bottles, a mirror, brushes…no baubles.

He tried another drawer and another until they'd all been searched. Perhaps she kept the necklace elsewhere. A parlor? The dining room? It could be anywhere, but this was the only room he'd never seen anyone but Mother Cummings enter. If the necklace was in the house, it must be in the library. A valuable necklace like that: Would she have left it here? It was widely known that Mother Cummings didn't live at Six George Street. Maybe she'd taken the necklace to her other home to keep it safe until she found a buyer.

Gideon scanned the room again, looking for a hiding spot, something he'd overlooked. The necklace had to be here. If it wasn't, his future was as lost as a pamphlet thrown into a fire.

He couldn't allow that to happen. He couldn't spend the rest of his life diving into pockets or cracking houses. He wanted out.

He leaned against the cold hearth and tapped his hands against his thighs as he meticulously studied every spot in the room. He had to be missing something. Why hadn't he found any ladies' fal-lals? Not a ring, not even an earbob. His foot kicked back, hitting the grate in the hearth, and he pulled his boot forward before the ash could coat it. But when he looked down, he didn't see any ash.

Gideon crouched and stroked his fingers over the grate. Stone cold.

No sign of wood or coal in the hearth. That was interesting. Even in summer, these houses were drafty. Surely Mother Cummings would want a warm fire while she inventoried her treasures. Gideon wished he had a glim-stick, but his eyes were so used to the dark, he figured he could see almost as well without one. Lying on his back, he shoved his shoulders into the hearth, wiggling until they fit. Then he reached up and felt the chimney stones. Bits of soot and ash dropped onto his face, but he ignored them as his deft fingers explored.

Brick, brick, brick, hole.

Gideon grinned in triumph, angled his wrist, and reached into the hole. His fingers closed on a velvet bag, and he tugged it out. Wrenching his shoulders from the hearth, he pulled the bag open. Inside, several rings tinkled, and a rum thimble ticked the minutes away.

Even better, something flashed and winked. Gideon lifted the diamond-and-emerald necklace. He whistled softly to himself.

"There you are," he murmured.

He thrust the bag into his coat and stood. Now all he had to do was cross the room, open the door, and make his escape.

Footsteps clomped without, and the door handle rattled.

Two

GIDEON CURSED. HE'D USED THE DUB TO OPEN THE door. Why the hell hadn't he locked it again?

He had two options: hide and be found or not hide and be found.

He patted the velvet bag, still hidden in his coat. The door creaked open.

"You took your time about getting here," Gideon said, hands on his hips. "I was beginning to think you wouldn't show."

The man and the woman in the doorway exchanged confused looks. That was better than having them try to kill him, so he kept talking. "Do you have any idea how late it is?" Not that Gideon knew either, but it sounded good. "I've been waiting for you for an hour."

Finally, the girl edged into the room. "Who are you?"

Gideon raised a brow in a way the ladies seemed to like. He'd perfected the art of brow raising.

"The question is, who are you? No one mentioned a rum duchess like you."

She giggled, and Gideon took that as a good sign. He moved forward, lifted her hand, and kissed it. "Pleasure you meet you. I'm Gideon."

She giggled again. "Alice."

The man she was with—little more than a cub, really—snatched her hand back. He probably had some prior claim on the girl. Gideon would have assumed he'd interrupted a romantic meeting, except he doubted Mother Cummings ever allowed anything of that sort down here. The rooms upstairs were for let. Everyone knew that.

"Ye're not supposed to be in here," the cub told him.

Gideon scrunched his face into a confused expression. "Then why'd you tell me to meet you here?"

Now might be a good time to think about escape. He spotted several brass door knockers on the floor nearby and sidled closer to them.

"I didn't."

"Mother Cummings don't let anyone in here," Alice told him.

"You're in here." He needed one door knocker. Just one.

"She trusts us."

"I see why." He made a show of looking her over, inching closer to the door knockers as he did. "Rum blowen like you. Are you hungry? Thirsty? Why don't we go outside and talk about the game?"

"There's no game with you," the boy said. "You think I'm some kind of nob?"

He swung his fist, and Gideon ducked, grabbing one of the door knockers. He came up swinging and caught the lad on the side of the temple. The cub went down with a yelp that was sure to attract attention. Gideon took Alice's hand again.

"Another time, sweet Alice."

With a kiss to her knuckles, he bolted from the room. He sprinted for the door to the house, ignoring the guard screeching at him to halt. He would flash her a grin and a wave when he flew through the door.

Except three short, thick men, fat as Norfolk dumplin's, thundered down the steps and cut off his exit.

Gideon skidded to a halt and went back the way he'd come. Unfortunately, the lad he'd smashed over the head had recovered and was coming for him, blood streaming from the new gash on his temple.

"Not going that way," Gideon muttered to himself and took the only option open to him, the door on his right. The handle turned, and Gideon ran through, slamming the door on his pursuers. That wouldn't keep them for long, and he turned in a circle, looking for a way to escape. The only exit he spotted was a glaze. He ran to it as the door burst open. Gideon pushed the pane up and jumped out.

He felt his coat again, making sure the necklace was still secure, and took off running. Behind him Mother Cummings's thugs climbed through the window.

They'd never catch him.

He pumped his legs, clearing the shadow of the house and screeching to a halt when Racer and Stub stepped in front of him.

"Gideon," Racer said, crossing his arms in front of him.

Gideon panted, looked over his shoulder.

"Where are you off to in such a hurry?" Racer demanded.

"Ye're not trying to chouse Beezle, are you?" Stub asked.

"Me? No." His lungs burned, and his legs twitched. His body screamed, *Run*. Voices exploded behind him.

"I was trying to get away from…them." He pointed to the Norfolk dumplin's coming through the jump. When Racer and Stub turned to look, Gideon gave them a shove and took off running.

He tore past the fencing ken where Mother Cummings kept her goods and onto George Street. Behind him, Racer and Stub yelled for Beezle. Racer was fast, and Gideon couldn't outrun him. He'd have to lose him. With that in mind, Gideon cut down an alley, leaping over a broken wheelbarrow and attracting the attention of a scavenging dog. He must have looked like a better meal than the dog had found, because the beast nipped at him and gave chase.

"Oh, come on!" Gideon said with a glance at the heavens. "A dog too?"

With the buffer nipping at his heels, he dove into a doorway, slammed the door on the mongrel, and stumbled up the stairs. His legs felt like lead bars. He was winded when he reached the roof, and he had to bend over and catch his breath. His legs cramped and threatened to fail him.

Panting, he peered over the edge and saw Racer entering the building. Beezle, Stub, and the rogues from Mother Cummings's weren't far behind. He needed an escape plan. Somewhere they'd never find him. Somewhere he'd be safe.

Fog and haze from coal fires shrouded the city. To the south, the river's countless ships' masts resembled bony fingers pointing to the sky.

Skeletons.

Not that way.

East led to more rookeries, more men to chase him. West—*west*. West meant Hyde Park, Piccadilly, Mayfair…

Gideon forced his beleaguered legs to attempt three large steps back, then tested his endurance. He ran across the roof and jumped across to the closest building, landing with a thud. The roof sloped, and he slid down and down.

Shit. He was dead.

His hand snagged a loose piece of wood that cut into his skin. He dangled, blood from his hand dripping into his eyes. Ignoring the pain, he slammed his feet against a glaze below him.

Shit again. The glass was too thick to break, and his fucking hand hurt like a hot iron had branded it.

Then the pane lifted, and a woman peered up at him. "What the bloody 'ell is going on?"

Good question.

A slug hit the building beside him.

Very good question.

Gideon peered over his shoulder. Mrs. Cummings's men hunched on the building he'd jumped from. With their heads together, they watched as one primed the barking iron again.

"This is bad. This is very bad."

Gideon looked up. Not that way. He looked down at the window and the not-insubstantial drop below.

Neither path was desirable, but out of all his options, being popped was the least desirable. With a muffled curse, Gideon released the piece of wood and slid down until his feet balanced on the window ledge. The woman had ducked back inside when the next pistol shot rang out, and he swung inside before the slug hit, right where his head had been a moment before.

"Hey!" From the safety of the room, he shook his fist at the thugs.

The blow to his head came from nowhere. Gideon staggered back and closed his eyes to stop the spinning.

"Get out!" the woman screamed, slapping at him.

Gideon held up his hands and danced around her.

"Just show me the door."

Still avoiding her blows, he reached the door, threw it open, and fell into the corridor.

"There's got to be an easier way," he muttered as he stumbled to his feet and down the stairs. He burst into the street outside the building, paused to find his bearings, and started west. He took off at a light run, ignoring his leaden legs. There'd be time to inventory his injuries later. He turned down a side street and smacked into a tall, lanky form.

Beezle stepped into the light. "Going somewhere?"

Gideon fell backward, recovered his balance. "I was looking for you."

He spread his hands in a gesture of surrender.

"Of course you were." Beezle held out a hand. "Give me the necklace."

The hand was dirty and scarred, much as Gideon's. The long, sharp nails had dirt underneath. Behind him, Stub and Racer called out.

"Give it to me now, and I'll kill you fast," Beezle said.

"A generous offer, but I'm not ready to die."

"Too late."

Beezle lunged, and Gideon caught the glint of the long, deadly dagger he held. Gideon shielded his face with his arm, crouching instinctively. The low growl made him flinch.

Beezle looked over his shoulder. "What was that?"

The mongrel stepped out from the shadows behind Beezle. His teeth were bared, the only white on his otherwise black form.

"Have you met my friend Killer?" Gideon asked.

Beezle swung the blade, and the dog lunged for him. Gideon shot away, running on fear as much as thrill. He exited the alley and tumbled into the street when he heard the dog's growls behind him.

"Not much of a meal, is he?" Gideon called over his shoulder.

The dog barked, and Gideon pushed his body to the limit.

"If you want to eat me, first you have to catch me!"

⌒≈⌒

"Why are you in here?" the Dowager Lady Dane asked, holding a lamp aloft.

Susanna turned from her father's bookshelves. She'd been tracing the spines of her father's collection in his darkened library. She hadn't bothered to light a lamp or to ask Crawford to stoke the fire in the hearth. She wanted the peace of the dark.

But peace was fleeting.

"I repeat, why are you in here?"

Susanna shrugged.

"Do not shrug. It is not ladylike."

"I'm sorry. I would choose a book to read."

Her mother huffed and held the lamp higher as though to view Susanna's choice. "And did you? Make sure I approve it first."

Susanna had tugged her shawl close, shivering in the coolness of the large library.

"I haven't chosen one yet. I...I was thinking about Dane." Oh, treacherous ground! She should scuttle away or risk being smashed underfoot.

She squinted her eyes closed and pressed on. "Have you had word from Dane and Marlowe?"

Her mother put a hand to her forehead. "Do not mention that woman's name to me. She is the reason we have no invitations tonight. Lord Braybrook is hosting a musicale, and do you think we were sent an invitation? No. We are little more than pariahs. That is what your brother and his mésalliance have done to us."

"We are hardly pariahs." She should shut up now, but then she would never know. And she would have to call herself *coward*. Again.

"We are not as popular as we might have been, Mama, but you cannot blame Dane for following his heart. He loves Marlowe."

"*Love*." Her mother fanned her face with a gloved hand. "What do you know of love? What about duty? What about honor? How could he shame us by marrying a...a common thief?"

"Haven't you ever been in love, Mama?" Susanna flinched back at the impertinence of her question.

Generally, she refrained from asking her mother even the most basic sorts of questions, but Lady Winthorpe's conversation at the garden party had made her inexcusably curious.

"Of course," her mother snapped. "I loved your father."

"There was never anyone else?"

Her mother's thin lips pressed together. "Why do you ask?"

Susanna almost shrugged. She caught herself in time. "I just wondered."

"You wondered?" Her mother stalked into the room, bringing the slash of light from the lamp with her. "There is nothing about me to wonder. I married your father and birthed three children. Why the three of you insist on plaguing me now is beyond me."

"Have you ever been to Vauxhall Gardens?" Susanna asked. Was it her imagination or did her mother's face go white?

"Of course. But it was a long time ago. The gardens have deteriorated since then. It is not safe, full of rakes and courtesans."

"I want to go."

"Out of the question." Her tone was imperious. Not even the Queen could have done as well.

"I'm out now, and it's a fashionable setting."

"Absolutely not," her mother said, her manner more forceful than Susanna felt the suggestion warranted. "It's not safe. Pickpockets and rogues of all sorts frequent Vauxhall. Even Lambeth is no longer safe."

Susanna would not back down, not after her triumph over Lady Litton. She wanted an adventure, and Vauxhall was the most romantic and daring place she could think of. If she didn't go now, her mother would keep her in the prison of this town house for the rest of her life. Even if Susanna married, she'd only move to another prison. For once, Susanna wanted to be free, to go somewhere of her own choosing, to go somewhere for her own amusement—not because she was obligated to.

"Then we should ask Brook to escort us," Susanna said. "We would be safe with an inspector who has his contacts at Bow Street."

Surely her mother could not object to that argument.

"Your brother is far too busy with his work to be called upon to escort us on such a frivolous journey."

Susanna's jaw dropped. "But you hate Brook's work! You always say he should go out in Society more. You said his insistence on associating with Runners is an embarrassment. You—"

"I know what I said, young lady," her mother snapped. "I do not need my words repeated by you. And what I am saying now is that we will not trouble your brother with this."

"But—"

The dowager held up a hand. "Furthermore, this is the last I want to hear of this. Not another word. Do you understand me, Susanna? We are not visiting Vauxhall Gardens. *Ever.*"

Susanna stepped back in surprise at the vehemence in her mother's voice. The dowager put a hand to her forehead. "Now look what you have done. I have a megrim. Edwards!" She took the lamp out of the library and called a second time for her lady's maid. "Edwards, I need a compress."

Susanna crossed the room and closed the door, muting her mother's voice. Then she returned to her father's desk—Dane's desk now. She felt for the chair, wobbled, and slid to the floor. A sob welled up in her throat. "I'll never be free of her."

She sounded pitiful, and she didn't even care. She was trapped, like the butterfly her brothers had once caught at Northbridge Abbey and imprisoned in a glass jar. The butterfly had flown about the jar, beating its wings on the glass until it finally ceased in exhaustion.

The boys soon grew tired of watching the butterfly and went to play other games. Susanna immediately released the poor creature, but by then it was too fatigued to fly out. Even when she dumped it on the grass, the butterfly did not move. It had given up.

She'd tried to be the perfect daughter. She'd tried to do everything her mother asked of her, but nothing was ever good enough. She didn't speak loudly enough or she spoke too loudly; she walked too slowly or too quickly; she ate too much or too little; her hair was too long or not long enough; she was too fat or too thin. Susanna felt like cowering, as she was now, every time she saw her mother, because she never knew what she would be criticized for next.

She was tired of fighting. She wanted to give up, lie down, fall asleep, and never wake up again. The weight of her exhaustion pressed down on her, and she leaned against the side of the desk, giving in to it.

Scrape.

Susanna stopped crying and listened.

⁂

"Very good, Edwards," Dorothea said when her lady's maid had taken her wrapper and assisted her into bed. The cool sheets felt good against her swollen feet. She'd spent too much time on them at the garden party. She'd had to search the entire house before she'd found Susanna in the music room, of all places.

But thank God she'd found her. Dorothea's heart had thumped wildly when her daughter hadn't been in the retiring room and no one could remember having seen her.

Edwards held up the compress. "Here you are, my lady."

"That is perfect, Edwards." She settled the compress on her forehead and closed her eyes.

After a few moments, Edwards turned the compress over. "Feeling better, my lady?"

"No, Edwards, unfortunately I am not. I do not think I shall be well until I see Susanna married and married well."

Edwards's mouth turned down sympathetically. "The girl does seem to put you out of sorts."

"Yes, she does. Did I tell you she disappeared at the marchioness's garden party today?"

"You did, my lady."

Dorothea eased herself back down onto the pillow and closed her eyes. "I worry about her. She resents it when I try to protect her. Am I not a mother? Should I not keep my daughter safe?"

"You love her, my lady."

"Of course I do. I love all of my children."

Edwards turned the compress again. "I have always sensed Lady Susanna was special to you, my lady."

Dorothea opened her eyes. "She is, Edwards. She is very special. I do not think she even knows how special she is to me."

"You should tell her, my lady."

Dorothea closed her eyes again. That was something she dared never to do.

❧

Scrape.

In the library, Susanna went still. There it was again.

The town house was old and had a tendency to creak and groan. But then she heard it again, and this time she knew it was not the house. It sounded like…a window. There were two windows behind Dane's desk, and both looked out upon the small garden. One was directly across from where she sat huddled on the floor. The draperies were closed, and nothing stirred behind them. Was she imagining the noise, or was something or—God forbid—*someone* trying to enter the house?

She peered around the corner of the desk and stared at the opposite window. Her breath caught when the draperies rustled with the breeze. The window had definitely *not* been open before. It had been cold enough in the room without allowing the night air inside.

Susanna jerked back, hidden on the far side of the desk again. Everyone knew London was rife with housebreakers, but would the thieves be so bold as to try and enter a house when the family was home? She heard a thump and trembled.

Apparently, the rogues *were* so bold. What would they do to her if they found her? Kill her? Rape her? Kidnap her for ransom?

She must escape, but how?

She peered around the desk again and saw two legs standing in front of the window. It was too late to run. The thief was already inside. She did a quick inventory of herself. She had nothing, absolutely nothing that would protect her from a ruffian.

She could hear the thief breathing now. He was breathing hard, as though he'd been running. She pressed her back against the oak of the desk and craned her neck. She spotted the shadow of a candlestick on the edge of the desk. She hadn't lit the candle in it. If she could pull it off the edge without the thief noticing, she could use it to protect herself.

She felt the edge of the desk with her fingertips. Closing her eyes, she stretched her fingers until she touched the cool silver of the candlestick. She eased her fingers around it and tugged it soundlessly over the edge of the desk.

The candlestick shook in her hands. The weight was more than she was prepared for, but she caught hold of it and clutched it to her chest just in time.

The thief clomped into the room. He wasn't worried about being quiet. She could hear him now. He lifted books and replaced them. She knew the sound the binding made when lifted and released. That meant his back was to her.

Her heart thundered so loudly she feared he could hear her, and she was at risk of swooning at any moment. She dug her fingers into the ornamentation around the candlestick until the silver cut into her palm.

She must be strong. She must be brave.

It didn't appear as though any other thieves were entering after this one. She could hit him with the candlestick and prove to her mother that she was an independent, capable young woman who should be allowed to go to Vauxhall Gardens—or anywhere she pleased!

Susanna trembled as she moved to her knees and slanted her eyes up and over the desk.

There he was!

He looked every inch the dangerous rogue! He was tall and powerfully built and had dark hair covered with a cap. And he was indeed pawing through her father's books. She had to stop him.

She ducked down and scooted along the edge of the desk until she reached the side closest to the shelves. She was exposed now. If he should but move a little to his left, he would see her. She forced herself to slide slowly and with exaggerated care until her back collided with the sharp edge of the far corner of the desk.

She could smell the thief now. She'd expected him to smell of something rank and evil, but he smelled of the night air and something else, perhaps sandalwood?

This close, she saw the rough hew of his clothing. The dirt on his boots. He did not belong here, and his actions left no question as to his intent. She grasped her skirts in one hand to keep them from tripping her, and held the heavy candlestick in the other. Soundlessly, she rose. He seemed to sense her movement, but right before he could turn, she rushed him and slammed the candlestick onto the back of his head.

With a groan, he went down, the cap tumbling from his head.

She'd done it! She'd really done it.

She gave a small gasp of surprise and horror when she saw the trickle of blood on his neck. Oh God. Had she killed him? What would happen to her if she'd killed him? Would she go to Newgate?

She wanted to wake Crawford, but she couldn't call the butler if she'd killed a man. He'd be forced to summon the magistrate. Better to ensure the thief was alive before calling for anyone.

Tentatively, she knelt down, and her hand wavered over the thief's neck. She'd seen her mother's physician touch the dowager's neck at this point to check her pulse. Susanna had never tried to check a pulse, and she'd never touched a man other than her father or her brothers. Her hand hovered above the man's neck, until finally she shut her eyes and forced herself to touch him.

He was still warm. His head was turned away from her, so she couldn't see if her hand was in the right position, but she didn't feel a pulse. She moved her fingers a fraction of an inch.

Still nothing.

She moved them again, and he groaned.

She snatched her hand away and scrambled backward. The man tried to rise, lifting his shoulders off the floor and cupping the back of his head. He groaned again and turned his head to look at her, just as she was about to raise the candlestick again. He raised his hand to ward off the blow, but she'd paused anyway.

His eyes held her. He faced the hearth behind her, and she could see the pain in his eyes but also the color.

They were green, a vivid, beautiful green that reminded her of forests and glades and the serenity of the country. And so she paused.

Later, she would come to realize that small hesitation had been a mistake.

Later, she would realize that was the moment everything had gone wrong.

But as she sat with the candlestick held aloft, the thief staring at her, all she could think was that he was beautiful. That she wanted to sketch him; that it would be impossible to find the right color for his eyes.

"Lady Susanna?"

Three

"How do you know my name?" she asked.

At least he thought that was her question. His head throbbed loud enough to wake the dead. What had she hit him with? That glim-stick?

Shit. She could have killed him.

She brandished the glim-stick again. "I said, how do you know my name?"

He sat back on his haunches, almost toppled over. He was stronger than this. He'd been soundly chafed more times than he cared to remember.

"Because I know you." His tongue felt thick and fuzzy.

"How dare you speak to me?"

He winced. Her voice was a knife cutting through his brain.

"*You* asked me a question," he answered. "Twice."

"How do you know me?" She pointed the glim-stick at him as though it were a tilter, and rose to her knees. Her eyes, dark and owlish in her small face, studied him like a wary animal might. She shook like a small, terrified animal. He'd seen his share cornered. She had the same look of fear.

"Because Marlowe's my crony." As soon as it was out of his mouth, he realized how the words made him sound. Lower class. "I mean, me and Marlowe are acquainted."

"Marlowe?"

The glim-stick lowered.

"You and Marlowe?"

He held out a hand. "I'm Gideon."

She jerked the glim-stick high again, shaking it. "I will use this."

His head throbbed in sympathy. "I know."

"What are you doing here?" She scrambled to her feet, still waving the glim-stick. "Marlowe and my brother aren't in residence at the moment."

This was news. "Where are they? If you send for her, she'll vouch for me."

"I can't. They're at Northbridge Abbey."

That was a wrinkle. He rose to his feet.

"Stay back!"

He wanted to snatch the glim-stick from her hand and toss it out the window—or, seeing it was silver, stuff it in his coat. Instead, he held up his hands.

"I won't hurt you. If Marlowe's not here, I'll be on my way." Keeping his hands raised in defense, he took three careful steps back and paused by the bookshelf where he'd stashed the bag with the necklace.

"What are you doing?" She was a pretty little thing but definitely a nob. Giving orders came naturally to her.

"Taking what's mine." He felt for the bag, his fingers grazing it when he heard the growl. There, in the window behind him, panted that mongrel dog. Its paws rested on the casement, and its devil eyes stared at him as though he were dinner.

How the hell had the buffer found him here?

"Shoo," he said, waving his hand at it.

It bared its teeth.

"Is that your dog?"

"No." If he'd had a dog, it wouldn't block his escape route. "If you don't mind, I'll exit through the front door."

"You stay right where you are. If you even—" She cocked her head. "Someone is coming!"

"Damn," he grumbled. He had the dog at his back, a daft mort with a glim-stick in front, and now someone else would join the party.

Gideon took the only recourse available at the moment: he dove under the desk.

"What are you doing?" she hissed.

He poked his head out. "Don't tell them I'm here." And he ducked back again just as the door opened.

Hiding was a gamble. He had no reason to trust the mort. She'd probably snitch on him, but he'd grasped at the chance, small as it was, that she wouldn't. Maybe the odds were in his favor tonight. He'd managed to lose Beezle and the other cubs, not to mention Mother Cummings's thugs. The damn dog was still on his heels, but he could deal with the buffer quickly enough. With that thought, he peered out at the window. The mongrel had disappeared.

One less wrinkle.

"My lady, is anything the matter?" It was a man, and he spoke like a slavey. His consonants were crisp, whereas Gideon's were woefully soft. The butler?

"Crawford! Hello."

She sounded nervous as hell. He bet she looked like she was ready to jump out of her skin.

That was it. He'd be in the iron doublet before morning.

"I thought I heard a sound."

"A sound?" Her voice was shrill and false. "I didn't hear anything."

The butler, Crawford, cleared his throat. "It sounded like yelling. Is anyone in here with you?"

"No. I was—I was talking to myself."

There was a long stretch of silence, and Gideon imagined the slavey debated whether or not to believe her. If he didn't believe the girl—and with pitiful deception skills like hers, who would?—this Crawford had to decide what he would do about it.

"Shall I call for your mother? I fear you might be too much alone at times, my lady."

Gideon twisted his face in disbelief. The slavey thought she might be lonely? He'd believed she'd been talking to herself? This gentry mort must really lack for friends.

Gideon had no idea what that would be like. He was never alone. He'd lived all his life in cramped quarters, first at the orphanage then in the flash ken with the rest of the rooks he knew. Why, the space under this desk was more room than he usually had to himself.

"Oh, no, no. I'm fine," she said. "In fact, I will select a book and then retire."

"Very well, my lady."

"Good night, Crawford."

"Good night, my lady."

Gideon waited until all was silent again, and then he poked his head out. His trained gaze had already picked out everything of any real value in the room. The silver glim-stick she insisted on using as a weapon would fetch a pretty penny, but the ormolu box on the mantel and the Sevres porcelain dish on the table by the door would be lighter to carry and just as easy to fence.

The necklace was worth ten times all that cargo.

"All clear?"

"He's gone," she said. She'd set the glim-stick on the desk, but she lifted it again now.

"Then I'll be on my way." Another glance at the window told him the dog was still gone. Now was his chance. He crossed to the bookshelf and reached for his cargo, but his hand came away empty. His heart jumped into his throat, and every last bit of air whooshed from his lungs. Gideon shoved books aside, toppled several on the floor.

The necklace was gone.

He rounded on the girl. Her face told all. She couldn't lie if her life depended on it.

"Where is it?" He advanced on her.

She brandished the glim-stick, but he was done playing games. The necklace was all that mattered. It was his life.

Gideon had choused Beezle. He'd be cargo for the Resurrection Men if he stayed in London, and he couldn't leave London without blunt.

"Don't come any closer." She clutched the glim-stick.

"Where is it?" he asked again, keeping his voice low. "I don't want to hurt you, but I will if you don't tell me what you did with it."

"It's hidden, and you'll never find it."

His gaze flicked over the room. A large vase on the table behind her made the most obvious hidey-hole.

"It's in that vase, isn't it?"

She would have made a pitiful rook. She dashed to the vase, dug the bag out, and stuck it into her bodice.

"If you wanted me to rip your clothes off, you only had to ask." He took a step forward.

"Touch me, and I'll scream so loudly I'll wake the whole house."

Gideon took another step forward. "You didn't tell the slavey I was hiding here. You won't scream."

She raised the glim-stick again. "I will. I promise I will."

He looked in her eyes. Damn it.

She didn't bluff. She was terrified, and if he touched her, he'd end his short, sad life dangling by the neck at the gallows. Either that or on one of the prison hulks. He didn't know which was worse.

Gideon crossed his arms. He could negotiate. He excelled at negotiations. Added to that, he had a way with women. He'd give her one of his charming smiles, and she'd be all his. He hadn't met a woman yet whose clothes didn't practically fall off when he gave her The Look. Gideon glanced down then back up, giving her the most potent form of The Look he could muster.

She glared at him. "Do not touch me," she said.

Gideon choked on his surprise. Why wasn't she melting? He must have done it wrong. He tried it again.

"What is wrong with your face?" she asked. "Your mouth looks odd."

"Damn!" The Look didn't work on the bloody mort. He clenched his hands to keep from shaking her. "What the devil do you want?"

"I want to go to Vauxhall Gardens."

"Vauxhall?" he stammered.

It was not the strangest request he'd ever heard, but he'd not been expecting it. Not from this rum duchess.

"Then go. What does Vauxhall have to do with my cargo?" He gestured to her chest. He could see the black velvet of the bag peeking out from between her cleavage. Under other circumstances, he might have even been interested in that cleavage. Right now, all he wanted was the cargo.

"I can't go," she said in a tone that implied this should be obvious. "I need someone to take me. I want *you* to take me." She said the last as though it were an order, not a wish.

Gideon raked a hand roughly through his hair. "I'm no jehu. Give me the bag, and you'll never have to see me again."

He reached for her chest, but she batted his hand away with the glim-stick.

"Ow!" He snatched his hand back, checking it for fresh bruises.

"I'll give you the bag after you take me to the pleasure gardens."

This was what the swells called *an impasse*. He stared at her, willing her to back down. She pressed her lips together in a show of stubbornness he had not expected.

"And if I refuse?"

"Then I turn this"—she gestured to the bag—"over to my brother. You do know Sir Brook Derring?"

Oh, he knew Sir Brook. The man was a bloody thief-taker. One of the best in the city.

Gideon wanted to hit something. He wanted to howl in frustration. Instead, he ground his jaw together.

"Fine," he finally spat. "Let's go."

She would see him killed and do herself in along the way. Hell, if she wanted to go to Vauxhall Gardens, they'd go.

"Fine?" Those owl-like eyes narrowed with suspicion. Or had they gone sharp now she'd settled on her prey? "You'll take me?"

"That's what I said." He grabbed her arm and tugged her toward the window, but she dug her heels in to the carpet.

"Now?"

"Yes, now. I want my cargo. I take you to Vauxhall, you give me the bag, and we part as friends."

She was shaking her head. Damn and hell!

"What *now*?"

"I can't wear this."

"What?"

The white gown with the blue sash was sweet, if one liked that sort of thing. He supposed the rich swells did like that sort of thing. They wanted their women untouched and pure. This one certainly looked that.

"What's wrong with it?"

"It's an afternoon dress. I must change into evening wear."

"No, no, no." Gideon slashed a hand between them. This was not happening. Time was the enemy.

"You look fine. We leave now."

But she was already inching toward the library door. "It won't take me but a moment to change."

He didn't believe that for a second. When he and Marlowe had been cronies in Satin's gang, he'd helped her dress more times than he could count. Women's garments were notoriously difficult to manage.

New tactic. "Fine. Go change. I'll wait here with the bag."

"I don't think so," she said with her hand on the door handle. "I'm keeping it with me."

"It doesn't leave my sight."

She waved the order away. "You can trust me with it. Besides, if I give it to you, you'll run away as soon as I step through this door."

He gasped in mock astonishment. "I beg your pardon. I would do no such thing."

"I don't believe you."

He pressed a hand to his heart. "That hurts. Where is the trust?"

She patted the bag nestled against her chest. "Right here. I'll be back in a moment."

And she was gone.

Gideon swore at the closed door for a good three minutes and then kicked the desk. It hurt his foot more than it hurt the desk, and he didn't feel even marginally better.

Vauxhall Bloody Shithole Gardens!

Why the hell did she want to go there?

The better question was how he would get her there without any of Beezle's cronies seeing him. They'd be all over London now, searching every last nook and den for him. Gideon needed to leave the city, not take a stroll through its popular pleasure gardens.

On the other hand, no one would expect him to go to Vauxhall. Maybe he'd be safe there for a little while. And maybe he could lift the necklace off her without her even noticing. He was a good diver, not as good as Marlowe had been, but he could take a bag off a nob.

He'd have to be close to her to reach into her dress. She didn't seem too keen to have him touch her.

Still, the night was young. His odds might change.

The hairs on the back of his neck rose at the low growl Gideon heard from the open window.

The blasted dog was back.

"Shit," he muttered as the beast jumped through the window and lunged at him.

❦

Susanna's heart beat so fast she could hardly catch her breath long enough to choose a gown. She would go to Vauxhall Gardens!

She would go with a thief who made her legs weak with terror, but she would go.

Her mother would kill her.

She might be dead with her throat slit in a dirty alley before her mother even noticed she had gone.

Her heart thudded painfully.

She couldn't think like that. The man was one of Marlowe's friends…who happened to be a criminal.

A criminal she'd outwitted.

She set down the candlestick and pulled the black bag from her bodice. He'd wanted it back rather desperately, but she'd managed to obtain the upper hand.

She scooted closer to the lamp and pulled the bag open. Inside, something sparkled. Holding her breath, Susanna reached into the soft velvet and pulled out a diamond-and-emerald necklace.

She stared at the piece for a full minute. If the jewels were more than glass and paste, the necklace was worth a fortune.

She held the bauble to the light. That was no paste.

Had the thief stolen it?

Of course he had. And now she'd stolen it from him. What would she do with it? She couldn't keep it. She might go to gaol for theft.

She'd hide it. She'd do them both a favor if she hid it. She would return it to the thief when he'd fulfilled his part of their bargain. All she required was escort to Vauxhall. It was foolish to think that anything there might give her some clue about her mother's past, but neither could she discount her mother's stern objection to her going. What didn't her mother want Susanna to see?

Thugs? Ruffians? Undesirables?

Well, Susanna had dealt with one of those downstairs, and she'd held her own. She couldn't afford to let her guard down though. Marlowe's friend was the most terrifying man she'd ever met. He made no secret of the fact that he was not a gentleman. His language was deplorable, and he'd tried to reach down her bodice!

Which reminded her of the need to change her clothing. She peered about her bedroom and decided to secret the little jewelry bag in her dressing table, in the same box where she kept her own jewels. No one would have reason to look there, as she didn't have anything of real value.

When that was done, she struggled out of her gown. She would have called her maid, but Maggie would ask questions. Susanna did not want to have to explain or make up a lie.

When she'd finally stripped to her underthings, she pawed through her gowns. She wanted to wear something that made her look older and more sophisticated. She felt like a green girl around the thief. She'd always thought she'd find men like him disgusting. Their manners were coarse and their bathing habits infrequent, but this Gideon was rather handsome, except for the wicked scar slicing his temple and eyebrow. She'd managed a good look at it when he was near the light. She might have touched it then if she hadn't been surprised by his pleasant scent—sandalwood and the night air and…

Freedom.

Maybe his eyes were what drew her. She'd never known anyone with such beautiful green eyes. She'd looked at his eyes and thought of emerald valleys and verdant woods. Could a truly evil man have eyes that beautiful?

She'd be safe with him. They'd go to Vauxhall Gardens tonight, and she'd be home in the morning. Her mother would never know her daughter had been away.

Susanna chose a deep pink gown to wear. She didn't have red. Her mother would not allow her so much as a russet gown, so this vibrant shade of pink was the most audacious she could manage. The neckline was modest for a ball gown, but the back plunged, which always made her feel daring. She was out of breath by the time she'd pinned all the fabric into place and pulled on her long, white gloves.

This dressing oneself was exhausting. She glanced at the clock. It had taken her almost a half hour. Gideon was probably furious.

Susanna grasped the candlestick again and hurried from her room, tiptoeing past her mother's chamber and down the stairs. She opened the door to the library soundlessly and closed it behind her. That was when she heard the growling. She turned and gasped at the sight of Gideon on the rug with a large brownish-black dog standing over him.

"What is this?"

The dog watched her, baring his teeth and deepening his growl. Susanna pushed her hands onto her hips. "Stop that."

The dog whimpered and quieted. She cut a look at the thief. Even his dog had bad manners.

"Why are you lying on the floor? This is no time for playing."

"I'm not playing," he said, his voice sounding tense and strained.

The dog growled again, and Gideon went silent.

"You should teach your dog some manners."

He muttered something, but she couldn't hear him over the dog's growling. "Sit," she ordered the dog. "Hush."

Obediently, it sat and stopped its noise.

"How are you doing that?" the thief asked, backing away from the dog.

"Doing what?"

"Controlling that dog. If you hadn't come in when

you did, it would have ripped my throat out." He moved to stand beside her, keeping his distance from the animal.

Susanna cringed at the image that statement produced in her mind. "Then this isn't your dog?"

"*No*, I already told you that. It started chasing me tonight and must have followed me here. It doesn't like me."

He sounded so hurt, so genuinely shocked, that she almost laughed. She would have laughed if it hadn't occurred to her that a strange dog was sitting just a few feet away from her. She'd always wanted a dog, but her mother had refused to allow her even that much companionship. Perhaps this was her chance to have the pet she'd always wanted.

"It's probably hungry," she said, moving closer to the animal.

Gideon grabbed her shoulder and pulled her back. "Don't get too close."

"It won't hurt me," she said, shrugging his hand off, although his skin was surprisingly warm. "Will you, puppy?" she asked. "Good puppy. Sweet dog."

The dog thumped its tail.

"We should find it something to eat."

"We should find a pistol and shoot it."

She gave him a shocked look. "Do not be ridiculous. I would not kill a dog."

"Yes, *I'm* the daft one here."

She sidled closer to the animal and held out her hand for it to smell. The dog sniffed and then licked her hand. Susanna laughed and patted the dog's head. The dog leaned into her touch, practically knocking her back in its enthusiasm.

"What a good dog you are," she said, scratching behind its ears. It really was filthy. Her gloved hand came away lightly dusted with grime. "I don't have time to fetch you anything to eat now, but we'll get you something soon."

"We're not taking that thing with us," Gideon protested.

"Well, we can't leave it here." She peered down, glancing at the dog's underside. Her cheeks flushed a bit pink, but she had wanted to know. "I mean to say, we can't leave *her* here. Do you think she has a name?"

"Fuck me," he muttered. "Now she'll name it."

Susanna's cheeks heated, and she pretended she hadn't heard his foul words. She scratched the dog under her chin. "How about Beauty?"

The dog cocked its head to the side, indicating either she liked the petting or she liked the name. Susanna chose to believe the latter. "You like that, do you? Then Beauty it is."

"What did I do to deserve this?" Gideon muttered.

Susanna gave him an arch look over her shoulder. "I'm sure you have committed all sorts of unpardonable sins, not the least of which was stealing that necklace."

"*You took it out of the bag?*"

"Yes." She nodded briskly. "And I hid it. You'll never find it, and I won't give it back until you take me to Vauxhall Gardens and return me safely."

He squinted at her. "It's in your jewelry box, isn't it?"

"Stop doing that!"

"You can't leave it here. Someone might find it."

"Nonsense. It's perfectly hidden in…in its hiding spot."

He pointed a threatening finger at her. Beauty growled again, and Gideon held up his hand.

"I'm not going without the necklace."

"Why not? So you can steal it back and leave me to fend for myself?"

He had the gall to look astonished and offended, but his response was just a moment too late.

"Leave you? I would never—"

"I don't believe you, and I certainly don't trust you."

He spread his arms wide. "I understand completely. Clearly, I'm not the best person to take you to Vauxhall. Give me the necklace, and we'll go our separate ways. You can even keep the dog. In fact, I insist you keep it."

"*Her*, and we will not go our separate ways. If you want that necklace back, you'd better take me to Vauxhall Gardens."

Beauty yipped her agreement.

Susanna glanced at the door and then at the open window. She could hardly lead a man, a dog, and herself out of the house undetected. Surely a footman was about and would inquire as to her actions. Hopefully, none of the servants had heard the barking or, if they had, assumed it wasn't coming from inside the house.

She started for the window, and Beauty followed. "We'll have to go this way," she said. She'd never climbed out of a window before, but it seemed the only recourse. She peered down at the ground. It wasn't far. They were already situated on the ground floor.

"I really think we should discuss this."

Susanna felt the sultry breeze in her hair and wondered if she did indeed need her wrap. Of course, the weather might change in an instant. She might have been better served by wearing her pelisse, but it was too late to go back and fetch it now. "You go first," she told Gideon.

"And if I insist ladies go first?"

She lifted the candlestick and caught sight of the dog. "Beauty wouldn't like that."

He didn't look worried she'd hit him with the candlestick again, but he clearly didn't want the dog to attack—she could see that much in the glare he tossed her before marching to the window and climbing nimbly through. She tried to observe how he accomplished the task, but he moved too quickly. She was left staring down at him and then trying to figure out how to get the candlestick and herself through the window. When she'd turned this way and that, Gideon sighed and said, "Tonight, Strawberry."

She stiffened. Had that been a reference to her hair color? "What did you call me?"

"Put one leg through and then the other."

"But you'll see my ankle."

He flashed her a grin. "Your calf too, I hope."

"A gentleman would never look."

"Too bad I'm not a gentleman."

Leaving the candlestick balanced on the sill, she moved sideways and awkwardly lifted one leg over the casement. Her dress rode up her leg, but she tried to pretend he wasn't looking at her exposed flesh. She held onto the casement and then wondered how she was supposed to pull the other leg over without falling. She lifted her foot from the floor, but then she wobbled, and she had to clutch the window even tighter with her hands.

"You won't fall," he told her, sounding bored.

"Swing your leg over and jump down. This would be much easier if you weren't wearing that ridiculous dress."

She couldn't move. It was mortifying, really, because she was such a coward. "I…"

"Do it."

"I can't!"

"Then give me the necklace and stay here."

"No." She straightened her shoulders as much as possible in the uncomfortable position.

"You said yourself that you can't do it. This is nothing compared to the rest of the night."

She didn't know what he meant by that, and she didn't want to know.

"You can't do it. You can't—"

In one swift motion, she swung her leg over and hopped down. She might have fallen forward, but he caught her in his arms. She fell against his chest—his broad, muscled chest. She inhaled sharply and looked up and into his face.

"Well done, Strawberry."

He set her down. Her legs trembled, and her breath hitched in and out. She wasn't certain what panicked her more—jumping out the window or being held by Gideon.

A yip sounded, and Beauty jumped neatly beside her.

Susanna patted her, grateful for the reason to keep her flushed face down. "Good job."

"Let's go, Strawberry!" Gideon called.

She grabbed the candlestick from the sill, and with a last look back at the darkened windows of her home, she followed him into the even darker night.

Four

GIDEON TOOK HOLD OF ONE OF HER WRISTS AND hauled her away from the town house. He kept to the shadows, moving quickly. Beezle's cronies could be anywhere, even in Mayfair. They'd cut across St. James's and reach Vauxhall by way of ferry. Not as direct a route as taking the new Vauxhall Bridge, but he had an aversion to Tothill Fields. The country made him nervous.

"Ouch!"

Strawberry stumbled, and he had to slow. Again. The gentry mort wore a silky, pink ball gown and long, white gloves. Where the hell did she think she was going?

Her pretty little pink slippers had peeked from her skirts when she'd climbed out the window. Those were the problem. Footwear not meant to be walked in. What the devil would these nobs think of next?

They'd made it as far as Berkeley Square, which was to say they'd gotten nowhere at all. But Strawberry pulled her wrist free and grabbed hold of a tree, steadying herself. She lifted her foot, presumably to feel the bottom of her slipper. The dog was still following them and found another tree to do its business.

Gideon kept watch on the street and park impatiently. By nob standards, the night was far from over. Carriages with bright lamps and glittering gilt paint on the doors clattered past them. He'd yet to spot anyone else on foot. Not everyone out tonight wanted to be seen.

"How much farther to your conveyance?" she asked.

"What?"

Her head jerked up. No way could she see anything in the dark, but she had her left foot raised for inspection. "Hasn't anyone ever told you it is rude to answer *what*? The correct phrase is either *pardon* or *excuse me*."

She was serious. She thought she could stand there and lecture him on asking for *pardons* and prattle on about *conveyances*.

He pinned her to the tree with a hand on her shoulder. She staggered, regained her balance, then gasped with fear. He could move quickly when he needed.

The buffer growled, and Gideon growled back.

"Listen, Strawberry." He bent close to her pretty face and those large brown eyes. "I don't give a damn about your rules. I'm in this for the goddamn necklace, not your lessons on…deportment."

Her body flinched in surprise. He had a few surprises left.

"Your language is deplorable. I must assume since you know words like *deportment*, you use profanities intentionally."

"Assume whatever the hell you want."

She made a sound of complete and utter disgust. He knew the feeling. "Take me to the conveyance. I want this night over forthwith."

God save him.

"I don't *forthwith* have a conveyance."

"What?"

He smirked. "You mean *pardon*?"

Her lips thinned. "Surely you have a dray of some sort."

"No."

"A pony cart?"

Silence was answer enough. A breeze wafted past them, and the scent of something sweet and feminine tickled his nose.

Her.

Their bodies were close, his arms trapping her within reach. His fingers itched to touch the swath of pale shoulder revealed when the flimsy garment she clutched around her slipped. He'd never touched a woman like her, all clean and pale and sweet-smelling.

"If you have no conveyance of any sort, how do you propose we travel to Vauxhall Gardens?"

"I didn't propose we travel anywhere."

"Semantics." She ducked under his arm and moved away. The dog was immediately at her side. Gideon felt the loss of her heat and scent keenly, and propped his shoulder on the tree lest he yank her back.

She patted the dog's head. "We will have to engage a hack to take us to…or how does one reach Vauxhall Gardens?"

"By bridge or ferry. Since we don't have a rattler, we go by ferry. They can be hired at either Whitehall or Westminster Stairs."

She began walking—in the wrong direction. After a half-dozen steps, she realized he wasn't following her. "Come on then."

"Where are you going? The river is that way." He jerked his head south.

A look of chagrin passed over her face. "The hackney driver will know where it is." She pointed along a dark street. "We should be able to engage one at Old Bond Street."

"How much blunt you got?"

Her brows came together. "Blunt?"

"Chink." He rubbed his thumb and forefinger together. "Yellow boys. Shillings."

"None." Her fingers curled into the dog's matted fur.

"Of course you don't." He stuck his hands in his pockets and sauntered closer to her. "You've probably *never* paid for anything yourself."

"That's not true." She ducked her head, pretending to look at the dog. If Gideon taught her nothing else, he would teach her how to lie convincingly.

"I have a secret." He leaned close, whispered the words beside her ear.

Her shoulder came up protectively, and she gave him a sideways look, her lashes lowered.

"I don't have any blunt either."

That wasn't true. He had a few shillings, enough to pay for a boat to Vauxhall, but not enough to pay for a hack, a boat, *and* the entry ticket.

Not that he planned to buy a ticket.

Her head jerked up, and the dog gave a warning bark. "What will we do? We need money."

He shrugged his shoulders, dug his hands deeper into his pockets. "I know somewhere we might find a diamond necklace. I could fence that. We'd have more blunt than we need."

And he'd be rid of her.

"No."

He gazed off into the distance, pretending to think. He'd give her time to realize his way was the only way.

"We'll have to walk then." He made a point of looking down at her hem. The pink material was ornamented by lace and fabric flowers. It was the most impractical gown he'd ever seen.

And he wanted to touch it, touch her warm skin underneath it—more than he cared to admit.

"I can't walk." She was nothing if not predictable. "My slippers already have a hole."

"Nothing for it then." He grasped her wrist, ignoring the dog's growl. "We fetch the necklace."

He didn't know how she managed to dig her slippery heels in, but she did. He couldn't tug harder without hurting her or without the buffer attacking. He rounded on her. "This was your plan, Strawberry. How did you expect to make it to Vauxhall Gardens without blunt or shoes?"

She didn't answer, but her eyes burned into him. "I'm going. With or without you."

She gave him her back and walked away. Actually, she hobbled. A rock must have dug into her foot. It was probably as new and uncallused as a baby's skin. He let her walk a half-dozen steps, gave her time to think it through, but when he expected her to turn back, she kept hobbling.

Foolish mort would be dead within the hour if she went alone.

He shrugged. That wasn't his problem. *She* wasn't his problem. He was a housebreaker. He could go back to the town house, crack it, and steal his necklace back. That was exactly what he should do.

But damn it if he could manage to walk away from her. It was like steering a toddling child into the middle of Piccadilly Street. And then there was Marlowe. Strawberry was Marlowe's relation now. Gideon had few he called friends, and even fewer friends he actually *liked*. Marlowe was one of those.

Strawberry was Marlowe's, and that made her his by default.

Damn.

He caught up to her in four long strides. She gave him that sidelong look again and continued walking. He looked straight ahead, slowing his pace to match hers.

"We need shoes or blunt or both," he said.

"You needn't trouble yourself about my slippers. I will make do."

He laughed. Now the princess pretended she wasn't pampered and spoiled. Let her do so when his neck wasn't in the noose.

"I don't think so. You're already limping, and I'm not about to carry you across London. Even if I could manage that, we'll have to pay passage on a boat and for entry to Vauxhall." He might manage to sneak into the pleasure gardens, but he wouldn't make it across the river without paying. He had no desire to go for a swim in the murky water of the Thames.

But perhaps he need never make it as far as the river.

"I won't go home. Not yet."

Not until she was good and frightened. Then she'd race him home and throw the necklace at his feet.

"Then we have no choice. Find me a bubble."

She halted. "I beg your pardon."

"That's what we call the swell whose pocket we'll pick."

Her face reddened with a mixture of shock and horror. "I will not be a party to theft!"

He folded his arms tightly over his chest. "You stole my necklace."

"It's not your—that's not the point! I won't stoop to thievery."

He let those words sink in until her face reddened further.

"I mean…I didn't intend to insult you." She tugged at her wrap, pulling it like a shield around her.

"We can't go back to your town house for blunt, and we can't do the trick. Do I have that about right, princess?"

"I'm not a princess."

Right. And he wasn't a thief.

"You will simply have to find another way to obtain the funds we need." She sniffed.

Of course he would because Princess Strawberry wasn't about to dirty her fingers. He'd been counting on it.

"There's one last option."

The hands fidgeting with the fringe on her wrap stilled, and she gave him her full attention. Easier to hook than a hungry fish. Or so he thought. He'd never been fishing. An oversight he planned to rectify when he was finally away from London and free from the life of Gideon Harrow.

"We see a crony of mine."

She pulled the wrap to cover her throat. "What sort of…of crony?"

"The sort who can help a man out when he needs shoes and blunt."

"Can we trust him?"

Of course they couldn't trust him. Gideon didn't trust anyone. Strawberry, on the other hand, was far too trusting. Else she wouldn't be away from her cozy, safe home with him.

"Trust him?" Gideon spread his arms. "I'd trust him with my life."

The dog woofed, and Gideon gave it a quelling look. Strawberry glanced at her too. "You'll keep us safe, won't you, Beauty?"

The dog wagged its tail.

"Shall we?" He made the sweeping bow he'd seen the rum dukes do a time or two. "This way, madam."

She followed like a little lamb.

The buffer whined but stood rooted in place. "Come, Beauty!" Strawberry called.

With a last plaintive whine, the dog followed.

∽

Walking the streets of London at night was a vastly different experience from flying along them in a coach and four. For one thing, the city stank. Unwashed bodies, refuse, horse manure, and the stagnant heat of summer combined to make her gag.

The thief laughed at her when she covered her nose with her silk, lavender-scented handkerchief.

"You think this is bad? Just you wait, Strawberry."

His words filled her with a mixture of dread and excitement. The dread she understood. The dread was the emotion she ought to feel. The excitement was all wrong. Her mother would have been appalled—which only made Susanna want to revel in the adventure even more.

She'd never have a chance at another adventure like this again. Soon she'd be leg-shackled to some stuffy gentleman or elderly lord. She'd spend her days embroidering and receiving callers who wanted to chat about the weather or the latest fashions.

Susanna enjoyed fashion and weather as much as anyone, but there must be more to life. The years stretched before her like an infinite carpet with an unvarying pattern. This foray into disobedience and risk began and ended her life.

Surprising how much she was enjoying this. The handsome rogue was not at all what she'd expected when she'd heard Marlowe speak of her life in Seven Dials. Oh, he was vulgar and ill-mannered, but those eyes and that chest…

When he'd pinned her to the tree, she hadn't been able to take a deep breath, partly out of fear and partly because he'd stood so close. He'd *touched* her. Without permission.

The crowds about her thickened, and she clutched her wrap tightly, brandishing her candlestick.

"Where are we?" she asked, grateful for the thief on one side and Beauty on the other. Hard-eyed women and thin children watched her from dirty doorways.

Rambunctious men turned to gawk and whistle when she passed. The thief had been right about the gown. She should have worn a sack.

"You never been to St. Giles?" he asked. "Little rookery just on the east side of Mayfair, and I warrant this is the first you've seen of your neighbors."

"Are you certain it's safe to be here?"

"Safe? No. And if you keep waving that silk wipe in front of your nose, someone will snatch it and might decide to take you with it."

She shoved the handkerchief back into her glove. The fingers of the once-pristine gloves were black from the dog and whatever else she'd touched. Apparently, there was a market for handkerchiefs, so she'd better keep her gloves close to her as well.

"This is it," the thief said, stopping abruptly in front of a battered wooden door covered with pamphlets and advertisements for miracle tonics. The owner must not have cared enough to remove them. The thief rapped on the door then glanced back at her over his shoulder. A fire burned nearby, encircled by a group of men who roasted meat on the flame. In the red glow, the thief's scar looked painfully angry. His eyes glittered like a cat's.

"Let me talk," he said.

She nodded, wrapping her fingers in the warm fur at the dog's neck. Her throat was dry, and her feet throbbed. The thin slipper soles hadn't protected her tender heels or arches from sharp stones. The slippers had been a miscalculation.

She looked at the thief. Perhaps he'd been a miscalculation as well.

The door creaked open, and one pale blue eye blinked at them.

"Gideon Harrow looking for Mr. Stryker."

Gideon. A Biblical name. Had his parents—he *did* have parents, didn't he?—been devout Christians? Methodists, perhaps. Her own mother attended church only when compelled and spoke of Methodists as though they were the devil incarnate.

"'Arrow? What do ye want?"

Susanna held her breath. She'd expected a welcome of some sort. Her hand burrowed deeper into Beauty's fur. The dog seemed to sense trouble, but as yet no low hum of warning rose in her throat.

"Just open the jigger, Stryker. I have a lady with me." Gideon used his boot to shove the door wider. A gaunt face surrounded by white hair and fuzzed with white bristles stared out at her. Another watery eye fastened on her.

"So ye do." Stryker's mouth turned down at the corners. "Ye sure you want to bring 'er in 'ere?"

"No choice." Gideon shouldered his way inside. "Strawberry?" He jerked his hand at her impatiently.

Susanna lifted one foot, rested it on the first of the three steps leading to the door. Beyond this Stryker, all was darkness. She cut a glance over her shoulder, where the men at the fire near the street watched her with predatory gazes.

"In or out, Strawberry? I'd suggest in, but you can take your chances with them if you want."

Beauty growled at the men behind her, and Susanna patted her head. She tucked her candlestick under her arm, lifted her skirts, and climbed the rest of the steps. Stryker's pale eyes shifted to the dog. "That thing stays outside."

"No." Susanna pulled Beauty closer.

Gideon closed his eyes as though in pain. "Strawberry, leave the mongrel on the stoop."

Wordlessly, Susanna shook her head. Where she went, Beauty followed.

"I'm not having that buffer in me place," Stryker said. "It's got fleas."

"Then it should be right at home," Gideon mumbled.

"Beauty doesn't have fleas!" Susanna argued, shocked at the vehemence in her voice. "I admit she needs a bath, but I haven't seen her scratch once."

Beauty jerked, craned her neck, and bit at her hindquarters. Susanna pressed her lips together and, with her eyes, dared the men to argue with her.

"The dog stays in the entry," Gideon negotiated. "We'll only be a moment."

Stryker emitted a growl of his own and jerked his chin. Gideon moved into the darkness, and Susanna shuffled after, keeping Beauty's warm body against her thigh.

The door closed behind her, and Stryker snapped lock after lock into place. He held a tallow candle in one hand and pointed a bony finger from the other hand at Beauty. "Down."

Beauty lowered her haunches and settled comfortably against the door.

"Where's your gang?" Gideon asked.

"Where else?" Stryker asked with a jerk of his shoulder. "Kitchen." He stroked the fuzz on his chin and narrowed his watery eyes. "Where'd you find her?"

"Long story."

"I've got time."

"I don't."

Gideon lifted the hem of her skirt, and Susanna slapped his hand away.

"What do you think you're doing?"

"Showing him your shoes."

"Them's shoes?" Stryker asked. He shook his head. "Useless."

Susanna's back straightened. The nerve of these men!

"That's why we want to trade them. She needs a solid pair of boots. Boots that fit so she can walk."

Stryker scrubbed his cheeks. "Trade 'em? What do I want with 'em slippers? No one in 'er right mind would buy 'em."

Susanna gasped. "I'll have you know these slippers were handmade by Madam Durand. If you know anything of fashion, which you obviously do not, you would know she's one of the finest modistes in London."

"Mod—what?" Stryker's face had scrunched into a fuzzy, wrinkled oval.

"Stryker." Gideon wrapped an arm around the other man's bony shoulders. "Those slippers are silk."

They were actually satin, but Susanna didn't correct him.

Gideon patted the other man familiarly. "The sole is the finest kid leather."

Susanna saw what he was about now, and slid a slipper out from under her hem so the pretty pink satin was visible. She was loathe to part with the slippers. They matched the gown perfectly, but neither could she traipse across London in them.

"The ribbons are in perfect condition," she added. "Not frayed or wrinkled." She had no idea if that was true. They'd been in perfect condition when she'd tied them on. "A lady would pay…" She had no idea what someone would pay for slippers like these. She'd never even seen the bill. "…would pay money for these."

Stryker stared at the slippers and stroked his jaw. "Problem is we don't 'ave many *ladies* round 'ere."

"Plenty of molls." Gideon said something low and quiet near the man's ear, and Stryker laughed.

Susanna's face grew hot. She didn't know anything about molls or the sorts of things men whispered when women were not present. Her ignorance now reminded her of when she'd been a child in the country, watching her brothers tromp through meadows while she had to stay close to home.

Stryker opened his bony hand. "Let me 'ave 'em."

Susanna waited for Gideon to nod. When he did, she looked for a chair to sit upon. "Is there somewhere I might sit to remove these?"

"Might as well come into the kitchen." Stryker slid deeper into the dark entry. "Ye can wait there while I find real shoes."

Gideon didn't move, and Susanna waited beside him. She didn't know what waited in the kitchen for her, and she dared not find out without Gideon beside her. When her legs trembled and wobbled, she reminded herself Gideon knew Marlowe. Marlowe would never allow anything to happen to her. Maybe Marlowe had sent Gideon. Before Marlowe had married Dane, she'd lost a wager and promised Susanna an adventure.

So far, this had been an adventure.

"Who's down there?" Gideon asked.

"The usual." Stryker's voice came from the murky blackness.

"Maybe I'd better wait here then."

Susanna gave him a sharp look. Did this Gideon have so many enemies?

"Coward," the voice in the darkness hissed. "If I know Gideon 'Arrow, ye want more than a pair of shoes. Better go down if you think to swindle me out of the rest."

"I never swindle," Gideon said, looking very much like offended royalty.

"Right."

Susanna heard a shuffling sound. Somehow she knew Stryker was gone. She stared into the black corridor then turned in a circle to study the entry. Not a chair in sight. She might be able to hold one wall and balance to remove the slippers, but it wouldn't be very ladylike.

Her throat was still dry. She desperately wanted a splash of tea.

"You have enemies in the kitchen?" she asked.

"I have enemies everywhere. You?" His green eyes assessed her with an unfamiliar look. Cynicism?

"None that I know of."

"Doesn't surprise me. You haven't lived enough life to make any enemies."

Susanna was unexpectedly offended by the remark. She couldn't have said why. It seemed like not having enemies should be a good thing, but Gideon acted as though it, once again, proved her immaturity.

He moved around the entryway, peering into the adjoining room, looking for God knew what. How he could see anything was beyond her. The place had no lamps or candles. Even Stryker's tallow candle emitted only a weak, pale light.

"I don't want to live a life that will make enemies."

"That's a sad fact." He moved from one corner to the next, inspecting the empty room. "The only people who don't have enemies are the ones who don't have any opinions. The ones who duck their heads and close their mouths to ensure they don't offend anyone. Them's the real cowards."

Susanna did not think she'd ever been more offended in her life. She gawked at him with her mouth hanging open. Beauty growled briefly.

Susanna crossed her arms. "If I'm the coward, why are we hiding up here?"

He paused in his search and crossed to her. "You want to see why we're *hiding* up here?"

When he put it that way, she didn't want to see at all. She almost shook her head no, but he'd only look down on her more. And she'd had quite enough of that.

"Take me to the kitchens," she said firmly. "Unless you're too afraid." *Please, please be too afraid.*

Gideon took her gloved hand and pulled her into the blackness.

❧

The moment he tugged her into the darkness, he regretted it. He'd never known a woman so innocent of the world. She was right to be frightened. She'd be even more frightened if she knew how completely vulnerable she actually was. She'd see now, when he took her to the kitchen. He'd protect her as best as he was able, but she'd wanted this adventure. Better before they went on that she knew the risks.

If she took one look at those risks and decided to run home, then his night was that much shorter.

He negotiated the dark floor of the house, leading her toward the steps down to the kitchen more from memory than sight. His eyes had adjusted to the darkness now, but the house was still damn dark.

The first sounds of the men below floated up from the kitchen, and her fingers tightened on his hand. Gideon pushed down the urge to squeeze her hand back in reassurance. He wanted her afraid, wanted her to give up this quest to travel to Vauxhall Gardens.

"I'd like to be able to use this hand later," he muttered, shoving the tender part of him down. "Loosen your claws, madam."

"I beg your pardon." She attempted to snatch her hand away, but he wouldn't allow it.

Another part of him wanted to take her in his arms and tell her she was safe. That he'd protect her. He'd slit his own throat before he said something so asinine. He blamed her for his confusion. The gentry mort looked as though a strong breeze would blow her over. She was slim and delicate, her skin pale and almost translucent. She was a doll who belonged in a toy shop, not in St. Giles.

She even had doll-like eyes. They were as wide as an owl's but a thousand times more beautiful—deep brown with a thick fringe of lashes that swept down and over her cheek when she was embarrassed.

"Careful here," Gideon said when they reached the staircase. "Take the steps slowly."

Dim light filtered through the gloom at the bottom of the stairs. The men in the kitchen had heard them coming and quieted. Gideon glanced over his shoulder at her and almost lost his own damn footing. Her cheeks were pink, her eyes dark brown, and her hair...

It looked more copper than strawberry blond in the dim light. She'd pinned it—or one of her slaveys had—in some twisted, coiled, plaited arrangement on the back of her head. The mass had stayed firmly in place, much to his disappointment. He wondered what it would look like down around her shoulders. Was it straight or curly? Soft or coarse? If he buried his nose in the tresses, would the scent match the light, clean fragrance that had tantalized his senses when the breeze blew the right way?

He caught his balance again and led her to the bottom of the steps. The men would take one look at her and eat her alive.

Five

"WELL, IF IT ISN'T THE COVE WHAT BIT THE COLE."

Gideon bowed to the half-dozen men standing around a scarred wooden table with one broken chair. A low fire burned in a hearth, where a large black pot hung over the flame. A dozen dirty bowls littered the floor and table as well as several empty jugs of ale. In one corner, a cat tore at a bone, seeking any morsel of meat remaining.

Dim light from two dirty lamps danced on the kitchen walls in eerie patterns. The glow illuminated the men's faces, making them look more like devils than men.

Gideon's gut clenched. The company couldn't have been much worse—Rum, Lighter, Jonesy, Dab, Corker, and Mill. Six devils of the underworld.

"Gentlemen," Gideon said with forced gallantry. "A pleasure as always."

"Ye're right about that," Corker, a bald man with one long eyebrow, said. "This is a pleasure. You got a price on yer 'ead. Don't know what you filched from Beezle and don't care. Jonesy"—he jerked his head at the small, thin man who constantly rubbed his palms together—"fetch Beezle."

Gideon held up his hands. "Now wait just a moment, gentlemen. Is that any way to treat a crony?"

"Crony?" Mill spat a dark, foul juice from his scruffy jaw. "Ye're no crony to naught but yerself."

"That's not true. Mill, last year you and me, we cracked that house together."

"And you ran off with the clank and sneakers. That were the only cargo worth anything," Mill said in his high-pitched voice.

This was bad. Gideon did a quick reckoning. He'd crossed all of them in one way or another. "A misunderstanding," Gideon told Mill.

"What about that time we was cornered by them pigs?" Rum said. His low words slurred together. "I 'ad to dispatch 'em meself."

"Rum," Gideon said, his voice and expression one of deep pain. "It's not my fault you couldn't climb through that glaze. But look   "

"No, *you* look," Lighter said, taking a step toward him. Lighter was a giant of a man. He walked in a perpetual crouch to keep from banging his head on ceilings.

Gideon would have stepped back, but Strawberry was cowering behind him. He was cornered. Lighter's meaty hand wrapped around Gideon's throat and lifted him. Dangling a foot off the ground, Gideon knew the exact moment Lighter got a look at Strawberry. The murderous expression on his face was snuffed out like the flame of a candle.

"Who's this?" Lighter asked, voice full of wonder.

Gideon couldn't turn his neck, incapacitated as it was between Lighter's beefy fingers, but he rolled his eyes in Strawberry's general direction. Even holding that blasted glim-stick, she gave a curtsy worthy of the queen.

"Gentlemen," she said, sweeping those thick lashes down. "It's a pleasure to meet you."

Lighter's jaw dropped. Gideon shook his body in an attempt to dislodge his throat from Lighter's grip, but the man would not release him. The hiss of the lamps sounded loud in the sudden silence. Like Lighter, Mill's chops hung open. Corker and Jonesy looked like they'd hit their nobs too hard. Mill blinked rapidly, and Rum fumbled to straighten his dirty neckcloth.

Corker recovered first. "Who are you?"

Gideon didn't know her well enough to deduce whether or not she was nervous, but if she was, she gave no sign. She smiled brightly, and she had the sort of smile that spread sunlight into the darkest reaches of the flash house. "I'm Susanna."

"Susanna," Mill squeaked reverently.

"You with *him*?" Lighter shook Gideon by the throat, and the world went black for a moment.

"Through a mutual friend. Perhaps you know her? Marlowe?"

"We know 'er," Rum mumbled. "She sent Satin to City College."

"Newgate," Gideon explained with a wheeze.

"And good riddance." Jonesy leaned forward to spit then seemed to think better of it and swallowed loudly.

"I don't know anything about those circum-stances," Strawberry said, moving forward and into the light. Her pale, pink-tinged skin and shiny hair made her look like an angel beside the dirty, dirt-stained men. Mill took a step back.

"I do know Mr. Harrow has agreed to assist me with a personal matter, and"—she bestowed a kind smile on Lighter—"I would be so grateful if you would set him down. He looks as though he cannot breathe."

Lighter stared at her then opened his hand. Gideon thudded on the floor.

"Thank you. I can see you gentlemen are busy. As soon as Mr. Stryker returns with my shoes, I shall take Mr. Harrow and be out of your way."

"You can't 'ave 'Arrow," Corker said.

Gideon rubbed the aching shoulder on which he'd fallen and rose to his feet. What the devil was this? Why wasn't Strawberry weeping in a corner or on the floor in a swoon? Of the six devils, she'd charmed at least three. But not Corker. Corker would scare her right back to Mayfair. He wouldn't hurt her. None of these rooks were the sort to harm a woman, but neither were they cock robins.

"I beg your pardon?" Susanna said pleasantly.

"'E's got a price on his head. We're taking him to Beezle."

"Oh dear." She looked down, her expression one of grief. Gideon could have sworn tears shimmered in her eyes. If they were authentic, he'd run back to Beezle himself.

She looked up, her brown eyes pleading. "That is dire news indeed."

"Why?" Mill asked. Rum nodded.

"Because I suppose that means the end of my dream."

Jonesy pointed to Gideon "'*E's* your dream?"

She flicked a glance at him. "No, no. Of course not."

Gideon crossed his arms, offended for some reason. She'd said it almost as though she thought the idea he could be anyone's dream ridiculous. Gideon could have told her there were any number of ladies—well, not *ladies* exactly, but women—who dreamed about him.

"He offered to take me to Vauxhall Gardens. *That's* my dream. You see—" She made a show of looking about for a seat.

Dab, who'd stayed in the back until now, rushed forward with the broken chair. "'Ere, miss."

"Thank you." She smiled at him, and his face went as red as a hot coal.

Gideon stared. He'd never seen anyone with the power she had. Once, when he'd been young, he'd sneaked in to see a traveling circus. Gideon had never forgotten the snake charmer—the power the man had over the deadly snakes, the way he entranced them and coaxed the serpents into a terrible but beautiful dance.

Strawberry was a snake charmer, and he hadn't even known it.

Gideon should have been relieved. The six snakes in Stryker's kitchen were extremely venomous. Instead, he was annoyed. Gideon was starting to think he would actually have to take her to Vauxhall.

Strawberry had seated herself daintily in the wobbly chair. She acted as though it were a throne, arranging her skirts around it and folding her hands together over the glim-stick. "My dream is to go to Vauxhall Gardens. Have you ever been?"

Several of the men shook their heads. Corker and Lighter nodded.

"Was it magical?" she asked, looking first at Corker then Lighter.

"It's not magical," Gideon interrupted. "It's one more place for the swells to show off their finery."

"I thought it was magical," Lighter said.

His voice was wistful, and his eyes far away. Gideon wanted to snap his fingers in front of Lighter's face and say, *Wake up.*

"Did you?" Strawberry asked.

Instead of elbowing the giant in the gut, the other rooks nodded encouragement for Lighter to continue.

"There was music and dancing. The music was the most beautiful thing you ever 'eard. Sounded like angels singing."

"*Angels singing?*" Gideon laughed.

Mill shushed him with a deadly look.

"Go on," Strawberry said, appearing as though she hung on Lighter's every word. Dab, who had stayed by her side, looked at her as though he'd finally met his god.

"I 'eard that music," Lighter said, "and I forgot all about dancing. I stood all night and listened."

"You didn't dance?" Strawberry asked.

Lighter looked down at his giant frame. "Who'd dance with me?"

"A big strapping gentleman like yourself? Who *wouldn't* dance with you?"

Gideon groaned. "Don't you see what she's doing?"

"I see ye're interrupting 'er telling us about 'er dream," Rum said, his voice a grumble. "Shut yer gob."

"Thank you," she said. "I've never been to Vauxhall Gardens, and I am sure I would enjoy the music as much as Mr...." She looked up at Lighter.

"Lighter," he said.

"As Mr. Lighter did. But you see, I have a more important reason for venturing into the pleasure gardens."

"What's that?" Jonesy asked.

Strawberry looked at each of them in turn—Dab, Jonesy, Lighter, Mill, Rum, and the only one who appeared skeptical, Corker. "Love," she said simply.

"Love?" Corker asked.

"No," Gideon moaned. "Not you too."

"Have you ever been in love, Mr...."

"Corker," Dab supplied. He pointed to each man in turn and said their names. If she thought they were unusual, she didn't show it.

"Have you, Mr. Corker?"

"I fell in love at Vauxhall," Corker said.

Gideon groaned.

Strawberry clapped her hands together. "Really?"

"Love." Gideon snorted. "Some moll who led you down The Dark Walk for a shilling."

Corker slammed a meaty fist on the table. The wood whined and shivered.

"It weren't like that, Gid. She weren't no buttock." He looked down at his hands. "Least I don't think she was." He laced his fingers together then unlaced them, the sausage-sized digits moving almost gracefully. "She were beautiful and kind."

Gideon rolled his eyes. Dab moved like lightning, slamming Gideon against the wall. With a muffled curse, Gideon threw him off.

"Ain't you ever had a dream?" Dab asked.

"Yes," Gideon said. "My dream is to get the hell out of this place. The hell away from Beezle. I don't give a damn about music or *love*." He sneered at Corker.

"Don't mind 'im," Mill squeaked. "Everyone knows 'e was in love with Marlowe for years. She didn't love 'im back."

"Go to hell!" Gideon lunged for Mill, but Lighter extended an arm, effectively blocking Gideon's path.

"If yer dream is to go to Vauxhall, then you should go," Jonesy said. "I'll take you meself."

He stepped forward, standing before Strawberry like a knight from the old stories.

"No!" Gideon ducked under Lighter's arm and shoved Jonesy aside. "I'm taking her."

Dab advanced. "Not if she don't want you to."

"Miss Susanna, I'd be honored to take you," Rum muttered, approaching Strawberry.

"So would I," Mill added.

Gideon ran a hand through his hair in frustration. At this rate, half the rookery would be escorting Strawberry, and he'd never get the necklace back. Unless she went with Stryker's rooks. Then he could sneak back to her house, rifle it, and—

"Gentlemen," Strawberry said finally, interrupting the argument as to who was better suited to escort her. "I'm afraid I promised Mr. Harrow he could escort me."

"'Arrow has a price on his pate," Corker said, his single eyebrow lowering to shade his eyes. "We're taking 'im to Beezle."

"And you cannot take him to this Beezle tomorrow? I need him for one night, and then he's all yours." She held her hand out, as though serving him on a platter.

Corker's eyebrow lowered further.

"Please, Mr. Corker. You, of all people, understand about the importance of love. And this dream I have of finding love at Vauxhall Garden, it isn't for me. It's"—she gave them all a pleading look that would have put the actors at Drury Lane to shame—"it's for my mother."

"Your mother?" Mill squeaked.

"Yes." She stood. "I'm afraid I've been something of a disappointment to my mother. I thought if I could find the man she'd once loved, then perhaps she might love me. Just a little."

"How could you be a disappointment?" Lighter said, planting his legs apart like tree trunks. "You're perfect."

"If only that were true. I'm afraid I'm not as accomplished as she'd hoped I would be. And I can be a bit impulsive and—"

"Stubborn," Gideon added.

Dab smacked him. "Shut yer potato trap."

"It's true. I can be stubborn." She looked at her toes, still clad in the flimsy slippers.

Gideon blew out a breath. Where the hell was Stryker already?

"But if you will just give me the chance to make this one dream come true, then I will be so very grateful."

Lighter looked at Dab, who looked at Mill, who looked at Rum, who looked at Jonesy, who looked at Corker. Corker blew out a long, tortured breath. "Go. Live your dream."

"What dream?" Stryker said from the steps. "It better be a dream about going out tonight and filching me cargo we can fence, or you'll be dreaming in someone else's flash ken." He lifted a pair of mud-caked boots. "'Ere you go. They're not pretty, but they don't 'ave no holes."

Susanna blinked, clearly appalled at the idea of wearing the scuffed, grimy beater cases. She must have thought better of objecting, because she sat, daintily removed her slippers, and took the boots from Stryker's hand. She slid her feet into them as though they were encrusted with jewels.

She rose, wiggled her toes to check the fit, and handed the slippers to Stryker. "Thank you, sir."

"I ain't no sir. Unless I miss my guess, the two of you are hungry." He jerked a thumb at Mill. "Give them some of that stew."

Mill hurriedly filled two bowls and set them out with a crust of bread. Gideon didn't even glance at the food before shoveling it into his mouth.

Susanna balked at the brown glop. "Perhaps I will save this for Beauty."

"The dog?" Stryker asked. "Gave her some kitchen scraps already. Her belly is full."

"Oh." Susanna looked down at the stew. "Then I will eat…this." She closed her eyes and spooned the stew into her mouth. Gideon was impressed. The stew didn't taste half as bad as it looked, but he didn't think she'd be able to stomach it.

Finally, she pushed her bowl away. "My compliments to the cook."

Stryker grinned. "I'll tell Nancy. Bet she never

had a lady compliment her cooking before. Now, my men have work to do, and the two of you better be on yer way. Looks like rain." He glanced at Corker and then the rest of his men. "Unless one of you 'as an objection?"

Corker bared his teeth but didn't protest.

"Well then," Gideon said, pushing Strawberry in front of him and up the stairs. "We'll just be going."

"You'd better watch your back," Jonesy called. "We're coming for you tomorrow."

"I'll miss you too," Gideon called.

"You'll see me soon enough," Rum said with a growl.

"You have to catch me first."

Gideon pushed Strawberry through the door at the top of the stairs and took her hand. Outside, distant lightning lit the skies and threw jagged slashes of brightness into the dark house. Gideon used the light to pull Strawberry through the rooms and back to the door where the dog rose and nuzzled her hand.

Once on the stoop, Gideon heard the snick of the lock slide back into place.

The streets were all but empty of the men and women who'd been lolling about earlier. The distant rumble of thunder had driven most of them to seek shelter. Gideon could smell rain in the air, and the towering clouds billowing in the night sky meant a storm was coming. If they were fortunate, they would beat the weather to Vauxhall Gardens. If not, it would be a long, cold, wet night.

✌

"As…grateful as I am to possess these boots," Susanna began, "we have solved only half our dilemma." She pulled her wrap close around her shoulders. The breeze snapped at her skirts, and refuse blew about the streets as though pushed by an invisible hand. The skies to the west had a rather ominous green tint to them, and lightning spiked through the low-hanging clouds. Beauty hugged her leg, hiding her face in Susanna's skirts.

Gideon started down the steps without waiting for her. "You mean we still don't have any blunt."

"Yes."

He didn't seem inclined to wait, and she did not want to be left behind, so she hurried to catch up to him.

"I don't think that will be a problem." The wind whipped at his thin coat and snatched his words away so she could hear only half of them.

"Why not?" she asked, raising her voice to be heard over the rattle of debris and the wind rushing through her ears.

"Because I had no idea you had such talent."

"Talent?" She must have heard him wrong.

He turned, pausing in the middle of the street, and pointed toward Stryker's house. "What the hell was *that*?"

"I don't—"

"What you did at Stryker's, convincing six men they should protect you from me. God knows, you're not the one who needs protection. *You* filched *my* necklace."

"It's not yours. You…filched it from some poor soul."

"Not the point!" He jabbed a finger at her, and thunder rumbled in the sky. Susanna looked up. The lightning seemed to be closer now.

"The point, Strawberry, is we don't need coin. I have faith you can charm any man into giving us exactly what we want."

"If you are implying I would use my female charms to entice a man to do my bidding, you have sorely misjudged me, sir."

Gideon closed his eyes, and the stark planes of his face were lit by the storm in the sky. The image would have made an amazing sketch if she'd only had paper and pencil.

The first big plop of rain fell on her neck.

And shelter.

"Not those sorts of charms, Susanna. God knows you've probably never even been kissed."

She was so shocked at the statement, she didn't have a ready retort. It was true, but how did he know that? How did he know she wasn't a wanton woman? After all, she'd stood up to six large thugs, and she had the mighty Gideon Harrow doing her bidding as well.

Kissing a man was nothing to her. She could do anything.

"We'd better start moving," Gideon said. A flash of hope appeared in his eyes. "Unless you've had enough and want to go home?"

"Never."

"I knew you would say that." He stomped off, and she had to run to follow.

By the time she caught her breath, she was hope-lessly lost. He'd led her through a rabbit's warren of narrow streets and alleys, old buildings, and even a graveyard. The slow plop of rain had become a constant drizzle, and she was damp and cold.

She'd never admit it to the thief, but the thought of going home was growing rather appealing as the thunder grew louder and lightning flashed above them. Then again, she'd made it this far. Vauxhall Gardens couldn't be much farther, and then all of her questions would be answered.

Unless they weren't.

There was no guarantee she would learn anything of her mother's past at the pleasure gardens. In fact, it was entirely unlikely. Knowing that, she still could not convince herself to turn around. She had to make this journey, even if she gained nothing from it.

The next clap of thunder was so loud, she jumped and Beauty whined. The boom was punctuated by a sheet of rain, as though the heavens had been split wide, and an ocean of water drained out. Keeping her hand on Beauty's neck, she trudged after Gideon, barely able to make out his form in the blinding rain. The streets had already begun to fill with water, soaking her feet through the boots.

"We'd better go inside," Gideon yelled, "or we'll find ourselves floating away."

She nodded and looked about them. The shops were all closed for the night, but there was a public house across the way. Ladies were not supposed to enter public houses, especially not the sort that looked like that one, but she really had little choice. "There?" She pointed to the lighted window.

"No. It's a gin shop. Too many people who might recognize me."

"Exactly how many enemies do you have?"

"You don't want the answer to that. Come on." He grabbed her hand and pulled her through the ankle-deep water and toward a cluster of buildings. She was glad he held on to her. Between the heavy rain and the rush of water at her feet, she might have stumbled or lost her way. He steered her away from the larger items of refuse floating in the street—a log, a board, a dead animal of some sort.

"Beauty!" Susanna called, although the dog was right on her heels. "Stay close."

Gideon tried the door of the building, but it was locked. Susanna pushed her back against the frame, trying to find what scant protection she could from the storm. Beauty huddled beside her. Gideon uttered an oath and shoved at the door. It didn't budge.

"Can't you pick the lock?" she yelled.

"Not in this weather." Water sluiced down his face, and his dark hair fell over his forehead and against his cheeks. The hair covered the angry scar on his temple, but he looked more dangerous than handsome at the moment.

He stepped back, turned sideways, and rushed at the door, hitting it with a shoulder. The door shook, but the lock held fast. Gideon rubbed his shoulder and winced.

"Perhaps we should try another building."

"I didn't ask for your advice," he barked. Beauty yipped at him in warning, and Susanna gave the dog a pat of appreciation.

He moved back, farther this time, crouched, and ran full tilt. Susanna closed her eyes and felt the jarring impact when he slammed into the door. Wood creaked and popped, and she opened her eyes. The thief had shoved the upper part of the door inward. It wasn't a large opening, but if he could squeeze through, he might be able to open the door from the inside. He rotated his shoulder and studied the door. Only problem was, he wouldn't fit.

"Give me your foot," he said.

"What?"

"You're going in. Give me your foot. I'll boost you."

"I'm not going in! What if someone is in there?"

"Then say hello and tell them to open the goddamn door next time."

That was it. She'd had enough. "Do not blaspheme. If we ever needed God's assistance, the time is now."

"Sweetheart, God won't open that door for us. You will. Give me your foot."

She stared at him, the water pounding down on her head and running into her eyes. He stared right back.

"Fine."

He bent and cupped his hands to form a stirrup.

"You'd better not try and catch a glimpse of my ankle."

He slammed a hand against the door. "You think all of this is about peeking under your skirts? Woman, I don't give a farthing about what's under your skirts. It's nothing I haven't seen."

He cupped his hands again and shook them. Susanna shoved her foot into the stirrup, grateful the pouring rain obscured her pink face. She was making a fool of herself with him. She couldn't wait to reach Vauxhall and be done with him.

He hoisted her up, and she grabbed at the door to brace herself. First she dropped her candlestick through the opening. She heard it thud on the floor. With a jump, she pushed her body into the narrow, rectangular hole, wincing as the jagged wood snagged on her dress and tore against her shoulder.

If she'd known it would be like this, she would have given him the damn necklace the first time he'd asked.

And now he had *her* swearing!

"Wiggle through!" he yelled at her.

She was trying. Her hips seemed to be stuck in the opening. She might have wiggled more vigorously, but the wood dug into her skin through the thin gown. She didn't want to tear the material.

"I can't. My gown will rip. Help me down."

She wasn't certain what his answer was, but it sounded like, "The hell I will."

She felt his hands on her bottom and screamed in outrage.

Far from causing him to remove his hands, he pushed harder.

"Take your hands off me this instant!" she yelled. Her voice disappeared into a boom of thunder and the driving rain.

He pushed again, and the floor rushed up at her face. She thrust her hands out quickly, catching herself. Her forehead smacked the floor, despite her efforts, and she groaned in pain when her elbow struck. She rolled over and whimpered, tugging her torn gloves off, finger by finger.

She stared at the dark ceiling, her ears ringing, her head pounding. Her leg burned, though she would have expected her forehead to be the most damaged.

"Strawberry!"

She snarled. It was the thief. He'd pushed her through that opening and tried to kill her. Now he wanted her to open the door to him.

"Open the bloody door."

She wanted to tell him to open the bloody door himself, but she remembered Beauty was out there. She couldn't let the dog shiver in the rain, and she couldn't trust the thief to take care of the animal.

"Strawberry!" he bellowed.

"I heard you!" she bellowed back. Her mother would have fainted dead away had she heard her daughter. Susanna sounded like a fishwife.

With a groan, she rose and stumbled to the door. She felt the wooden surface with both hands until she found the thick bar across the center. No wonder the thief hadn't been able to break it down. He wouldn't have been able to pick this lock either.

She shoved at the wooden bar, but it didn't shift. She pushed up again, straining her muscles. Leaning her head against the door, Susanna blinked tears away. She would not cry. She'd faced six terrifying men in that kitchen just an hour before. She was strong. She didn't cry.

Her leg throbbed terribly, and she reached down and pressed a hand against it. Her hand came away slick with something thicker than water.

Blood.

No wonder it hurt so badly.

"Susanna?"

He'd used her name. He must have been quite concerned she would leave him out there. She would have too, if not for Beauty.

"There's a bar across the door," she called. "I'm trying to lift it."

"Use your shoulder for leverage," he answered. "It's probably stuck."

"Use my shoulder," she grumbled. Her shoulder hurt because he'd shoved her through the jagged opening, and she'd cut it on the splintered wood. But she bent down and situated her shoulder under the beam anyway. She pushed up, using her legs, ignoring the pain slicing through her shin. She blew out a breath, ready to give up, when the beam moved.

"I've got it!" she called, excitement pulsing through her.

She didn't feel the pain now as she pushed up and up, lifting the bar then catching it in her hands and tossing it on the ground. The door swung open, and a flash of lightning illuminated the shapes of Gideon and Beauty dripping in the downpour.

"I did it!" she said. Her teeth chattered as she spoke. The summer shower had brought cooler temperatures. She shivered and stumbled.

Gideon lunged forward, and he caught her in his arms. "What the bloody hell happened to you?"

"Nothing. I—"

She glanced down, saw the blood on her skirts, and swayed. Gideon's arms stayed around her, holding her up.

From somewhere she heard a dog bark, and then she was falling, falling, falling.

Six

"OH NO YOU DON'T."

Strawberry's eyes closed, and her limbs slackened. But he wasn't having it. Gideon didn't allow fainting. He carried her inside the building and lowered her against a wall, propping her upright. The rookeries always flooded with a hard rain, and anyone without lodging or who rented a room in a cellar would seek shelter.

The dog went to her and whined as it licked her face. He liked the mongrel a little better for that.

Gideon shoved the door closed and lowered the heavy bar over it. The splintered wood at the top left a gap. There wasn't much to do about that. But he wanted the outside door closed as much as possible to keep the rain—and any unwelcome visitors—out.

The dog was still whining, but in the darkness, Gideon could make out Strawberry's raised hand keeping the dog at arm's length to prevent any more licking.

"Almost lost you for a moment."

"The blood…" Her teeth chattered so much he had to lean close to understand her.

"I'm not used to seeing so much blood."

"Blood?" Gideon grabbed her arm and felt the chilled skin. The flesh was wet but not slick with blood. He knew the difference.

"Take your hands off me," she demanded.

"Where are you hurt?" He ignored the way her small hands pushed ineffectually at his larger ones. When he touched her leg, she stiffened and cried out. Gideon pushed layers of sodden silk out of the way until he touched the bare flesh above her ankle.

"Unhand me."

"Shut your gob for a minute."

The dog growled. Gideon growled back.

"And I was just starting to like you," he said.

Blood ran down her leg, thicker and heavier than the rainwater, but it might have been mixed with mud. He sure as hell hoped she wasn't bleeding as heavily as it seemed. What he wouldn't give for a candle or a lamp or a warm blanket.

Beneath his hands, she shivered violently, and Gideon cursed under his breath. This was another reason he didn't want to be saddled with this girl. She might be a fair-roe-buck, but she was the sort to catch a chill and roll over dead. Then his feet would dangle in the breeze for murder.

"Stay here," he told her. "I'll be back in a quarter of an hour."

"You're leaving me?" She sounded almost panicked.

"Can't bear to be without me, can you?"

"I'd be happy never to see you again!" she spat.

He was glad to hear the warmth in her voice. She had fight left in her.

"But you will. I'm for the gin shop. We need supplies."

"The gin shop! I thought you said you had too many enemies there."

"I do."

She started to argue further, but he was done listening. "Keep the dog beside you. I don't think anyone is fool enough to be out in this weather, but don't take chances."

"You can't leave me!"

He crossed to the door and lifted the damn bar again. The rain still poured down in sheets. More rain made no difference to his dripping clothes, but he pulled the collar of his coat up and over his head anyway. It might not keep him dry, but it would hide his face.

Gideon navigated his way through the flooding streets. Debris floated past him, everything from a child's doll to a broken bowl to a dresser drawer. In his zeal to avoid the trash threatening to knock him over, he almost missed the entrance to the gin shop. He doubled back, climbed the two short steps to the entrance, and stepped inside.

He almost preferred the muddy, rank streets. The smell of unwashed bodies, vomit, and gin struck him like a fist. He struck back, plowing forward with Herculean force of will. Keeping his collar up and his head down, Gideon made his way to the bar.

He didn't care for Blue Ruin. He'd drunk it often enough, especially when he'd given up on Marlowe, but he always regretted it in the morning. A sour stomach and a pounding head weren't worth a few hours' oblivion.

No one paid him much attention. He was one of two dozen wet, dirty men huddled inside. Some of the men had drunk so much gin, they were past caring. Gideon shoved one unconscious ragamuffin out of his way and placed a croker on the bar. It was all he had. He'd better get that necklace back. In the meantime, he'd steal what he couldn't buy.

The dash behind the bar slid his hand over the coins. "What?"

"Bottle of gin, slice of bread."

"This ain't no inn. Don't have no bread."

Gideon held his hand out. "Then I want my chink back."

The dash snorted. His jowls shook when he laughed. He jingled the coins in his fist. "I'll see what I can do."

He slammed a small bottle of gin on the bar, and Gideon rolled it between his palms, darting his gaze surreptitiously to his right.

Damn. Jack Gipson was at the table to Gideon's right. He owed Gipson money. Gideon ducked his chin into the coat collar and looked to the left.

Perfect. There was Dagget. The arch rogue of the Fleet Street Cubs hated Gideon almost as much as Gideon had hated Satin. It was an old dispute over territory—which the Covent Garden Cubs had won. Dagget had never forgotten, and his gang regularly abused Satin's boys when they had the chance. Of course, Satin was in the stone jug now, thanks to Marlowe. That left Gideon to spur Dagget's wrath.

Gideon looked past Dagget toward the steps leading to the upstairs rooms. He wanted light to get a look at Strawberry's wounds. The gin would warm her and the bread feed them, but he needed light. He could steal a lamp or a tinderbox, but both would be drenched and useless before he made it back to the vacant building. But if he could acquire a piece of hot coal, he could light a fire from the dry printed bills lining the floors of their temporary shelter.

Gideon had no idea if the shop had coal. Coal was a luxury in the rookeries, but the gin shop was doing brisk business. If he sidled up the steps—

"Here."

A brick thumped on the bar before him.

"What's that?" Gideon asked.

"Bread." The dash grabbed another bottle of gin and slid it to a man on the far side of the bar.

"Is it fresh?"

The dash's jowls jiggled right before he swiped a paw at Gideon. Once again, Gideon's quick reflexes saved him. He snatched the bread and jumped back, feeling the thick tips of the dash's fingers brush his chin. Gideon flashed the man a triumphant grin right before he stumbled over a large foot. Gideon sprawled on his arse, the bread clunking him in the cheek.

"That will leave a bruise," he muttered and looked up and into Dagget's ugly mug.

Dagget's bulbous eyes widened with pleasure, and his wide nostrils flared. "Gideon Harrow," Dagget said in his coarse, grainy voice. Rumor was Dagget had once escaped the noose, but not before it had all but crushed his throat. He certainly sounded like a man who'd been half-strangled to death.

"Well, well, well," Dagget snarled. "Look what the cat dragged in."

"It was a dog, actually," Gideon said, using his palms to back away in an imitation of a beached crab.

"Speaking of which, the pup is hungry. Have to go." He jumped up and arrowed for the stairs. He still needed that coal.

"Harrow!" Dagget hollered.

Gideon winced. Who would have thought the rogue could make so much noise?

"Harrow?" another voice chorused.

Gideon would have bet ten pounds, if he had it, the voice belonged to Jack Gipson. He didn't dare pause to look over his shoulder, because he could smell Dagget's foul breath on the back of his neck. Gideon bolted.

"You ain't allowed up there!" the dash called.

Gideon took the rest of the steps two at a time and shot into the first open door he found. He slammed the door shut, slid a rickety chair that wouldn't hold worth shit in front of it, and skidded into the next room. A large woman, naked but for her shoes, sat astride a man in a small bed in one corner. She rode him vigorously, sweat pouring down her back.

"Don't mind me," Gideon said.

The woman screamed and threw one of her shoes. Gideon ducked and slid toward the coal stove. The door in the adjoining room splintered as Gideon grabbed a white slip of fabric from the floor—the woman's cap—and used it to protect his hand as he reached inside for a piece of coal.

"Got it."

The other shoe hit him in the temple, and he stumbled back with a curse. Hand to his temple, Gideon shook off the pain and searched for an escape. Dagget blocked the door he'd come through, and the large naked woman yelled at him in front of the other door.

Gideon spun in a circle, attempting to locate a window, and finding none, began to plan how he would survive the beating. Dagget laughed and lifted his hands menacingly.

"Now, Dagget—" Gideon began.

The door behind the woman slammed open, and the dash shouldered his way inside.

"Jean!" the dash hollered upon seeing the naked woman. The dash lunged for the man in the—presumably his—bed, and the woman threw herself on her husband's back.

Gideon went for the door.

Dagget met him halfway. Gideon ducked to avoid the fist aimed at his nose and slammed the rocklike loaf into the man's breadbasket. Dagget doubled over, and Gideon shoved past him. He ran for the stairs, skidding to a stop on the middle step when he spotted Jack Gipson lounging at the bottom.

"I was betting you'd be back this way," Gipson said.

"Then you win the prize," Gideon said between shallow breaths.

"Prize? What prize?"

"Here!" Gideon tossed the cap holding the hot coals inside, and Gipson caught the bundle. With a scream, he tossed the cap from hand to hand then dropped it on the floor and ran into the rain to cool his reddened hands. Gideon jumped down the steps, lifted the cap by the strings, and plunged into the rain.

⁓

Gideon sheltered the cap from the rain as best as he could. He was blinded by the downpour as before, the winds were cold, and the thunder was closer than ever. The storm would persist tonight. They'd have to hole up in the building until the weather cleared, so he'd better make sure the coal stayed hot.

He zigzagged through the eddies and streams that now comprised the streets and finally ducked into the shelter. He'd no more than shook the rain off his face than the dog emitted a menacing growl.

"Don't come any closer!" Strawberry warned. "I am armed."

"With what?" Gideon asked. "A fan?"

"Gideon?" Her voice sounded hopeful, and when lightning crackled in the sky, he found her huddled in a corner with the glim-stick.

His old friend the glim-stick. His head still hurt from their first meeting, and now his face hurt from the moll's shoe. Hell of a night he was having.

"Yes, it's me, so call off the attack dog."

"Beauty. It's Gideon."

Gideon moved to shove the bar back down over the door and lock them both in—and others out. The damn dog knew who he was. It just didn't like him.

"I was afraid something had happened. You were gone an eternity."

"Met with some old cronies."

The next flash of lightning illuminated the room again. Gideon moved toward the back where the dilapidated remains of a staircase crumbled.

She huffed. "So you were carousing while I sat here in the dark and worried."

"Something like that." He bent and scooped up a stack of old pamphlets and newspapers.

"What are you doing?" Strawberry asked.

"Gathering material to burn."

A long silence ensued, and he filled his arms. Some of the bills were so old they'd disintegrate as soon as the coal touched them.

"But there's no fireplace. No stove."

Gideon dropped the papers in the center of the room. "Don't need one."

The strings of the cap hung from his wrist. He grasped the edges and turned it over so the coal fell into the pile of papers. For a long moment, nothing happened. Gideon crouched down and blew on the coal, encouraging a fire. Smoke wafted into his nostrils, making him cough, but he blew again, gently. One old paper began to smolder and then another. A small fire leaped from one of the papers, and Gideon cupped his hands around it and shoved another paper into it. He fed the fire like that until it was stronger, and then gathered a handful of more pamphlets. These he rolled into logs to make them last longer. He laid several on the hungry fire and stacked others nearby. He could feed the fire for an hour or so before he ran out of tinder.

He paused, took a breath, and pulled the gin from his coat. His gaze met Strawberry's across the flames. Lifting the bottle to his mouth, he took a sip, grimaced, and took another.

"You're drinking? At a time like this."

"Let me give you some advice, Strawberry," he said, his throat burning. "When a man brings you fire, drink, and food"—he tossed the brick-like loaf onto the ground—"say thank you and stubble it."

She pressed her lips together in what looked like a silent struggle. "Thank you," she finally said quietly. He toasted her with the bottle.

"You're welcome. Now, drink a little of this."

"No. I can smell that foul brew from here."

He shoved another paper log on the fire and moved to sit beside her, resting his back against a wall. "A sip won't kill you, and it might warm you up. Just a sip. I'll use the rest to clean your leg."

"You intend to pour that on my leg?"

He made a sound of acknowledgment. "Saw a doctor do that once. He said it cleans a wound better than water." He held the bottle to her. "Come on, Strawberry. Drink to your health."

She wrinkled her nose. "I can't!"

"Don't smell it. Drink it. Here."

He pinched her nose and held the bottle to her lips. She gave him a murderous look, which was less than effective when he held her nose, and sipped. Immediately, she attempted to spit it out. Gideon clamped a hand over her mouth.

"Swallow."

With fury in her eyes, she did. He released her mouth, and she coughed violently. "Eh! Awful man!"

"Give it a few moments. You'll feel warmer. Now, let me see your leg."

Her back went rigid. "I will not!"

He had the strong urge to down the rest of the gin and put himself out of this misery for a few hours.

"Strawberry," he said, trying for a patient tone, "the fire won't last all night. Let me see how badly you're hurt."

"I can't show you my legs."

The buffer yipped its agreement.

"I've seen legs before. Yours are nothing new."

She eyed him skeptically.

"Don't you think if I were planning to ravish you, I would have done it by now? Showing me your dirty, bloodstained leg won't throw me into a wild frenzy of lust."

She smiled at that.

"Oh, so you can smile." Gideon smiled back. "Was it the *wild frenzy of lust*? I thought that was a clever one."

She gave a short, breathy laugh. "You're not at all what I expected."

"Pull up your skirts," he said. Bet no man had ever said that to her before.

She closed her eyes and dragged her hem to her knee. Her stockings were shredded, and blood caked one shin from ankle to knee. She had a nasty scrape, as he'd expected.

What he hadn't expected was the hot flash of lust he felt when he saw her pale, undamaged leg. Yes, he had seen women's legs before, but he'd never seen any like these. They were the color of cream, and shapely, neither too plump nor too skinny. Her skin had a pinkish-gold tinge to it. The color might have been an effect of the fire, but Gideon didn't think so. Small ankles peeked from the ugly boots she wore. Their delicate bones were visible, and he had the strangest need to kiss her anklebone, to touch that fragile flesh and bone.

"Oh, dear Lord."

His gaze shot to her face, which had grown pale. Her lips trembled. "I can't look again. I think I shall faint."

"No swooning. No vapors." He shoved the gin bottle into her hands, forced it to her mouth.

Reluctantly, she sipped it. This time she swallowed without protest.

"It's not so bad," he said, taking one of her frilly underthings between his fingers and using it to wipe away some of the blood and dirt. She gasped.

"It will hurt more when I clean it. Better take one more drink and brace yourself."

"No." She shook her head. "Leave me alone."

Gideon raised his hands, the bottle in one hand glinting in the firelight. "That's your choice, but if infection sets in, who knows what might happen. I've seen cubs with cuts like this. After a few days, yellow-green stuff runs from the wound, and then it turns all black and falls off. Cubs lose legs and arms like that all the time. I think I saw one floating by on my way back."

"You're lying."

He cocked his head to the side. "It's your leg. A pretty one too."

She inhaled sharply. "You said you would not ogle me."

"No, I said I wouldn't ravish you. Now, am I pouring gin on the wound, or will you risk it turning black and rotting off?"

"Give me that bottle," she demanded.

He handed it over.

She took a long swallow, and Gideon had to yank it away from her mouth. "That's enough. I only have one bottle."

She was coughing so hard she probably didn't hear him. Finally, she looked up, hand to her throat. "Do it," she whispered.

"Are you su—?"

"Just do it!" Her voice was raspy but held a note of determination.

He placed one hand on her uninjured leg to hold her still, and raised the bottle with his other hand. He'd meant to pour the gin immediately, but the warm, silky flesh under his palm caught his attention. He glanced down to be certain he touched bare skin, not her gown.

His dark hand rested on her pale flesh, his palm wrapping almost all the way around her calf. How the hell did she have skin so soft? Even with the mud and the rainwater, he thought he could detect the slightest hint of flowers. Some sort of soap? Was it her gown? Her skin? He'd never known a woman who smelled like that, so sweet and clean.

"Gideon?"

"Oh, right." He lifted the bottle again and poured.

She screamed and kneed him in the jaw. He yelled and fell back, rubbing his jaw with one hand. "Bloody hell and back to bloody hell again!" His jaw hurt like one of the cubs had taken a poker to it. First his head, then his temple, now his chin.

"I am sorry." She reached for him, clutching his arm. "I am so sorry."

Gideon sat. "I'm fine." He shook her hands off him. He didn't want her sympathy. "I think we're even."

Her skirts had fallen over her legs again, and he gestured to the hem. "May I?"

She nodded. He lifted the hem again and examined his work. The leg was much cleaner now, and the wound free of most of the dirt and grime. He couldn't see well in the firelight, but it didn't appear to be a deep wound.

"Just a scratch," he told her, dropping her skirts.

"A *scratch*?"

Gideon drew back. His face couldn't withstand another hit. "A serious scratch."

"I hate you." She leaned back, resting her head against the wall of the building. Gideon tossed another paper log on the fire and forced his gaze to remain on the flames. It didn't help. He could see the curves of those shapely legs in his mind. His fingers tingled with the need to caress her impossibly soft skin.

"The feeling is mutual, I assure you." Except if he hated her, why did he want to see that leg again? She wasn't the sort of woman he usually found attractive. Not that he ever had cause to be in close contact with her sort before.

Marlowe was what Gideon considered his ideal. She had dark hair and striking blue eyes and a round, voluptuous body she'd been clever to conceal. Marlowe had been a cunning rook with a quick wit and more balls than most of the men he knew.

This girl…

Gideon glanced at Strawberry.

She was no Marlowe.

Strawberry was tall and thin. She had curves—he'd seen that well enough when he'd lifted the hem of her skirts—but the curves were gentle and sloping. Not like the rounded, generous curves he preferred on a woman. Her hair hung about her shoulders, half of it pinned and the rest damp and tangled across her back. She had red hair, not the bright red of the Scots or Irish, but a delicate blond with pale red infused throughout.

Or perhaps that was the fire playing tricks on his sight.

The fire could not deceive him as to the length or the thickness though. The locks must have fallen to her waist, at least, and they were so thick he could have fashioned a sturdy rope from them.

She opened her eyes. Gideon looked away quickly, a habit and not a necessary one, considering the unfocused quality of her usually clear gaze. She would be feeling the effects of the gin now. Maybe the gin was playing tricks on his mind too. Else why would he still be thinking about the silky length of leg under her skirt or what he might find if he lifted those skirts higher?

The dog nuzzled her hand, and she rolled her head to look down at the creature. Suddenly she straightened, looking as though she'd seen a rat. "Gideon!"

"Where is it?" he asked, looking around. Rats were nasty little buggers. He'd been bitten enough times to form a personal dislike.

"She's white. Underneath all that dirt and grime, she's white!"

It took him a moment to realize she spoke of the dog. Sure enough, the rain had washed some of the dirt away. He would have called her color more of a gray, but with the application of soap and another rinse, the dog's fur would have been white as snow. Gideon threw another paper log onto the fire.

"Guess she goes to prove appearances can be deceiving."

Strawberry cocked her head, another lock of hair falling over her shoulder, and gave him a long look. "My brother Brook always says not to judge based on appearances."

Gideon grunted. Brook Derring again—inspector, friend of the Bow Street Runners, and a master thief-taker. Gideon had no love for pigs, but when he'd had cause to work with Derring, the man had earned his trust.

That was not an easy feat.

"I suppose he'd know better than anyone. One too many men turned on him and tried to stab him in the back."

Strawberry shook her head. "That's not what he meant. At least, I don't think that's what he meant."

Her words slurred slightly, and she'd stopped hugging her arms. The gin had warmed her. The fire and the dog at her side helped too.

"Don't tell me the famous Sir Derring told you that underneath all the shit and stink of Saffron Hill or Bethnal Green, the rooks have hearts of gold. I've lived in the rookeries most of my life, and any man or woman with a heart of gold would have sold it the first chance they had."

"Even you?" she asked.

"Especially me. Don't start thinking I'm some sort of hero like your brother. I'm only taking you to Vauxhall to get my necklace back."

"It's not your neck—"

"I don't care about you or all the jabbering you did about dreams. That might work with Lighter and Corker"—why the hell had all her nonsense persuaded Lighter and Corker?—"but it don't work with me."

"So underneath all your dirt and grime"—she gestured to his chest—"your heart is just as black."

Gideon peered down at his shirt. It was still passing white. "Who are you calling dirty?"

"I meant it figert-figur-fig—" She lifted her hands in exasperation. "It was a metaphor. A metaphor is—"

"I know what a metaphor is. I know what figuratively means too. I may be a thief, but I'm not ignorant. I can read."

"You can?"

He pushed back from her in disgust and tossed another paper log on the fire. He didn't have many left, and the rain continued outside. They might be forced to stay here all night. Hell, this was London. It might rain for a week.

"I apologize," she said. "I was judging based on appearance again."

"Makes no difference to me."

Which was a lie. It did make a difference. He cared how she saw him. He didn't know why he should care what some little girl in pink silk—who'd never had a care in her life—should think about him.

But he did.

The fire crackled in the silence, and outside the shushing of the rain continued as it sluiced off roofs and sliced through the coal-thick skies. Strawberry's eyes drooped, and he expected her to snore in a few minutes.

"Is it true what the boys said about Marlowe?"

The question startled him, not only because he'd thought her close to sleep, but because it was so unexpected. "The *boys*? I promise you, Stryker's crew haven't been *boys* in a long time. If ever."

He'd evaded her question, picking a quarrel over her words. The strategy was tried and true, and one he employed often.

"The men then," she said. With a light wave of her hand, she brushed aside his defenses. "Is it true about Marlowe and you? You were lovers."

Again, she'd pierced the heart of a subject he'd rather keep wholly to himself. Gideon wasn't renowned for his prowess in fisticuffs. He was fast and smart because he didn't always win when he fought. But he knew a few ducks and jibes.

"Will you run to Lord Dane and tell him if I say I…" He paused and remembered his audience. She was leaning forward slightly, intent on his words, her bubbies swelling slightly at the bodice of the gown.

Don't start ogling her bubbies. It was bad enough he couldn't force the image of her legs out of his head.

"If I say I bedded her?"

Even though he'd used the least offensive term he knew, her cheeks still heated and flamed. She must be as innocent as a sunrise. He liked seeing that blush creep across her cheeks, liked the color it added to her pale face. He almost wanted to shock her again.

"No. I don't report to the earl. My brother loves Marlowe. I don't think he'd care what she did or did not do"—she gave him a steely stare as though in challenge—"before they wed."

Gideon snorted and shoved at the smoldering papers with a boot. "He cares. Men always care where a woman's been. Especially his sort—the swells. They want their wives untouched by another man's dirty paws." He held up his hands and wiggled his fingers at her.

"And you don't care as much?" Her eyes widened as though she'd shocked herself at the audacity of her question. He had no doubt this was the first conversation she'd had on the subject of tupping.

"This ain't about me," he said. He wouldn't be her tutor—appealing as that image was—and he didn't want to think about Marlowe and her new husband together in bed. Even if the thought of the two of them didn't seem to niggle him tonight as much as usual.

"But it is about you," she countered. "I asked if it was true that you were in love with Marlowe."

"Love." He sneered the word. "That's another of the words you swells invented to make the beast with two backs seem…" He considered his words carefully. He rarely had any use for his rusty vocabulary. It felt good to pull old words out of his memory and use them again. "Seem lofty and chaste. I don't even know what love is."

He jumped when her warm hand touched the skin of his wrist.

Fucking hell.

He would have bet a guinea she pitied him. It was his own damn fault.

Against his every instinct and despite his defenses, he'd revealed far more than he'd ever intended.

Seven

"GET YOUR FINGERS OFF ME." HE SHOOK OFF HER HAND
and leaped to his feet.

He didn't want to talk about Marlowe. Even
through the heavy warmth pressing down on her
limbs and the pleasant buzzing in her head, she
knew Gideon had loved Marlowe. He probably still
loved Marlowe.

No wonder he was bitter about love. Had anyone
ever loved him? Had anyone ever held him and
stroked his hair and kissed his forehead? He must have
had a mother who'd loved him.

She thought of her own mother and the distinct
lack of hair stroking and forehead kissing in her child-
hood. Perhaps he did not know what love was.

Maybe she didn't know either.

Gideon prowled along the perimeter of the dark
room. He was amazingly fluid and agile. He reminded
her of an acrobat she'd once seen when a troupe of
performers had come to a fair near the family's country
estate. Her mother had not allowed her to watch the
show, but she'd caught sight of the men leaping and

twirling and balancing precariously on a thin rope strung between two poles high off the ground.

Susanna had been astounded before her mother had yanked her away from the window and sent her to her bed without dinner. A few weeks later, when her mother had found a sketch Susanna had done, she'd thrown it into the fire.

In contrast, her brothers had gone out to watch the performance with their father. She'd heard their excited voices as they passed her door on their way to the courtyard. Over breakfast the next morning, she'd listened sullenly as they'd recounted the amazing feats they'd witnessed the night before. Neither her brothers nor her father had seemed to wonder at her absence or care that she had missed all the fun, as usual.

She'd always envied the men's freedom to go and to do as they liked, while she was confined to the house and constantly admonished not to fidget. She'd prayed to God to turn her into a boy more times than she could count. And when she was old enough to realize that could never happen, she cursed him in her prayers for making her a girl.

At the moment, she regretted a few of those whispered curses. She was cold, wet, and hungry— miserable enough to wonder if her brothers' freedom hadn't been quite as perfect as she'd imagined.

She tried to rise and almost pitched headfirst into the fire. Beauty yipped and nudged her back.

"You're foxed," Gideon said, coming back into the circle of light.

"I am not!" she protested. Ladies did not ever overimbibe.

"You drank a quarter of a bottle of gin at least. Unless you drink gin regularly, you're foxed."

"Ladies do not drink gin," she informed him.

"Whatever you say."

He lifted the brick he'd thrown down earlier. It was wrapped in a thin cloth she realized was a handkerchief. Under the handkerchief lay a brown, hard square.

"What is that?"

"Bread."

She laughed. When he didn't even smile, she sobered. "Oh, you're serious."

She touched the hard loaf with one finger. The bread did not give at all. "That baker should look for another profession." She giggled.

She hadn't meant to giggle. She hadn't even said anything very humorous.

Gideon tried to pull off a hunk of the bread, and when his efforts failed, he banged the edge on the ground. Finally, he was able to pry loose a sizable chunk. He offered it to her on his extended palm.

Susanna shook her head. "You go ahead."

"You need something besides Blue Ruin in your stomach. That stew Stryker served us was watery and thin."

"Why is it called Blue Ruin? I've never understood that." She managed to stand on the second try, and swayed, the circle of flames coming dangerously close to her again, but this time Beauty didn't nudge her back.

This time Gideon caught her.

Oh dear.

The moment he touched her, she was in trouble.

His arms were muscular and enfolded her, warming her immediately. He was bigger than she'd realized.

Her head reached only his chin. She knew this because she stared directly at the exposed flesh of his throat. She knew this because she could smell that bare flesh, the light scent of rain and smoke and man. The scent of man was heady.

The feel of man was intoxicating. Her hands rested, flat palmed, over his lungs. His hard chest was a fortified wall, his broad shoulders the battlements. She raised her eyes to the patch of stubble above his Adam's apple. The dark hair was coarse, and she imagined it might scratch at the delicate flesh of her fingertips. It might feel wonderfully decadent against her tender lips.

She couldn't resist looking at his lips. As hard as he claimed to be, his lips looked soft and supple. They were pink, in contrast to his bronze skin and the night's growth of beard. Susanna looked higher, into his eyes. She couldn't see the vibrant green color in the dim light, but she could imagine it. The firelight flickered off his skin, making his cheeks look golden, making the scar slashing across his eyebrow look angry red.

"What happened?" she asked, reaching up to touch it. He caught her wrist midway and pushed her hand against the wall of the building. The coarse wood chafed her sensitive flesh. His fingers laced with hers and burned her skin. She couldn't tear her gaze from his. She couldn't take a deep breath. She couldn't stop the world from spinning like a wooden top.

"You step too close to the flames, you will be burned," he said, his voice low and thick.

She swallowed.

"Do you want to be burned?"

"No," she said. But a small part of her did. The fire might destroy her, but the heat would feel so lovely and warm on her cold limbs.

"Now you answer a question for me."

She allowed her head to fall back so it rested on the wall behind her and she could look up at him easily. He was far too close to her. He should move back. She should insist he release her and step away.

Except if he drew away, she feared she'd pull him to her again. And if she did that, she would not be able to stop herself from touching him.

"What question?" she whispered.

"Is it true what you said to the *boys* at Stryker's? Is this trek to Vauxhall to find your mother's lover?"

"Yes. And no. And…I don't know. I can't think with you standing this close to me. I can't think when you're touching me."

His lips quirked slightly. The heat from his hand on her wrist shot from her arm to the center of her chest, and her heart pounded hard as that heat radiated out and through her entire body. Her nipples puckered and hardened, though she no longer felt cold.

"Do I distract you, Strawberry?" he whispered.

They were both whispering now. That was unwise. Friends whispered. Confidants whispered. Lovers whispered.

He was none of these to her.

"If you could step back…"

"I don't want to step back."

"I won't fall into the fire. I'm steady again."

He laughed, a sound deep and velvet. "Are you? I could make your head spin."

"You already have." Had she said that? "I mean, it is. Your hand…" She looked to the side, where his hand pinned hers to the wall. "You're so warm."

"And you're so incredibly soft." He freed one finger and stroked it along the inside flesh of her corresponding finger. She shivered. The heat bubbling in her chest dropped to her belly. How could he do that to her with just a touch of one finger on hers?

"I've never felt skin like yours," he said.

His finger dipped lower to stroke her palm. She gasped and swayed. Now her entire body tingled, the heat dipping very low indeed. She needed to press her thighs together to stem the way her body had begun to pulse.

"I must have drunk more than I thought," she breathed. "I'm not quite as steady as I ought to be."

"You've never even been kissed, have you?" he asked.

Her gaze had dipped to his lips, but now it flew back to his eyes. He'd asked an impertinent question, one she should chastise him for even thinking, much less voicing aloud. The words died in her throat. His eyes were so dark, too shadowed for her to see anything, and yet she *knew* if she had been able to see them clearly, they would have been full of desire.

Gideon wanted her.

No one had ever wanted her. She might have seen desire reflected in a man's eyes before, but she'd never felt it in return. She'd never even had a conversation about a subject more personal than the weather with any man save her male relatives.

She'd never been kissed. Why should she have been kissed? She'd been carefully chaperoned, her virtue protected for her future husband.

It occurred to her, belatedly, that she'd now put that virtue in danger. She should have considered that before she ever left the town house with him. She'd thought she was safe with him, but she wasn't safe at all.

And she didn't want to be safe.

His lips were only a few inches from hers, and it thrilled her. She wanted him to kiss her. She wanted him to press her hard against that wall and kiss her until she was dizzy with the sort of desire she'd only read about in books smuggled into her room and hidden away from her mother. She'd blushed at several of Shakespeare's sonnets, but she'd never blushed as fiercely as she did now.

"No one has ever *tried* to kiss me," she confided.

His brows rose as though he were genuinely surprised. "Would you have allowed it?"

"No." Her gaze lowered to his lips again. She could barely remain upright. Her heart was so loud in her ears, the press of blood against her eardrums making her sway.

"Would you allow me to kiss you?"

"No."

He chuckled. "You lie."

She did. She'd heard the lie in her voice, though it hadn't sounded like her voice at all. She'd sounded like a breathless, desperate woman.

He lifted the hand resting on the wall beside her and slid a piece of her hair behind her ear, his finger caressing her cheek. She drew in a sharp breath. "Don't." The plea escaped in a strangled gasp.

"Do I frighten you?"

She didn't answer. How to explain that it was her own reaction that frightened her far more than he ever could? He drew her hand away from the rough wood of the wall.

His fingers slid down her palm, teasing the lines on the skin, making his own path across the pink surface. Her blood pulsed in rhythm with his movements. She burned with heat and desire. Her lower belly was hot with something she knew must be arousal. She wanted desperately to press her hand against that private part of herself to relieve the tension.

He caught her wrist, two fingers circling it. Keeping his gaze on hers, he lifted her palm to his lips. He didn't touch his mouth to her, but the warm rasp of his breath feathered against the underside of her fingers. Her back was chilled and still damp, but where their bodies all but touched, she was deliciously warm. The fire crackled, the light fading and the orange reflection dancing on the walls and ceiling. Dimly, she heard the soft patter of London rain outside.

He dipped his head, his gaze meeting hers from under thick, lowered lashes. "May I kiss your hand, my lady?"

He was mocking her. Surely he was mocking her. And yet she found herself nodding in agreement. A line from one of the sonnets of Shakespeare she'd dared read only in the dark of night flickered in her memory.

To kiss the tender inward of thy hand.

She'd never known how erotic those eight words were. Her entire being hovered on the precipice of need as he slowly lowered his mouth to her middle finger. He brushed his lips against the crease where her finger intersected with her palm.

The stubble on his chin teased her skin, scraping it lightly, making her flesh itch and flame and tingle.

His lips moved to her third finger, his touch so light she barely knew it was there. And then his mouth slid over the inside of her smallest finger. He pressed his lips against that small finger, kissing her for the first time in earnest. She tried to pull away, but he didn't release her. Instead, his mouth opened slightly, and he touched her skin with the tip of his tongue.

She moaned.

Mortified, she emitted a shocked gasp. He didn't seem to notice. His tongue traced the lines of her finger, teasing and swirling against the tip. His mouth slid down and rested in the center of her palm. She squirmed. The stubble tickled her and sensitized her. It was as though every particle in her body was alive, and she could feel not only the press of his lips but the linen of her shift where it pressed against her belly, the hard leather of the boots digging into her ankle, the wispy silk of her gown on the back of her thigh.

Gideon kissed her palm, and Susanna closed her eyes. Sweetness flooded through her at the tenderness. Her first kiss, and it was impossibly perfect, impossibly arousing, impossibly unfulfilling.

He stepped back, his fingers still resting lightly on the pulse pounding against the thin skin of her wrist. With infinite care, he released her hand and dropped his. Susanna stared at her hand. It looked the same, though she would have sworn the flesh was hot to the touch. It seemed to flame and burn.

He bent, lifted something, and held the bread out to her again. This time she took it without argument. She bit into the hard crust, tearing at it with her teeth and swallowing the dry clump with difficulty. Her gaze was on the dying fire, where Beauty snoozed peacefully. How had the dog slept through the turmoil of the past few minutes?

Susanna slid down the wall and sat beside the pup, who raised her head. She opened her hand and gave the eager dog the rest of the bread. Beauty jumped to her feet and wolfed the morsel down in a single bite.

"Don't give the dog our food!" Gideon moaned.

"She likes it." Susanna broke off another chunk of bread with no little effort. Beauty gulped that down too. Gideon snatched the loaf away from her.

"This isn't for the mongrel."

"Well it isn't fit for human consumption."

She was glad for the distraction the dog provided. She didn't want to talk any more about kissing. She didn't want to discuss what had just happened between them and what she wished might happen if Gideon ever put his hands on her again. She wanted to close her eyes and sleep for a week and think of nothing and no one.

Gideon pushed her gently back against the wall. "You're fading, Strawberry. Go ahead and rest. The rain isn't stopping anytime soon."

"I'm not tired," she said with a yawn. Her heavy eyes seemed to drift closed without her consent. She allowed it, telling herself she would rest only a moment.

❧

"Give it 'ere, or I'll make yer mother sorry she ever birthed you."

"She were already sorry!"

Susanna sat so quickly, the earth tilted and her head turned over and over. She closed her eyes and pressed a hand to the bridge of her nose. Beauty growled. A sharp hiss came from behind her, silencing Beauty. The thief's legs were stretched before her. She frowned in puzzlement, her face heating when the obvious became clear.

She'd been resting on Gideon. No wonder she wasn't chilled. She'd probably been lying against his chest. At the thought, her belly tensed. The feeling should have been uncomfortable, but the sensation only made her warmer.

"I told you I was good fer it. Now give it over."

Susanna glanced over her shoulder at Gideon. "What's going—"

His hand clamped over her mouth, silencing her. She tried jabbing him in the stomach, but it was muscled and lean. His hand smelled faintly of the smoke from the fire last night. When he leaned close, she shivered from the tickle of his hair brushing against her cheek.

"Not a word. Not a sound."

She nodded, but he didn't release her. Light slanted through the cracks in the wood, knifing gold onto the floor around her. The patter of the rain falling had lulled her to sleep, but if the cries of hawkers and rattle of wheels on the streets were any indication, the rain had stopped.

And then there was the argument brewing outside.

"I want the coin in my hand, Mint," one of the men said.

"How do I know you won't sell it to someone else afore I return?" the second one whined.

"You don't. Best be quick, or you'll lose her to another bidder."

Susanna straightened. *Her?*

"Not a word," Gideon whispered again.

She grabbed his wrist and tugged his hand down. "What are they arguing about?" she whispered.

"It's not our concern. Our concern is staying hidden until they leave," he whispered back. A knife of light shot across his face, slicing across the smooth white skin of his scar.

"But—"

He raised one finger and gave her a look that would have terrified her the day before. But she wasn't so scared of him anymore.

"Give me two hours," the buyer outside the building was saying. "I can get the blunt."

"Two hours. Not a minute more."

Susanna heard the sound of boots moving.

"Meet me at Coffin Joe's."

More shuffling of feet, and then a sound like a child's whimper. Susanna was on her feet, candlestick in hand, before Gideon could catch her. He tried. His hand snaked out, but she was faster, and his fingers did little but grasp the fabric of her sleeve before she pulled free. She ran to the door, her legs weak and wobbly, like a newborn filly's. She hoisted herself high enough to see through the broken wood at the top of the door.

At first she saw nothing but the building across the muddy street and the debris piled against its stoop. She looked to the right and caught sight of a man's hat.

A hand came around her waist, but she shoved the thief back and levered herself higher. The man had moved farther away, far enough that she could see he had the arm of a small child clamped in his hand.

She gasped and jumped down, fumbling with the bar on the door.

Gideon slammed a hand over it. "What are you doing?"

"There's a child!" She pointed at the door. "He's selling a child."

"If you go out there, he might very well decide to sell you."

She shoved him aside and pushed the bar up. "You won't allow that to happen."

For some reason, he didn't slam the bar back down before she lifted it. The heavy wood thudded on the floor, and Susanna pulled the door wide. She took the steps in one leap and called, "Stop! You!"

The man turned, and her heart plummeted into her belly. Perhaps this had not been the best idea.

Gideon stared at the dark rectangle where the beam had been. Her words had completely stunned him.

She trusted him.

She believed he'd protect her.

No one had ever believed that about him before. Not even Marlowe had trusted him or expected him to protect her from all of Satin's cruelty.

Marlowe was cunning.

Strawberry was not.

"Give me that child!"

It was as though she wanted to be killed. Either she was incredibly brave or incredibly stupid. Maybe they were the same thing.

Beauty scampered to the doorway and barked, then looked back at him.

"I'm going," Gideon said. He was neither brave nor stupid, but for some reason her words latched on to that part of him deep inside. The part he kept carefully protected. He couldn't abandon her. Not when she believed in him.

Gideon ducked through the doorway and caught up to Strawberry. For all her bravado, she hadn't gone far.

"Who's going to make me?" a man asked. Assured that Strawberry was unharmed—so far—Gideon took a look at the man she'd confronted. He made a low growl in the back of his throat.

It had to be Daniel Gilfroy.

Or as he was better known, Dagger Dan. The man was known for the handmade daggers he always carried. Deadly daggers he wasn't afraid to use to gut a man or carve out an eye or lop off an ear.

Gideon grabbed Strawberry's arm and pulled her toward him and safety.

And then his gaze lowered to the child. The girl couldn't have been much older than three, though he was no judge of children's ages. She might have been five or six and small for her age. She had smudges of dirt on her face and matted brown hair, but her blue eyes were large and frightened. No tears. She'd lived a short life in the rookeries and probably had already learned tears wouldn't save her.

"I'll make you," Gideon said.

Dagger Dan flicked a wrist, and one of his long, crude daggers flashed into his hand. "Come on, then." The man motioned with the dagger, keeping one hand tightly on the child's upper arm.

"I don't want a fight."

"You got one now. And I won't even kill you, 'Arrow. I'll leave you alive so Beezle can 'ave that privilege. 'E's looking for you."

Gideon raised his hands, trying to seem reasonable, though he knew it would do little good. "You want your gin. Go get it. I'll take the child back home to her mother." He nodded to the girl. "Bess Castle, right?"

"You know the mother?" Strawberry asked.

Gideon ignored her, unwilling to take his eyes off Dan for even a moment.

"You want 'er?" Dan asked with a sneer. "Pay for 'er."

"You can't sell her!" Strawberry said, glim-stick waving about in righteous anger. She pulled away from Gideon and moved closer to the child. The woman was truly half-daft. Another step or two, and Dagger Dan would slice her open. "She's a person, not a…a piece of furniture."

Dan's eyes narrowed, then his gaze swept down Strawberry's gown. Clearly, her speech had alerted him to the fact that she was one of the swells.

"Well now." He shoved the little girl against the wall of a building. "What do we 'ave 'ere?"

"I am Susanna Derring. And you are?"

Gideon put another slash in the Daft column. She wasn't even sane enough to take a step back when Dagger Dan advanced.

"You want the little girl?" Dan asked.

Susanna nodded.

"Then I propose a trade. You for 'er."

"Absolutely not."

Gideon grabbed Strawberry back and shoved her behind him before Dan moved close enough to snatch her. "No trade, Dan."

"I ain't giving you the brat for free. She's mine. Payment for services rendered."

"What services?" Strawberry demanded.

"Bess would never give you her child," Gideon argued. He knew the woman, and she doted on the little girl. She was one of the few examples of motherhood he'd seen in the rookeries. Too many women were willing to sell their children for the next glass of gin or a full belly.

Dan flipped the dagger from one hand to the other. "The brat is mine to sell or trade. If you want 'er, you pay."

"That's reprehensible!" Strawberry shouted over his shoulder.

"Fancy words," Dan said with another flip of his dagger from one hand to the next. "Come closer, and I'll teach you a few new ones."

He lunged, and with Strawberry hugging his back, Gideon couldn't move fast enough. He saw the blade of the dagger coming for him, knew it would slice his face. He could only hope it wouldn't strike his eyes. He shut his eyes in protection, but the blow never came.

Instead, something large and warm knocked him on his arse.

He rolled away, his legs tangled with Strawberry's. Kicking free, he jumped to his feet and rounded on Dan with fists ready for a fight.

The mongrel had Dan's wrist clamped between its jaw. Dan tried to shake off the dog, but that damn dog wouldn't release his hand. Dan punched the dog, but she held on.

"Don't hurt her!" Strawberry yelled.

Gideon grabbed her arm and pushed her into the street. He finally noticed the small crowd that had gathered to watch. If Beezle hadn't known where he was, he probably knew now and was on his way. They had to run and hide before the Covent Garden Cubs made an appearance.

"Grab the brat and run," Gideon ordered Strawberry. "I'll catch up with you."

"But Beauty—"

"I'll see to her. Go!" He shoved her forward.

For once, the mort actually listened to him and grabbed her skirts with her hand. She ran, making a wide arc around Dan, and reached the child. Gideon saw her bend to speak to the brat, and then Dan finally shook the dog free. Beauty landed with a yelp of pain against the wall of the building. Blood dripped from Dan's wrist, but it was a mere flesh wound. He reached into his waistcoat and extracted another dagger.

"I'll cut you first, 'Arrow, then the dog." Dan moved closer.

Gideon held his position. He had to distract Dan until Strawberry was away.

"And then I'll find that little bitch and carve her pretty face!"

His hand snaked out, and Gideon feinted to the right. Pain lanced through his upper arm as Dan's thrust sliced through his coat. It wasn't deep, but Dan was just beginning.

Beezle would finish the job if Gideon didn't run soon. Gideon twisted to face Dan again. Behind the man, the dog shook her head and rose to her feet. She growled softly.

One chance, Gideon thought as Dan advanced and the dagger loomed large.

One last chance.

Dan slashed at Gideon, who stumbled back, tucking his midsection in to protect himself. Gideon's boot slammed into the wall of the building. Dan laughed and moved closer. Would he strike right or left? Gideon had to duck, and if he chose poorly, he was as good as dead. Dan raised the dagger, and Gideon tensed.

A gray blur shot before him, knocking Dan aside. The dog and man rolled, and the dog stood victorious on Dagger Dan's chest. She growled and snapped her jaws with menace. Gideon didn't wait. He took off in the direction Strawberry had gone. Before he could round the corner, he whistled.

The dog's head jerked in his direction.

"Come, Beauty!"

With a yip, she bounded after him.

With the dog at his side, Gideon dodged men and carts and the greedy hands of pickpockets.

His blood pounded with the thrill of another successful escape. He had only one problem.

Strawberry was gone.

Eight

"You're safe, sweetheart," Susanna said, pulling the child down a set of steps and pressing her back against them so the two would be hidden from view on the street. Whereas Mayfair tended to smell sweet and clean after a hard rain, this place had a distinct stench. All of the refuse had washed down into the doorway at the bottom of the stairs, and it stunk now that the sun had risen.

The little girl whimpered, and Susanna stroked her tangled hair.

"I won't hurt you. I would take you home."

"Mamma," the girl cried.

"Yes, to your mamma." Susanna knelt and looked the child in the face. "But you must be very quiet right now. We don't want the bad man to find us."

The girl's blue eyes widened, and she shook her head until her mop of curls fell over her forehead.

"Good girl. What's your name?" Susanna whispered.

"Jemima," the girl whispered back. "But Mamma calls me Jemma."

"My name is Susanna. Let's stay here and be very quiet until my friend Gideon can find us. He'll take you back to your mamma, Jemma. Yes?"

"Yes."

Susanna rose on tiptoes and slanted a look at the streets. She saw dozens of feet. She doubted she'd recognize Gideon's boots if he walked by. She rose a bit higher and glanced at faces. No one looked familiar. A man spotted her and frowned, and she ducked back down again, clutching her candlestick closer. Even though she looked a complete wreck, she didn't fit in here.

Her gown, now wrinkled and stained, was made of silk. Her gloves had long since been lost. Anyone who looked at her hands would note they were white and uncallused. She couldn't imagine what her hair looked like. If her mother saw her now…

Her mother!

Susanna drew a sharp breath, and the little girl looked up at her in concern. Susanna managed a reassuring smile she didn't feel.

Susanna had never considered that she might be away all night. She'd never thought about what might happen when Maggie went to wake her and found her bed empty and unused. She could imagine her mother's panic when it was discovered Susanna was not in the house. If he wasn't already at home, her brother, Brook, would be sent an urgent summons. He would do whatever it was inspectors did and determine she'd run away from home.

Her mother's heart would break.

Susanna's heart felt close to breaking. She was a terrible daughter. How could she cause her mother so much worry?

Why hadn't she considered this might happen before she'd made the rash decision to force the thief to take her to Vauxhall Gardens? She should return home immediately.

Except she didn't want to return home.

She still wanted to go to Vauxhall. If she returned home now, she'd ease her mother's worry, but she'd never be allowed out of her sight again. This was her last chance at freedom.

Would she be in any more trouble if she returned tomorrow instead of today? She hated to cause her mother more worry, but what was one more day?

Oh, she was a horrible daughter. She should tell Gideon to take her back.

And then he'd never have the chance to kiss her. He'd kissed only her hand, but tonight he might kiss her on the lips. Her belly tensed, and she drew a quick breath at the thought.

She shouldn't want such things.

But why couldn't she have one kiss before she was consigned to matrimony with a man she didn't even know? What was the harm, now that the harm had been done?

Jemma blinked up at her, quiet and still, and Susanna turned to peek out again. The streets were clogged with people now. Even if she left to search for Gideon, she'd never find him. She had been sheltered all her life, but she knew enough of London to realize a woman alone on the streets was not safe. She had nowhere to hide, nowhere safe to go.

Susanna felt Jemma press into her side, leaning against her. The child's thumb had found its way into her mouth, and she looked exhausted. How was Susanna supposed to protect this child when she couldn't even protect herself?

"Watch out!" a man yelled, and Susanna rose on tiptoes to gauge the street again. A man ran by. She could see only his legs and his shoes, but he must have been in a hurry, because he shoved aside anyone in his way. A gray dog trailed behind him.

"Beauty!"

Jemma pulled her thumb from her mouth and stared up at her.

"Wait right here," Susanna said, holding up her hand. "I will be right back."

The girl's lip quivered as though she had been told this before by a person who turned out to be unreliable.

Susanna bent. "I promise, Jemma. And when I promise something, I never ever break that promise."

Jemma's eyes widened until they were the size and almost the color of robin's eggs.

Susanna placed her hand on Jemma's bony shoulder. "I promise I'll be right back. Do you believe me?"

The child nodded wordlessly.

"Good." Susanna lifted her skirts almost to her knees and raced to the stop of the steps. "Gideon! Gideon!" If she lost him now, she was doomed.

Several men turned to look at her, but none were Gideon. She couldn't see him through the people and the twists of the winding street. He'd had Beauty with him.

"Beauty. Come, girl! Beauty!"

The door at the bottom of the steps where Jemma stood opened. "Wot's all the noise?" a woman yelled.

A man leered at her from across the street and started toward her.

"Beauty!" Susanna screamed, her voice sounding desperate even to her ears.

"Do you need 'elp, dearie?" the man coming toward her asked, his dirty hands held wide.

"No!" She backed toward the steps. "Jemma, come here." Susanna held out her hand and wiggled her fingers at Jemma.

Jemma's little hand gripped hers tightly, and Susanna pulled the girl close.

"Just leave us alone."

"Just leave us alone," the man said, mocking her accent. "Ye're new around 'ere, aren't you?" He'd crossed the street, showing no sign of respecting her requests. She could run, but when she looked right, she saw others watching with interest. She looked left, and a small group of boys advanced. Dash it all!

"Come 'ere, dearie." The man was close enough she could smell the sweat on him. He held out his hand, and she knocked it away.

"Hey!"

A low growl silenced him. Susanna broke into a smile. Between the man's legs, she spotted Beauty with her teeth bared. Jemma gasped and began to whine.

"No, no! Jemma, she's my dog. She won't hurt you." Susanna cut her gaze to the would-be attacker. "But she *will* hurt *you*. Step away, or I'll order her to attack."

Susanna had no idea if the dog would attack or not.

Fortunately, the man stepped away. Another man ran toward them, and Susanna braced for attack.

"Whoa!" Gideon held his hands high. "Call off the attack, Strawberry. I've come to rescue you."

She leveled a glare at him. She hoped it was as powerful as the one her mother always gave her. "If you wanted to rescue me, you should have been here three minutes ago."

He gave a one-shouldered shrug. "Hey, if you want me to go…" His words trailed off as he sauntered away.

"No! Gideon!"

He grinned at her over his shoulder, and she could have kicked him. She might have just as easily kissed him. He looked like a naughty boy when he gave her that smile.

"I need you to take Jemma home."

His gaze dropped to the child, and then he glanced over his shoulder like a man being followed. The man who'd taken Jemma and the men at Stryker's flash ken had mentioned a Beetle.

No, that wasn't it.

Beezle.

She didn't know what sort of name Beezle was, but she was willing to wager he was the man Gideon feared seeing over his shoulder.

"Let's go, then." Gideon gave a mock bow to the small crowd that had gathered. "Gentlemen, if you'll excuse me." He held out an arm, and Susanna took it. She didn't particularly want to allow him to escort her, but under the circumstances, it seemed the wisest course of action. She held out an arm to Jemma, who slipped her small hand around two of Susanna's fingers. Beauty gave a final warning growl and pranced after them.

"You're Bess Castle's bantling?" Gideon asked Jemma, keeping his gaze on the people they passed.

"Yes," the little girl said, her voice quiet.

"How did Dagger Dan get you?"

"Is that his name?" Susanna asked, forgetting to walk for a moment. "His parents named him Dagger?"

Gideon snorted with laughter, and even Jemma smiled shyly.

"His cronies named him Dagger. His real name is Daniel Gilfroy—at least that's the one he tells everyone." Gideon craned his neck to peer at Jemma. "Did your mum sell you?"

"No!" Jemma's voice was loud and clear. "He took me."

"As payment for what?"

Jemma didn't answer. They turned into a dark alley where dilapidated tenements rose above them.

"She probably doesn't know," Susanna said. "Does that happen often?"

"Every day, but I wouldn't expect it from Bess."

Horrid, Susanna thought. It was all absolutely horrid. The conditions the people lived in, the lows to which they stooped to survive. Dingy clothing hung from clotheslines, flapping like forlorn kites in the summer breeze. Women sat on stoops with crying babes in their arms, and men loitered on corners, dark looks of desperation on their faces. At the end of the street, a group of children crouched in a circle, and Susanna realized they were probably gambling.

She looked down at Jemma. What kind of life

did the little girl have to look forward to? How long before Dagger Dan came for her again, and this time Susanna would not be there to stop him?

Jemma pointed at a building.

"Right. This is it," Gideon said.

Susanna looked up. It appeared indistinguishable from the other buildings, but she supposed the child knew her own home.

"Beauty, stay here," she commanded, pointing to the stoop outside the entrance. The dog sat, head high, looking like an Egyptian depiction of Anubis.

Gideon led them into a dark entryway that smelled of urine. Something—please God let it be a cat—scampered away, claws clicking on the floor.

"This way." Gideon led them up a flight of creaking stairs with no rail. Susanna tried hard not to touch the wall, but she kept close to it in case one of the steps should give way. The place was dark and dank. Water from the recent rains dripped, echoing through the building.

Jemma pushed past both of them on the third landing. She knew her way, even in the dark. She scampered down the corridor and pounded on a door at the end.

Susanna followed quickly, her sleeve against her nose to mask the smell of rotting fish and boiled cabbage. Inside one of the flats they passed, a man and woman argued loudly, their angry voices carrying through the thin walls.

"What do ye want?" a voice called through the door Jemma had pounded on.

"Mamma."

Susanna reached the door. The woman who'd

called out hadn't spoken again. Then the door flung open, and a young girl knelt down with arms wide open. Jemma rushed into her mother's arms and burst into tears. The mother whispered words of comfort, lifting her child and cradling her close. She looked up, one hand on the back of the child's dark hair, her eyes wide with amazement.

Susanna gasped in shock. Jemma's mother was nothing more than a girl. She was nineteen at most, barely old enough to be out. And yet she had a child?

Bess's gaze lingered on Susanna and then darted to Gideon. When she saw him, her body slumped. "You brought her back. Thank you."

"Don't thank me. It was all her." He jerked his head in Susanna's direction.

Bess gave her a curious glance again. "Please, come in." She stepped back, and Gideon gestured for Susanna to precede him. Uneasily, she entered the room, trying not to gawk but vastly interested in where Bess and Jemma lived.

And not a little bit afraid to find out.

The flat was worse than she'd anticipated. It was tiny, barely large enough to fit the four of them. A pallet lay on the floor, and Susanna assumed from the thin blanket on top it was the bed. A chipped cup and a kettle sat on a wooden crate that served as a table. There was no stove to speak of, and not even a hearth to keep them warm in the winter. In the corner hung a dress. Beside it was a similar gown in a child's size.

"It's not much," Bess said. Her gaze was on Susanna's silk gown.

Susanna gave a quick curtsy. "I apologize. I should have introduced myself." She threw Gideon a look. He should have introduced her. "I'm Susanna Derring. Mr. Harrow is a friend."

Gideon quirked his lips in obvious amusement at that statement.

"Thank you for bringing Jemma back. I told him I'd pay as soon as I could, but he didn't want to wait."

"Dagger Dan owns the flat?" Gideon asked.

Bess nodded. "He owns most of them on this floor. I've always paid him promptly before, but I lost my position."

"What position?" Susanna asked.

Bess rubbed her daughter's thin back. "I was a seamstress at a shop on St. Martin's Lane. I worked hard, I did. I was never late, but the owner's niece needed money. Mrs. Gordon couldn't pay all three of us, so she let me go."

"When was that?" Gideon asked.

"A fortnight ago. I haven't found another position yet."

"Dagger Dan will be back," Gideon said. "You can't stay here."

Tears shown in Bess's eyes. "I know."

Gideon nodded at Jemma. "Take care of her." He took Susanna's elbow and moved toward the door. Susanna shook him off. How could she leave without trying to help this woman?

"Is there somewhere else you can go?" she asked Bess. "A friend or relative?"

Bess shook her head. "There's no one."

"Where will you live?"

Bess didn't answer, just clutched her child tighter.

Gideon nudged her arm. "Strawberry, let's go before Dan returns."

When she didn't move, he took her elbow and tugged. She took two steps and dug in her heels.

"No. I'm not leaving."

❦

Gideon groaned aloud. He'd known this was a mistake. Everything with Strawberry was a mistake. They should be safe in the building where they'd spent last night, not in Seven Dials at Bess Castle's flat, where Dagger Dan—Gideon's newest enemy—was likely to make an appearance at any moment.

Beezle might very well be on his way too, if he'd gotten word of Gideon's activities this morning. And Beezle always knew everyone's comings and goings. Gideon didn't have time for Strawberry's tender heart—not if he wanted to save his own arse.

"Yes, you are," Gideon said, grabbing her arm again and pulling her.

"No!" She turned her big brown eyes on him.

Oh no. Not the eyes. Gideon bit the inside of his cheek until it hurt. He would not fall prey to that pleading look in her eyes again.

"We can't leave Jemma and Bess here for Dagger Dan. And we certainly cannot force them out on the streets."

Gideon pointed at Bess, whose eyes were as wide as Strawberry's now. Even the brat was watching them with surprise and shock. "You heard her. She owes Dan blunt. You got any blunt?"

"No." Strawberry looked down.

"And even if you did, Dan will want revenge now. The only way she'll survive is on the streets." It was a ludicrous statement. No one survived long on the streets.

"We have to do something!"

"*You* do something. I'm leaving before Dan or someone worse shows up."

"Beezle," Bess murmured. "I heard he was after you."

He reached for the door, but Strawberry skirted around him and closed it. "Who is this Beezle everyone keeps talking about? Why does he want you?"

Gideon started to reply and found he had nothing to say. "You don't want to know, and if we don't leave now, you're apt to find out."

"Fine," she agreed. The bloody woman did not have any sense!

"But I'm not leaving until I give her a letter of introduction."

"A letter of—what the hell are you talking about?" he yelled. Gideon knew he was yelling, and he knew that was a mistake. He'd lost his temper, which was a bad sign. He never lost his temper, but the woman was talking about letters. *Letters*, for God's sake!

"This is not the time for fucking correspondence."

She pointed a finger at him. "Watch your mouth. There's a child present."

Gideon couldn't even form words. He tried to speak, but his mouth would not work. Finally, he covered his eyes with his hands and banged his head against the wall. "We're doomed. This is it. Done in by letter writing."

"I'll be quick," she said.

She'd be quick. She'd better hope Beezle killed her quickly, because death was the only thing coming to them quickly.

"Do you have a pen and paper?" she asked.

Gideon let out a weak laugh.

"No, miss. Well, actually, I do have this old pamphlet."

Gideon opened his eyes. Bess had set the brat back on her feet and rushed to a cupboard. She opened it and drew out a paper advertising a play. "I sewed some of the costumes for the production," she said proudly.

Strawberry turned it over. "This will work. I need something to write with. Do you have anything that will leave a mark?"

The brat tugged her mother's sleeve. "Mamma, your sewing kit."

Bess's brow creased, and then her face lit up. "Yes! My marking pencil. You could use that." She rushed to the pallet, pushed it forward, and pulled out her sewing kit. She'd obviously kept this one thing of value hidden. She set it on the bed, knelt before it, and took out a marking pencil.

"Perfect." Susanna set her blasted glim-stick on the floor, took the pencil, and flattened the pamphlet on the crate. She spoke as she wrote. "You are to take this to the Derring town house in Mayfair." She gave the address. "Ask to see the dowager countess, and tell her you come with a message from me."

"A countess?" Bess shook her head. "I couldn't."

Seeing his chance at escape, Gideon waved a hand.

"Yes, you can. This is her daughter. She'll welcome news of her."

Bess's eyes grew even larger as she looked at Susanna from head to toe. Strawberry continued to write. "Tell her I asked her to give you a position in the household. I'm writing it all here." She lifted her hand and indicated the pamphlet. "You'll be safe there, and we can always use a good seamstress."

"I-I don't know what to say," Bess stammered.

Gideon yanked Strawberry to his side as soon as she lowered the pencil and snatched the glim-stick.

"Say good-bye. We're leaving." She stumbled as he pulled her into the corridor.

Gideon hadn't survived in the rookeries this long without knowing how to keep his head down when a Bow Street Runner or the arch rogue of another gang was looking for him. Beezle knew most of his hidey-holes, but he had one or two he'd kept to himself. He needed to go underground until nightfall, when he and Strawberry would be less conspicuous. They'd hide for a few hours, allow the trail to go cold, and when it grew dark, make their way to Vauxhall Gardens. He'd have his necklace back tonight and be gone by dawn tomorrow.

Gideon led Strawberry and Beauty through every rabbit hole, back alley, and cut-through he knew. No one could have tracked him, not even one of his fellow rooks. The problem was that Strawberry stood out like a diamond or, considering her hair, a ruby, glinting in the dirt.

Men stopped to ogle her. Women whispered about her. Children swarmed her, trying to touch her gown or her hair. Beauty gently dissuaded the most curious. Gideon never thought he'd be grateful for the dog. But even the dog brought them more attention. He heaved a sigh of relief when he tapped on the back door of a fencing ken in Field Lane.

Strawberry leaned against the wall beside the door. The fact that she didn't ask any questions demonstrated how exhausted she must have been. They'd traveled from Mayfair to St. Giles to north of Holborn Hill. They'd had almost nothing to eat and very little sleep.

Gideon would have expected Strawberry to complain and whine by now, but she'd not said a word.

He also would have expected her to look like a well-used mop. Instead, she was more beautiful than when he'd first seen her all clean and tidy in the town house library. Her beauty was dangerous in that way. He'd accustom himself to her large brown eyes or her thick red-blond hair, and then the next time he caught a glimpse of her, it was like seeing her for the first time again.

She stole his breath away, even with a torn dress and her hair a mass of tangled curls down her back.

She seemed to have no idea of her allure. She leaned against the building with her head tilted back and her eyes closed. For the moment, Gideon had his fill of her. The shadow of lashes on a marble cheek, marred with a streak of ash. The long, graceful sweep of her neck. The swell of her breasts rising from the vee at the bodice of the gown. He imagined hooking one finger into that neckline and ripping it away, exposing her flesh to his eyes and his hands and his mouth…

Beauty yipped at him, and Gideon focused on the warped wood of the door. He rapped again, harder this time. Fencing was a profession largely conducted under cover of darkness, and he would be surprised if Des was out of bed before noon.

The dog knew what she was about, protecting her adopted mistress. Gideon wanted her, and the realization of it hit him hard enough that he slammed his fist into the door again. When had he begun to crave tasting her, touching her? He couldn't pinpoint one exact time, but there were a thousand little slips on the slope of desire.

He'd kissed her hand last night, and the sweet taste of her flesh had been intoxicating.

She'd fallen asleep with her head on his shoulder, and rather than shove her off, he'd wrapped an arm about her to keep her warm, and listened to her quiet breathing for hours.

He'd watched her march to confront Dagger Dan with absolutely no trace of fear. That had been sheer ignorance. She wouldn't have been so foolish if she'd known what the man could do. The way she'd stood, the way her face had colored, the way she'd tossed her hair in anger—just remembering it made his cock harden with need.

"Des!" Gideon yelled. "Open the fucking door!"

Beauty barked several times in support, reaching up to scratch the door with her front paws. The rains had revealed white fur underneath all the dirt, and with a good bath, the mongrel would actually be a handsome beast. She had a slim snout and bright eyes and a way of prancing that said she was too good for the other dogs huddled under carts or scavenging in rubbish.

"Perhaps he's not at home," Strawberry said. She stood straight now, her eyes on the upper windows of the fencing ken.

"He's home, and he'll let me in. He owes me."

"What does he owe you?"

Gideon heard heavy footsteps behind the door. "A favor."

The door cracked open, and Gideon pushed it wider, causing Des to stumble back. The man looked like he'd been up all night. He probably had. His blond hair stood out at all angles, and the stubble on his chin glinted gold in the sunlight. His eyes were shot through with red, making the blue color even brighter.

"Wot the fuck do you want?" he growled.

"Watch your language," Gideon said with a grin. He jerked a thumb at Strawberry. "There's a lady present."

"What lady?"

The door opened wider to reveal a buxom brunette in a shift that hid absolutely nothing of her lush curves. In fact, she might have looked more respectable naked.

"A real lady, Brenna. Move aside so we can come in."

Strawberry didn't move, her gaze riveted on Brenna, so Gideon prodded her forward. When Beauty tried to follow, Des held up a hand.

"The dog stays outside."

Strawberry's chin notched up two inches, and Gideon wanted to weep. They'd been so close. *So close.*

"If Beauty stays outside, so do I," she said, her tone haughty.

Des's blue eyes all but popped out of his head. He looked at Gideon, the unspoken question so loud, Gideon almost winced.

"Miss Susanna Derring, meet Des…what the hell is your surname anyway?"

Brenna pushed Des out of the way. "Where are your manners? Let's make the introductions inside. You can bring the dog, love." The hint of an Irish accent hung about Brenna's words. The London accent hadn't quite overtaken it.

Inside, Brenna lit a lamp and bid everyone to sit on the mismatched chairs scattered about the tiny living quarters behind the shop. The shop was shuttered at the moment, but Des would open it later, displaying the silk wipes prominently and exchanging blunt for goods quick as lightning.

While Brenna bustled about making tea, Gideon tried the introductions again.

"Desmond Stewart, but everyone calls me Des," he interrupted. "This is Brenna, and you, Miss Susanna Derring, are new to Field Lane."

"She is, and we're in a bit of trouble."

Des laughed. "When are you not in trouble? I suppose you want to hole up here for the day. Well, I don't need your trouble coming in here—"

"Des!" Brenna slammed a cup on the table with enough force that Gideon worried it would shatter.

"Of course they're welcome. We can't put this girl out on the streets."

"Ye're certainly free with the invitations, considering this isn't even yer home."

Susanna's eyes widened, and Gideon figured she'd just then realized Des and Brenna weren't married.

Gideon leaned back in his chair, his tired muscles glad for the respite. "I didn't want to have to mention this, but you do owe me a favor."

"Then don't mention it," Des snapped.

"Now what's this?" Brenna crossed her arms over her chest, causing the shift to dip even lower.

"A trifle," Des answered. "You can stay until nightfall, and we're even. There's room in the cellar."

"The cellar!" Brenna sloshed the tea she'd been pouring on the table, and Gideon had to yank his hand away to prevent it from being burned. "Look at these poor folk. We'll give them the bedroom."

She set the kettle down, but before she could reach for the bread she'd set out, Des pulled her into his lap. "I thought we were using the bedroom."

She giggled and waved a hand at him. "Time enough for that later."

"There'd better be." Des gave her a playful kiss and tugged her bodice down, revealing one bulbous breast. He tweaked it, then set her on her feet and lightly swatted her bottom. Brenna laughed, adjusted her shift, and set out bread and jam.

Gideon reached for the bread, but Strawberry didn't so much as breathe. "Aren't you hungry?"

Her face was as red as her hair, and her mouth shaped into a small O. No doubt she was shocked by the display of affection she'd just witnessed.

Gideon rather liked the idea of shocking her further.

When they'd eaten, Beauty curled up by the stove to stretch her full belly, and Brenna led Strawberry upstairs to wash and change. Gideon recounted the events of the past night and morning to Des, and by the time he was done, Brenna tiptoed down the stairs, wearing Strawberry's silk ball gown.

"She's asleep. Poor love is exhausted."

Gideon indicated the too-small gown that stretched to the point of ripping over her hips and breasts. "Did you steal her clothes?"

"I gave her one of my dresses. If you're to continue dragging her through London, Gideon Harrow, this isn't the most practical attire."

"It looks fetching on you," Des said with a look in his eyes Gideon knew well.

"How did you find her?" Brenna asked. "I vow she's innocent as a babe. Asked if Des and me were married." She guffawed at that thought. "Blushed to the roots of her hair when I stripped this gown off her." She pointed at Gideon. "You'd better be careful with her. She's a virgin or I'm not Brenna O'Shea."

Gideon raked a hand through his hair. His eyelids were heavy, and he envied Strawberry her slumbers. "I wouldn't touch her," he said. "The sooner I'm rid of her, the better."

"Good," Brenna said with a nod.

"Very good," Des said. "Come sit on my lap, Brenna love."

"Oh, I'm Brenna love now, am I? Before, I was too free with the invitations."

"My mistake." Des tugged her down, and Gideon rose.

"I'll just…" But they weren't paying him any heed. He made his way upstairs, leaving Brenna's giggles behind. The door of the one room above had been left cracked. Strawberry lay on the bed, one hand curled under her chin. She wore one of Brenna's dresses, a pretty green material that swirled around her legs. The smudge of ash was gone from her cheek, and her hair fanned out around her head like a halo of fire.

Gideon wanted to crawl into bed beside her.

He wanted to wake her with kisses and slow caresses.

He wanted… He wanted what he knew he could never have.

Nine

"Oh, Dorothea!" Lady Chesterly said as she promenaded into the Dowager Countess of Dane's boudoir and swept the dowager into an embrace reeking of cologne. Dorothea tried to breathe shallowly so as not to be overcome by the scent of rose petals.

Finally Florentia released her and settled on the cream silk-upholstered chair beside the lavender chaise longue where Dorothea reclined.

Florentia's small hazel eyes swept over her friend, and then she snapped her fingers at Edwards. "Tell the housekeeper we need tea sweetened with brandy right away."

"Yes, my lady," Edwards said.

"And some of those delicious biscuits as well." Florentia patted Dorothea's shoulder. "You must keep up your strength, dear."

No matter that the biscuits were Florentia's personal favorite. Dorothea didn't want a biscuit. She didn't want tea. She didn't even want her dear friend.

She wanted her daughter.

"I came as soon as I received your note," Florentia said. "You wrote the matter was urgent, but I must confess I did not expect to see you like this. My dear, I'm worried."

Dorothea reflected that was because she had rarely ever felt this close to losing her composure. She hadn't wept and railed when Erasmus had died. She had cried silent, private tears over the babes she'd lost all those many years ago. And she'd almost wept at Dane's wedding to that horribly unsuitable Marlowe. But she'd been strong. She'd had to be strong, because there was no place in this world for a weak woman.

That's what she'd tried to teach Susanna. And now the child was missing.

"Please tell me what ails you. Shall I call for the doctor?" Florentia asked.

"No," Dorothea said.

Florentia peered around the small but well-appointed boudoir. It contained a small desk, two chairs and the chaise longue, and a tulipwood table on which to serve tea. The windows faced the gardens, but Dorothea had ordered the curtains shut. The light hurt her eyes this afternoon.

"Where is Susanna?" Florentia asked. "Is she not attending you?"

Dorothea pressed her lips together. "Susanna is the reason I begged you to come," Dorothea said in a whisper. "She's…" She could not seem to say the words aloud. She'd heard them said. Crawford had said them and then Brook had, after he'd done a cursory search. But Dorothea feared if she spoke the words, the situation would become real.

Florentia leaned close. "She's...?"

Dorothea dug her nails into the soft flesh of her palm, willing the tears back. She swallowed, humiliated by the sound her gulp made in the back of her throat.

"She's ill?" Florentia guessed.

"No." Dorothea shook her head. She should speak and not force her poor, dear friend to conjecture.

"She's engaged?"

Dorothea closed her eyes against the sting of tears. If Susanna's disappearance became known, her daughter would never find a husband.

"She's with child!" Florentia whispered.

"No!" Dorothea shrieked. She could not bear to think of that consequence as a result of her daughter's foolish actions. She closed her eyes and attempted to calm herself. "She's run away."

Florentia gasped. "Surely not! You must be mistaken."

Dorothea shook her head. "I'm not. I slept late this morning. The storms last night woke me, and I did not rest well."

Florentia made a sound of agreement. "Yes, it was quite a storm. We lost a yew tree."

Dorothea gave her friend a severe look, and Florentia pursed her lips together, chastised.

"Edwards woke me because Susanna's maid was concerned. Susanna was not in her bedchamber, and her bed had not been slept in."

"Was she home with you last night?" Florentia asked.

"Yes, yes."

Brook had already asked her all of these questions.

"Oh dear," Florentia said quietly. Her tone sent a shiver of apprehension through Dorothea. Certainly, Dorothea had imagined every possible scenario, but she could not quell the urge to ask her friend to elaborate. "Do you think it possible Susanna eloped?" Florentia asked.

"Certainly not. I have kept her safe and secure, away from any men of that sort." Dorothea wanted to add that Susanna would never do such a thing to her devoted mother. Her daughter had to know it would break her mother's heart. She did not add the statement though, because if Susanna cared about not breaking her mother's heart, she would be here now.

"What does Sir Brook say?" Florentia inquired. "Surely, he will have her home at any moment."

"I would have thought so, but he has been gone for hours," Dorothea said, her voice beginning to shake. "He found no sign of forced entry or violence. In fact, the only missing article is a candlestick."

"One candlestick?"

Dorothea nodded.

"Odd. What does Sir Brook make of it?"

Dorothea dabbed at her eyes with her handkerchief. "You know Brook. He never speculates. So here I sit and wait. My darling Susanna could be in trouble, and I can do nothing to help her."

"Calm yourself, my dear Dorrie." Florentia patted her shoulder. It did nothing but irritate Dorothea, and she regretted asking the woman to come. She did not want to be patted. Florentia continued to pat away.

"You should not blame yourself."

Dorothea jumped to her feet, grabbing the edge of the chaise longue for support. "Why on earth would I blame myself?"

Florentia hunched her shoulders, looking very much like a turtle that wanted to disappear into its shell. "You should not. I misspoke."

"No, you didn't. You think this is my fault. Don't you?" She pointed an accusatory finger at Florentia. "Don't you?"

Florentia made a show of peering at the door behind Dorothea. "Is that the tea?"

"Damn the tea."

Florentia's small eyes widened.

"You think I protect her too much."

"She is your daughter. Of course you must protect her."

But Dorothea knew when she was being appeased. "But you think I protect her too much."

Florentia slumped and creased the material of her gown between two fingers. "I think you love her very dearly. After the losses you suffered, how could you not?"

Dorothea sank onto the chaise longue. All the air in her lungs seemed to whoosh out. "Exactly."

"But…"

Dorothea's chin jerked up.

"She might not have understood your motivations. Children sometimes rebel against being held too tightly."

"And you would know this because of your vast parenting experience?"

Florentia's cheeks reddened, and Dorothea immediately felt ashamed of her outburst.

"I am not helping." Florentia rose. "I should go."

"Wait." Dorothea held out a hand, and Florentia took it reluctantly.

"Perhaps I have been a bit strict with her. I didn't want her to make the same mistakes I did."

"Of course you didn't."

"I was too hard on her. I should have been more loving. I should have showed her more affection. God knows Erasmus could hardly bear to look at her."

"Do you think he knew?"

"He was no fool. I don't think he would have blamed me, if it hadn't been for Susanna." Dorothea buried her head in her hands. "And now," she said, her voice muffled, "she asks me to take her to Vauxhall Gardens. The girl has no notion what she asks of me."

"Surely you would be safe going now."

Dorothea shook her head. She refused to raise it. She would not be seen crying. "I will never be safe there."

She would never be safe anywhere. For all her efforts to keep her daughter safe, Susanna was lost to her. She might never see the girl again. And she hadn't even told her that she loved her.

And now it was too late.

"My lady?" The butler tapped on the door.

Dorothea wiped her eyes and straightened her shoulders. "Yes, Crawford. Come in."

He entered, his lips pinched with strain. He nodded at Lady Chesterly and presented a polished silver salver, perched on top of his white-gloved hands. A yellowed, crumpled playbill lay in the center.

"A woman and a child arrived at the servants' entrance just now, my lady. I would have sent them away, but the woman produced this…" He eyed the dirty paper, seeming uncertain how to describe it. "This playbill."

"I fail to see how this concerns me. We do not feed beggars. Send her on her way."

"The woman, a Mrs. Castle, claims Lady Susanna wrote a message on the back."

"Susanna?" Dorothea snatched the dirty paper off the tray and turned it over. Indeed, on the back in what looked to be marking pencil, was a short note in Susanna's handwriting.

Dear Mama,

Bess Castle is an exceptional seamstress who has shown me great kindness. I would be most grateful if you would ask Crawford to employ her and her daughter at Derring House. You are always saying a good seamstress is invaluable.

Your daughter,
Susanna

A postscript had been added, the words squeezed together.

I will be home soon.

"She will be home soon!" Dorothea thundered. "She will be home soon! Does she think she is on holiday? Where is this woman, Crawford? I want to speak with her. I want to know where she last saw my daughter."

"I thought you might, my lady. In fact, I have taken the liberty of sending Nathaniel to fetch Sir Brook and bring him here."

"Very good, Crawford," Florentia said.

"And I inquired of Mrs. Castle from whence she hailed."

Dorothea leaned forward. "And?"

"The address she gave me is in St. Giles, my lady. Seven Dials, to be precise."

Dorothea sank to the chaise.

Seven Dials. Her dear, sweet daughter had been in Seven Dials. Dorothea would kill her.

If she wasn't already dead.

Ten

Susanna jolted awake, momentarily disoriented by the unfamiliar sounds of a hoarse woman hawking meat pies and a group of men arguing about someone called Sir John Barleycorn. Opening her eyes did not reassure her. The room was unfamiliar, and it took her seven fast, hard heartbeats to remember where she was.

Unfortunately, those were followed by four or five painful clenches in her chest when she felt the warm, solid figure beside her. The curtains on the windows in the room were so thin she could see through them, and Gideon's dark hair on the pillow beside her gleamed in the filtered sunlight. Strands of light brown and gold were woven among the darker hair.

His arms were wrapped around his chest in a protective gesture. Either that or he wanted to touch her as little as possible. She could have spent hours studying his long, nimble fingers or his lean, powerful frame.

But her gaze drifted immediately to his face. That aspect of him she could not freely examine any other time. His eyelids hid his beautiful green eyes, and his mouth was slack with sleep. He looked quite young without his lips twisted in a mocking grin.

His head was angled in such a way she could easily scrutinize his scar. It must have been red at one time, but age had faded it to white. It started at his temple, just at the hairline, and slashed across an inch of skin to bisect his dark eyebrow. He was fortunate he hadn't lost an eye.

"Are you done gawking at me?"

Susanna squealed and jumped back. The bed was not wide enough to accommodate her startled movement, and she would have fallen had Gideon not reacted quickly. His hand wrapped around her wrist, and he yanked her back.

He yanked a bit too hard though. She ended up sprawled on top of his chest. When she tried to lever herself up and away, he held her in place with his hands pressed against her back.

"Take a good look," he said. "It's repulsive and yet strangely fascinating."

Susanna shook her head. "It's not repulsive."

His eyes narrowed, and he seemed to study her for a long moment. He'd said she was a terrible liar. Could he see that she did not lie now?

Could he see she didn't find anything about him repulsive in the least?

Quite the opposite, in fact.

Gideon shoved her aside. Sitting, he ran a hand through his hair, disheveling it further. "You want to know how I got it, don't you?"

"I don't mean to pry."

He laughed without humor. "No. You want to stare at me while I sleep, but you don't want to pry."

She looked down and noted the bodice of the dress Brenna had given her dipped rather low. Susanna tugged it up. "You are correct. My behavior was unpardonable. It won't happen again."

He stared at her with a look of complete bewilderment on his face. "You really mean it, don't you?" He stroked a finger down her cheek, and she tried very hard not to shy away from his touch. "You're so prim and proper." His hand dipped lower to the hollow of her throat. "Makes me want to corrupt you."

His finger trailed the neckline of the bodice she'd just yanked up.

"What if I don't want to be corrupted?" She grasped his finger in her hands and drew it away from her chest.

"What if you do?"

She tried to pull her hand away, but he had managed to twist his wrist. Now he held *her* hand captive.

"All I want is for you to act as my guide to Vauxhall Gardens. Nothing more."

"Nothing?"

When his eyes met hers, her throat tightened. She couldn't speak, and shook her head feebly.

"Not even a kiss?"

"No!" she choked out.

"Huh." He nodded as though her answer surprised him. "I'll tell you how I received my scar."

"You will?"

"If you tell me why it's so important for you to go to Vauxhall."

She ought to have known. He was a thief, after all. Nothing was free.

"Then again, it's your choice. You don't have to tell me," he said, finally releasing her hand. His green eyes cut to the thinly veiled window. "If you do, I might be more willing to risk my neck when night falls."

"Can't we go now? My mother must be out of her head with worry, and my brother is most certainly searching for me."

"Vauxhall isn't open during the day." Gideon stood and stretched, exposing a flat swath of bronzed skin at his waist. "Furthermore, Sir Brook can go to the devil. He may be the best investigator in the country. He may have found people no one else could find. But he doesn't know the rookeries like I do. He won't catch me unless I want to be caught."

"And Beezle?"

"He's another reason we wait until dark. You're too conspicuous in the daylight." His gaze settled on her, and Susanna felt heat rise in her cheeks. She notched her bodice higher again, which caused him to grin.

"Me? What have I to do with this Beezle?"

"You've been seen with me."

"Would that I could undo that."

He grinned, unapologetic. "I warned you."

Since he had indeed warned her, and she'd taken no heed, she ignored his statement. "So we wait until dark and then travel to Vauxhall."

"That's the plan." He sank down on the bed, and she tilted toward him before regaining her balance.

"And what do we do all day?"

Something crashed on the ground floor, and Brenna's giggle floated up to them.

"I can think of a few ideas." Another wicked grin. The man had an unlimited supply.

"Won't your friend want his room back?"

Another crash and another giggle.

"I think they're doing quite well without it."

Susanna ducked her head before he could see her cheeks. She feared they'd changed from pink with embarrassment to red with mortification. She heard more giggling and then a soft moan.

The heat from her face traveled down through her body and settled in her lower belly, causing an unfamiliar and somewhat urgent ache.

Oh dear. A distraction. That was it. She needed a distraction.

"You were about to tell me how you acquired your scar," she said loudly to cover the noise from below.

"Was I?" The undamaged brow rose. "Then you agree to my terms?"

Another moan.

"Yes, yes. I agree. Go on then."

"Are you feeling ill, Strawberry? Your face looks a bit flushed."

"I'm fine," she hissed, turning her face away from him. "It's warm in here."

"I hadn't noticed." He rose and went to the window, parting the curtains slightly and peering down. Susanna couldn't resist studying him while he stood with his back to her. He wore a coarse shirt that had once been white, and faded black trousers.

His coat had been abandoned on a chair. Despite the shabbiness of his attire, he wore it well. He stood tall and straight, looking almost regal. He might have been a deposed monarch attempting to adjust to life as a commoner.

What if that was part of the story behind the scar? What if he was actually the lost son of a duke or a baron who'd gambled away his fortune?

Or what if he was exactly what he appeared to be, and she was trying to make him into something he was not because...

Because she liked him.

Because despite everything—or perhaps *because of* some things—she liked him. And just now she'd been imagining herself married to him. Which was ridiculous. She could never marry a man of his station, and she was a foolish, naive girl to pretend he was anything other than what he appeared to be.

But how could she be anything other than foolish and naive when she had no experience of the world? Gideon Harrow was the first man who'd touched her bare skin. The first man she'd spoken to about any topic not prescribed by her mother. The first man who'd made her belly flutter and her heart gallop when he looked at her for a moment longer than was appropriate.

Susanna knew all of this when she considered the matter logically. Unfortunately, whenever those bold green eyes focused on her, she forgot all about logic.

As though he knew what she was thinking, he turned and caught her staring. If he was annoyed by her blatant perusal, he didn't show it. His expression remained both bemused and smug.

"You won't believe this, but I wasn't born a thief." He pulled the ineffective curtains closed and strolled back to the bed, standing at the foot and looking down at her.

"On the contrary, I find that very easy to believe."

Now was the moment he'd tell her he was actually a viscount in disguise. Hadn't Brook gained his current reputation for finding the lost brother of some viscount or other in an opium den? It was not impossible.

"My parents weren't wealthy."

She sagged with disappointment. When he didn't continue, she glanced at his face and caught the bewildered expression. No doubt he wondered what had disheartened her.

"Sure you want to hear this?" he asked.

"Yes. Please, go on. Your family was not wealthy."

"No, but we had a home, and I didn't go to bed hungry. There wasn't any money for school, but my grandmother taught me to read and write."

"Oh." She hadn't meant to show him her surprise, but when he'd said he could read, she'd thought he lied. She hadn't expected him to be educated. She supposed she should have expected it. He spoke better than most of his ilk, though his lower-class accent crept in once in a while. But then men like he were always tricksters and cheats. They could imitate their betters.

But perhaps Gideon hadn't been imitating.

"My grandmother had come down in the world. Her father had been a gentleman, but she was his only offspring. When he died, the property went to a distant cousin."

"It was entailed."

He pointed to her. "That's the word. When her husband died, her son—my father—had to learn a trade. He worked for a printing press and kept me supplied with plenty of reading material."

"What did the press print?"

"Religious pamphlets, political literature. Anything a man was willing to pay to have printed. My mother was a seamstress. She sewed all my clothing."

"You were well dressed and well-read." She pulled her legs to her chest and wrapped her arms around her knees. She would have never guessed any of this about him. It fascinated her to think of this man as a boy with parents and a grandmother. He seemed so alone now, so self-sufficient. He didn't seem to need anyone.

"It sounds as though your parents loved you a great deal."

He let out a short laugh and stared at a spot on the wall. "It does, don't it?"

The silence settled in, and thankfully there really was silence, as whatever Brenna and Des had been doing was over, and she waited for him to continue. When he didn't, she lowered her hands and rose to her knees.

"They didn't love you?" she prodded.

"They died." His gaze cut to her again, and for an instant she saw the boy he'd been. The hard, green eyes had been softened, and the arrogant set of his mouth replaced by a genuine smile.

But now the hardened thief was back.

"How?" she whispered.

"Fever. Took my grandmother and my mother." He shrugged as though he didn't care, even though she knew recalling their deaths must have been painful. "Took a lot of people that winter."

"I'm sorry," she murmured and reached out to touch his arm, to offer comfort.

He stepped back. "So was I, but I was even sorrier when my father started drinking."

Susanna could see where the story would go now. Why had she asked him to tell her this?

"Did he give you that scar?" she asked.

Gideon shook his head. "No. He gave me others. The drink made him mean. And then one night he didn't come home. I was an orphan at seven."

Susanna put her arms around herself because she knew he wouldn't let her hold him. He wasn't that little boy any longer, and yet she wished she could hold that child and soothe his fears.

"You want to know who Beezle is? He's the arch rogue of the Covent Garden Cubs. That's my gang—or was. Satin started the gang and brought me in when I was about ten or eleven. Beezle came later and proved himself just as ruthless as Satin. Now Satin's in the stone pitcher, thanks to our friend Marlowe, and Beezle's the new Prince Prig."

Susanna gestured to his temple. "And Satin did this to you?"

He touched it absently, almost as though he'd forgotten it. "In a manner of speaking. I fought with a cub from a rival gang over a trifle—a silk wipe maybe. He pulled a knife and did this." He traced the white scar with his tanned fingers. "Almost took my eye out."

"You were lucky," she said.

"Right. That's what I keep telling myself. I'm lucky."

He hadn't told her everything, and she was afraid to ask questions. How would she feel if she knew more about his life? Would she like him more? Hate him?

She was afraid she'd admire him, and she didn't want to care about him, to want to hold him, to wish she could save him.

She couldn't save him.

She couldn't even save herself.

Besides, he didn't need her to save him. He'd been doing quite well on his own, until she'd taken him from his path and forced him onto hers. "I'll make you a promise," she said. "As soon as you take me home from Vauxhall, I'll give you the necklace back. I won't break my word."

"No, you won't." His eyes hardened. "And now fair is fair," he said, resting one knee on the bed. It was so small that even that slight weight pushed her forward and all but into him. "I received my scar in a fight with another cub. Your turn."

He took her hand and pulled her up on her knees until she was facing him. The other hand slid around her back and drew her closer.

"What are you about?" she demanded.

Unconcerned, he settled her inside the leg braced on the bed, his chest almost touching hers, and his heat making her skin tingle.

"Taking my payment."

"I was to tell you why I want to go to Vauxhall."

"And you will." He released her hand and sank his fingers into her hair. A gentle tug and her neck ached until she looked him in the eye. "You agreed to my terms. You didn't ask what they were."

"I assumed—"

"That was your third mistake. Your first was asking me to be your guide, and your second"—he lowered his head until their faces were inches apart—"was telling me you'd never been kissed."

&c&

Her deep brown eyes widened, and he might have feared he'd scared her if she hadn't parted her lips and touched the tip of her tongue to the top. She wanted to be kissed. She should have been kissed before now, perhaps by some inexperienced youth who slobbered all over her or stuck his tongue down her throat.

His hand tightened in her thick strawberry-blond hair. He didn't want to think of any other man kissing her. He wanted to be the first.

"Why was telling you I'd never been kissed a mistake?" she asked, her voice breathy and low.

"Because it's an oversight I must rectify."

Her hair tickled his bare wrist. It felt like he imagined a skein of silk might feel before being woven into an exquisite garment. Her long lashes fluttered, then lifted again, giving him a look into her wide eyes—eyes that were dark with arousal.

"You shouldn't."

"You're right. I shouldn't. I shouldn't dare to touch you. And I'll kiss you because I shouldn't dare. Call it my contrary nature. I have a bad habit of doing what I shouldn't."

He lowered his lips and brushed them lightly across hers. Her lashes fluttered down, and he felt her tremble ever so slightly in his arms.

When he lifted his lips, her lashes lifted again. "Was that the kiss?"

He tried to hide his smile. "No."

The hand on her back drifted down to caress the curve of her waist. She was slim, but she had curves. He wanted to slide his fingers lower to discover whether her arse was as round and firm as he thought. But he'd save that for later.

He knew without question there would be a later.

"I plan to corrupt you, Strawberry."

"I told you I don't want to be corrupted."

"Little by little." His fingers edged down to her waist. "Bit by bit." He brushed the swell of her arse. "Minute by minute."

He gave her flesh a light squeeze, and she jumped.

"You don't want to be corrupted." He brushed her lips with his again. "Give me the necklace."

"I can't," she whispered. "Not until…"

His tongue traced the seam of her lip. She was impossibly sweet. Her lips were lush and full, and the taste of her like honey.

"What are you doing?" she whispered, sounding scandalized.

"I told you." He nibbled her lower lip. "Corrupting you."

He pressed his lips to hers, kissing her gently, allowing her to accustom herself to the feel of him.

"Don't," she whispered.

"Then tell me to stop." He paused, his lips so close to hers all he needed to do was breathe to touch her.

He waited. Gideon was a lot of things—a thief, a liar, a cheat. But he was no bully. He'd stop if she asked.

His heart pounded in his chest, and his body tensed. His cock grew hard as the seconds passed. Neither of them moved or breathed. And just when he thought they might be at another impasse, her hand pressed lightly against his chest.

That light, tentative touch almost undid him. He was tempted beyond reason to ease her back onto the bed, cover her with his body, kiss her the way she should be kissed. It would be nothing to accomplish. One leg was braced on the bed, and he held her to him. He needed only to lower her to the bedspread.

But Gideon wasn't Beezle's best rook because he gave in to urges. He knew how to be patient. He knew how to wait.

He bore the heat and the light brush of her fingers as her hand explored the contours of his chest. He fought not to jerk when her faltering fingers tickled him. He gritted his teeth when she skated over a particularly sensitive spot.

He waited until she raised her eyes to him again. The invitation was in her eyes, but he wanted to hear it.

"Say it," he murmured, his lips almost touching hers when he spoke the words.

"Kiss me," she whispered so quietly he almost couldn't hear her.

"Gideon." He pressed his lips against hers gently, teasing her. "Kiss me, Gideon."

She tried to shake her head, but his hand in her hair held her steady.

"I can't say that." He could feel the heat of her embarrassment where their skin touched. If he'd pulled back to see, he knew her face would have been the color of a beet.

"You can say it."

He pressed his lips to hers again, taking her lower lip between his teeth and sucking lightly.

"You want to say it."

"I don't…"

"Say it, Susanna. *Kiss me, Gideon.* Say it, and I'll slide my tongue inside you. I'll kiss you until you forget my name and your name and your fucking money and title. Say it."

Her body went rigid at his curse. It was impossible for him to temper his language when he was this aroused. And if she pulled back now, he'd make a vow never to curse again.

But she leaned closer, her breasts brushing against his chest. Small, firm breasts that would fit his hands perfectly.

Desire raged through his body, and his efforts at restraint taxed his muscles until they felt like they might pop with the exertion. He'd never wanted anything this badly. Never wanted a woman so much. Never waited for a woman like this.

Any other woman, and he would have walked away, decided she wasn't worth the effort.

But Gideon didn't move.

Her dark eyes focused on his. "Kiss me, Gideon."

He checked the urge to take her with the fierceness his body craved. Instead, he opted for torturous slowness. His lips slid over hers again and again until he knew her shape and was drunk on the satiny texture. She tried to kiss him back, an awkward attempt that only made him want her more.

He tasted her with his tongue, prompting her to part her lips. When she did, he slid inside her warmth.

She gasped and tried to withdraw, but he held her close. His tongue stroked hers, tangled with it, thrust and retreated. After a moment, she stopped fighting him. She moaned low in her throat, her body relaxing into his. He slanted his mouth over hers again and again, kissing her deeper and with more urgency.

He knew the moment she surrendered. Her body slid against his in an instinctive movement, and her tongue tangled with his. She was a quick student, and though her kisses were still unpracticed, Gideon's cock throbbed in response to her efforts.

He buried both hands in her hair and finally summoned the willpower to break the kiss. It was either that or take her on the bed.

God knew he wanted to take her. And God knew he had no right to take her virginity. He was a common thief and she a lady, and he wasn't good enough to kiss her feet, much less touch her like this.

"Strawberry," he said, pulling back and giving her a cocky grin. "I think my work here is done. I'd venture to say you're one step closer to corruption."

He gave her a wink because it was the sort of thing he'd seen lechers do.

Her hand stung his face when she slapped him. He released her. Obviously, the wink had been too much.

She pushed him back—unnecessary, really, considering he was already moving away to avoid another slap—and jumped off the bed.

"Do not ever touch me again, you—you *rogue*!"

He flinched, only half in jest.

Head held high, she whirled and marched to the door. Throwing it open, she tossed a withering look over her shoulder and slammed it shut behind her.

Eleven

IT HAD BEEN A GLORIOUS EXIT, SUSANNA DECIDED when she paused on the stairs and continued her retreat. Her return would not be as glorious. She should have considered the amorous activities of the couple downstairs before she'd marched away.

She should have ordered Gideon to leave. Let him interrupt the moaning and grunting.

What on earth were they doing anyway?

She had some idea. She'd moaned herself when he'd kissed her a few moments before. She hadn't known a kiss could be like that. She'd only ever experienced the dry, papery-light pecks her mother had given her. Her brothers occasionally bussed her on the forehead, but that was even less personal.

She'd seen Dane kiss his wife, of course. But she hadn't dared watch them too closely. Did Dane kiss Marlowe the way Gideon had just kissed her? Did everyone kiss that way?

It was scandalous!

It was startling.

She wanted to do it again.

But not with Gideon Harrow.

She never wanted to see him again. In fact, she wished she could force him to go to Vauxhall Gardens right now so she could be rid of him sooner. Instead, she would have to walk back into that room and bear his mocking grin.

Swallowing the bile rising in her throat along with her pride, she opened the door and stepped back inside. Gideon was at the window again, and to her surprise, he didn't look around.

"I hope you've come to apologize."

"Apologize!" she sputtered. "You possess the unmitigated gall to suggest—"

"That's a no then." He leaned a shoulder against the window, still not turning to face her. Below, something crashed to the floor. Susanna closed her eyes in mortification.

"Like rabbits, aren't they?"

She didn't answer. She did not want to encourage conversation. Instead, she went to the bed and sat primly on the edge. She folded her hands together and waited for him to make fun of her, but he continued to stare out the window.

What did he see out there that held his interest? He was probably plotting a new crime. That was fine with her, as long as he conducted his criminal activity *after* he'd escorted her to Vauxhall. She was through pitying him. Yes, his mother and grandmother had died from fever. It did not seem that his father had been a very kind or compassionate man.

Many men had unkind fathers.

Many women too.

That didn't mean one had to resign oneself to a life of crime. He might have stayed at the orphanage, tried to learn a trade…

Oh, she was being ridiculous now. Even sheltered as she was, she knew orphanages treated their wards little better than gaolers treated prisoners. She'd once asked her mother if she might join a philanthropic society to aid orphans, but her mother had forbid it.

"Philanthropy is for married women," she'd said. Apparently, the plight of orphans was too shocking for young misses.

She pulled a lock of her hair down and examined the ends, partly to have something to do and partly to shield her face in case Gideon turned to look at her.

She did not pity him. He'd made his choices. He had few of them, but he had survived and made a life for himself. Too bad his way of living dictated he take advantage of her when she'd offered him the meager comfort any compassionate person would have. She would have to be strong and unfeeling to survive the night ahead.

She peeked through the strands of red. He still stood at the window. One of his hands tapped his thigh, the fingers beating a rapid pace. What *was* he planning?

This long silence made her uncomfortable. How long would she be trapped in this room with him?

"I believe I mentioned I wanted to go to Vauxhall Gardens because of my mother."

"Actually, you called it your dream."

"It is, or rather, what it represents is."

The fingers tapping on his thigh paused. "I'm listening."

"Dreams may seem silly to you."

"Now why would you think that?" he drawled.

She paused at his sarcasm. She should have expected it. "But I assure you my life has not been without its own travails."

"Travails?" he said with a disparaging look over his shoulder. "Right. Like the day you sacked your slavey and had to dress *yourself* in silk and diamonds."

"Well, yes, that was a difficult day."

He rounded on her, and she smiled.

Slowly, a smile crept over his features too. "You don't take yourself as seriously as I thought."

"I take myself very seriously. I must go to Vauxhall. After this, I'll never have another chance. I have to know why my mother behaves as she does."

"And how is that?" He rolled one of his sleeves up, exposing a muscled, bronzed forearm.

"Protective."

He looked up from his sleeve. "Yes, that must be awful."

"It is when it's taken too far. I'm not even allowed to go to the ladies' retiring room by myself!"

"The what?"

Her cheeks burst with heat. "You know, the private chamber for ladies."

"Oh, you mean to piss?" He grinned. "Sorry. But the look on your face was worth the crass words." He put a hand over his heart. "I'll be the perfect gentleman for the rest of the day."

"That I would like to see."

He gave her a rather dashing bow. "As you wish." He started on the other sleeve. "So your dear mama is overprotective."

"Yes. She's always been thus with me. My brothers were allowed to do as they wished, but I was locked away."

"Would it be impertinent to point out that you are a girl and they are boys?"

She checked a smile at the lofty way he gestured with his hand. "No, and even taking that into account, she all but smothered me. I don't understand why. I've done nothing to lose her trust."

"Until now."

"Yes, until now. And I've taken this step only as a last resort. You see, I was finally allowed to go to the ladies' retiring room alone, and when I was there, I had the oddest conversation."

He raised a finger. "I want credit for the fact that I have not voiced one comment that has crossed my mind these last few moments."

"You have it. Lady Winthorpe mentioned my mother had once been in love. And the man she had loved was not my father."

Gideon gasped. "No!"

Susanna looked about for something to throw. Where was her candlestick? Drat! She'd left it downstairs. "I know that is not unusual, but if you knew my mother, it would surprise you. She's…not the sort to fall in love."

"You mean she is a cold bitch?" At her stare, he held his hands up protectively. "I mean that in the most polite and gentlemanly way possible."

"No matter." Susanna stood. "Nothing you say can shock me anymore."

"Oh, I very much doubt that."

"You promised to be on your best behavior."

"It's just so damn tempting." His fingers danced on his thigh again. "Tell me more about *Lady Winthorpe*."

Susanna smiled at the way he made her name sound like she was on par with the Queen. "My mother has never loved anyone. Or at least that has not been my observation. Not me, not my brothers, not my father. Who is this man she did love?"

"The man *Lady Winthorpe* thinks she loved."

"Yes, it is the countess's recollection, but she mentioned picnics and late-night rendezvous at Vauxhall Gardens. She intimated my mother and…this man were lovers."

"Shocking. Immoral behavior among the upper classes."

Susanna strode to the window and stared out, seeing nothing. "Mock me if you will, but I couldn't help but think if I went to Vauxhall Gardens, I might discover something about her past."

"I don't mean to wake you from this dream—no, yes, I do mean to do exactly that. These meetings at Vauxhall were how many years ago? Twenty? Thirty?"

A group of boys carrying sticks chased a distorted ball into an alley then returned again, swatting it through the legs of passersby.

"I agree. I had thought of that, but then when I mentioned the possibility of her taking me to the pleasure gardens, she acted so strangely, so adamant that I not go. I began to wonder if maybe there was something there she wanted to hide from me."

He leaned one shoulder on the window casing, standing very close to her. "Let me get this straight. Your mother told you not to go to Vauxhall Gardens,

and the very next thing you do is run off with me to…
Vauxhall Gardens. I no longer wonder at your mother
following you to the retreating room."

"It's a retiring room, and that has nothing to do with
it. This is the first time I have ever disobeyed her."

"The last time too, I imagine, when she has you back."

"I'll be married immediately or sent to a convent
in France."

"A convent?" He lifted a strand of her hair to his
nose. "The life of a nun wouldn't suit you."

"How do you know?" she asked in challenge.
"You don't know anything about me."

"I know that inside that prissy exterior, there's a
woman with needs and desires waiting to come out."

"That's what you want to believe because you want
to corrupt me."

"On the contrary. I want to corrupt you because I
see the potential in you. You're a wanton, Strawberry."

She slapped his hand, freeing her hair. "I most
certainly am not."

"The way you kissed me earlier suggests otherwise.
There's passion in you. Don't tell me you didn't
feel anything."

"I won't discuss this." She directed her gaze out the
window again.

"Why? Don't want to admit you're a flesh-and-
blood woman, not a virgin sacrifice? Your mother
will marry you to the highest bidder, most likely an
old man with a title and enough blunt to fill a house.
That's what swells do to their children, isn't it? Marry
them for connections or blunt?"

"My brother did neither."

He lifted her hair again, and this time she allowed it. "That puts more pressure on you to be good, to go to your marriage bed as the sacrificial lamb. Tell me this"—he leaned close and whispered in her ear—"do you think your old, feeble husband will make you feel like I did?"

She shuddered, uncertain whether the gesture was from lust at the memory of Gideon's kisses or revulsion at the prospect of her future husband.

"Do you think it's like that every time two people come together? It's not. I felt something too, Susanna."

She turned her head sharply, causing him to tug on the lock of hair he still held. "You felt something?" She studied his face, trying to determine if he was telling the truth. His green eyes were clear and guileless, but she could not afford to believe he meant what he'd said.

She couldn't trust him.

"Something you've never felt before?" she asked softly. "Something different than every other woman you've ever been with? I'm special, is that correct?"

"You seem skeptical."

"My brothers warned me about men like you. You just want to trick me into falling into your bed." As soon as the words escaped her mouth, she felt the heat rise from her bosom to the top of her forehead.

He leaned close, one finger playing with the yellowed lace on her sleeve. "Do you really think I'd have to trick you to take you to bed?"

No, no she did not. One look at those gorgeous eyes. One look at those sinful lips. He did not need to persuade her much at all. She stepped back, stationed herself on the other side of the window. "Why are we having this conversation? Again? This is about why I need to go to Vauxhall. I want you to understand why I must go."

"Oh, I understand."

"You say that as though you understand something I haven't stated."

"See, I knew you were clever." He winked at her.

"I have no hidden agenda."

"Oh, yes you do. You just don't know it."

"Really?" She folded her arms over her chest and thrust a hip out. "Then what is it?"

"You have seized upon this trek to Vauxhall because it offers you what you really want."

"Which is to see Vauxhall Gardens."

"No. What you really want is a change, an escape from the life you've led until now. A way out before you're married to Lord Doddering, and you're trapped."

Her arms seemed to unfold themselves.

"In which case," he added with a wicked grin, "why not seize your freedom while you have the chance?"

❧

He didn't reach for her, but she stepped back nonetheless. "Don't even think about it, Mr. Harrow."

He laughed. "I do believe you're the only lady that's ever called me *Mr. Harrow*. I like it. I like you."

"Why?" Her brow furrowed, the slender eyebrows dipping down. "You shouldn't like me."

"Shouldn't I? You did steal my necklace."

"It's not your—"

"And you have an annoying tendency to argue with me."

She tossed her head.

"And stick your nose in the air as though the air the rest of us breathe isn't good enough for you."

Her head jerked down, and she poked him in the chest. "That's not true. I've never thought that."

"You're an earl's daughter. You think it without even realizing it."

Her face flushed again, this time with anger. "Of all the gall—"

"That's right." He paced away from her, pretending to warm to his topic. "You use words like *gall* and *unpardonable*." He imitated her accent and waved a pinky finger.

"You're jealous because your vocabulary consists solely of words like *arse* and *fuck*."

The moment the word escaped her lips, she clamped both hands over them. Her eyes, huge and owlish, darted from side to side, as though she feared someone had overheard.

Gideon grinned like a fool. He grabbed her hands and pulled them down. "What did you say, Lady Susanna?"

"Leave me alone." She tried to pull away, but he was having too much fun.

"Did I hear the word *arse* escape those pretty pink lips?" He touched a finger to her lips, and she promptly tried to bite him. He was too quick for that. "Arse," he mimicked in her rounded vowels. "It sounds so refined. But the other…"

"Do not say it," she warned him.

"Say what?" He gave her an imploring look. "What was the other word you used?"

"It was a mistake."

"Never say so." He caught her around the waist. "I liked it."

"You would! Let me go."

"Say it again, Strawberry," he murmured in her ear, and she stilled.

Her body trembled almost imperceptibly as he brushed his lips over the shell of her small ear. He caught a lock of her hair and tucked it out of the way then put his mouth on the sensitive spot behind her ear. She smelled of a mixture of soap and a light, flowery perfume. So sweet, so innocent.

He was a bastard to even consider half the thoughts running through his mind at that moment.

"I don't like red hair," he whispered against her jaw.

"And here I thought this was a litany of what you do like about me." She sounded breathless, her voice ragged and low with need.

"I'll get to that. I'm trying to remind myself of what I don't like first." He tasted the skin just below her jawbone, traced the delicate curve with his lips. "You're too thin."

Except she felt perfect in his arms. She was warm and soft and round and exactly the right height. He hadn't thought he liked tall women, but now he realized he would never have to bend or stoop to kiss Strawberry.

"So are you." She ran a hand over his back. She might have meant to point out how little extra flesh he had, but her hand slowed, and her fingers began to stroke him. His cock, which had been half-awake, came to attention then.

"We both need to eat more." He pulled her closer, tended to her long, pale neck. "Do you know what I think?"

"You actually think?"

He grinned. Her words might be saucy, but the catch in her voice betrayed her. She wanted him, even if she didn't know precisely what it was she wanted.

"I think quite a lot. I think about you and me eating in bed."

"That sounds quite decadent."

"Oh, you don't know the half of it." He swept her into his arms and carried her three steps to the bed. Tossing her down, he was over her, his hands holding her wrists captive before she could protest. She stared up at him, her eyes dark with arousal, her breasts heaving. Brenna's dress was too large in the bosom, and it had dipped down again, exposing Susanna's snow-white shift.

How he ached to rip the fragile linen in half and expose her pale flesh. He wanted to kiss her, touch her, bury himself in her. His breath came in ragged gasps, reminding him of a beast poised to pounce on its victim.

"Do you know what I like about you?" he asked between breaths.

She shook her head.

"You're kind."

Her eyes flickered with confusion. "Pardon?"

He laughed and had to lower his head beside hers on the bed. Releasing her, he rolled onto his back and lay beside her. The ceiling had a large crack in it in the shape of an *S*. When he stopped laughing, he met her gaze. She stared at him as though he were a lunatic.

It wasn't far from the truth.

"I'm *kind*?"

"Yeah." He wanted to touch her lips, brush a finger along her cheek, lift her hair to his nose. Instead, he lay perfectly still. "You're kind to mongrel dogs and lost children and women who need employment."

"Oh, that." She looked up at the ceiling. Her eyes narrowed. "I didn't even think you liked Beauty."

"I don't. *I'm* not kind."

She flicked her eyes at him. "I don't believe that."

When she looked at him like that, with those big brown eyes that had seen so little of the world and none of the cruelties he witnessed daily, he wanted it to be true. He wanted to be kind for her. He wanted to be the sort of man who deserved to lie beside her, touch her, breathe her rarified air.

"Of course you don't. You're one of them what believes the best about everybody."

"No, I don't. I don't believe you're innocent of theft."

"Bet you think you can reform me."

She looked away. "Everyone deserves a second chance."

"Do they?" He propped his chin on an elbow. "Care to prove that?"

She frowned at him and narrowed her eyes with suspicion. "I don't know."

Smart girl.

"I want another chance to kiss you."

He didn't think she could help the color that rose in her cheeks at his suggestion.

"Because I'm so kind?"

"Because I like you."

"Despite the hair?"

Their gazes were locked, and he could feel his heart thundering in his chest.

"Mmm-hmm."

"Despite my bony frame?"

"A man's tastes can change." He ran a hand down her arm, the bare skin so soft it was like that of a newborn's.

She curled her hands around his neck and tugged him down. "So can a woman's."

She pressed her lips to his, her touch tentative. Her stiff lips reminded him to hold back. She wasn't for him. He would only sample, and he shouldn't do even that.

But he wasn't a gentleman. He wasn't bound by duty and honor. In his world, men took what they wanted because life was short and they might have only one chance.

And so he kissed her. He kissed her because he shouldn't, because Beezle would probably kill him this night, because once he saw her to Vauxhall Gardens he'd never see her again.

Because he'd never wanted to kiss a woman so badly.

Her fingers slid into his hair, and her mouth opened under his. Gideon registered surprise, but he'd been trained to take. She freely offered her mouth, her lips, and he plundered them. He slid over her, his body molding to hers, his hands cupping her cheeks.

His tongue touched hers, teased hers, then took possession. He slanted his mouth over hers, kissing her as though this was the last kiss either of them would ever have. He kissed her until he could feel her heart thudding just as hard as his against his chest.

He wanted to touch her, to show her what was possible between a man and a woman, but he kept his hands on her face, cradling her gently. He'd wait until she asked, and he knew that would be never.

And still, if this was all he would ever have of her, it was more than he deserved. It was more than enough.

"Gideon," she said on a moan and arched her body to press into his. He didn't even think she knew what she was doing. She had no idea how much she tested him and his self discipline.

He nipped her lips lightly. "What do you want, sweetheart? Should I stop?"

"No!"

He grinned until she kissed him, and he forgot to grin, forgot to breathe, forgot to keep his hands off. Her small, shapely breasts filled his hands, the taut peaks pressing against his palms. They were the size of ripe peaches, and he imagined just as succulent. She moaned again then gasped when he tweaked one of her hard nipples.

Gideon froze. He knew he should remove his hands, but a man had only so much control. He raised his gaze to hers, expecting to see censure or anger.

"I didn't know I could feel like that." Her voice and her eyes were full of wonder and something else that resembled curiosity.

Oh, he could make her feel a hell of a lot more.

"Should I stop?"

"Oh, you are trying very hard to be the gentleman, aren't you?"

"Not as hard as I should be."

She arched her back, pushing herself fully into his hands. "Then don't try. I like the rogue."

She'd barely said the words when his mouth claimed hers again. He fully intended to kiss her senseless, but it was *his* senses that seemed to take leave when she met his kisses with her own, which were just as passionate, just as full of need.

He yanked down her stays and her shift, revealing the warm, round flesh of her breast to his callused hand. She was perfect, and he reluctantly broke the kiss to put his mouth on her flesh. The curve of her breast was as soft as satin, the flesh like a snow-laden rise before his eyes. Her pink nipple jutted proudly at the center, and he trailed his tongue across her breast until he could circle it. She made a sound of pleasure, and he lapped at her then blew cool air, causing her to dig her fingers into the back of his neck.

He flicked his gaze to hers, but her eyes were closed, her face flushed, her lips parted. Oh, he was a saint. He'd never been so tempted. His cock had never throbbed and demanded the way it did now at the view of womanly beauty and desirability offered before him.

Gideon put his lips on her nipple and gently sucked it into his mouth. He rolled it over his tongue, swirled the tip of his tongue around the hard bead, then sucked almost imperceptibly harder. He repeated the motions two then three times until at the final suck she cried out and thrust her hips so her core met his hard cock.

His vision dimmed slightly with the hard jolt of desire.

"Wh-what are you doing to me?" she asked, her words slurred with pleasure. Gideon felt a surge of triumph hard in his gut. He would never have believed her so receptive. If he but touched her between the legs, she would come apart. He slid a hand down her waist and over the swell of her hip—one firm press, even over the material of the gown. He had to see her face, watch her climax. Gideon wanted to know if she would be as beautiful as he imagined.

He cupped her warmth, and the door creaked open.

"No time for that, love," Brenna said, her voice quick and hard. "We have trouble."

Twelve

SUSANNA SCRAMBLED TO TUG HER CHEMISE OVER HER bare skin and extricate herself from Gideon's arms. She jumped to her feet in a tangle of hair and skirts and immediately felt foolish. Brenna wasn't looking at them. She kept watch over her shoulder. Now that the blood wasn't thrumming in her ears, Susanna heard voices below. Another woman and…Des? No. His voice was higher than the low rumble rising up the stairs.

"Who?" Gideon asked without preamble. He stood and scraped his hair back off his forehead, all the more handsome for being disheveled.

"Mrs. Cummings," Brenna said, cutting her gaze to him then back over her shoulder.

"Shit."

"She is, and ye weren't none too wise to make an enemy of her. What'd ye do? Steal from her?"

Gideon didn't answer, and Brenna laughed. "Ye've got balls, I'll say that. First Beezle, now Mrs. Cummings. Do ye want to die?"

"Not particularly." He pushed past Susanna and shoved the curtains aside.

Brenna stomped into the room and slammed the curtains closed again. "Don't be daft. Ye're not going out that way."

"It's the only way."

Brenna hooked a thumb at Susanna. "Not with her. She can't climb in those skirts. Couldn't climb in trousers either, I wager." She gave Susanna an assessing look and then glared at Gideon. "Or were ye thinking to leave her?"

"Mrs. Cummings doesn't know her," Gideon began.

Susanna clutched her chest when a sudden pain shot through her. He would have left her. A moment before, he'd been holding her, kissing her as though she were the only other person in the world. Now the coward was more than willing to be rid of her.

She must have made some sound, because Gideon turned his green eyes on her. "You would have been fine, and I would have come back for you when she was gone."

Because she had the necklace. That was the only thing he cared about.

"A fine plan," Brenna interrupted, "but she's looking for both of you. Next we'll have Beezle at the door."

"Goddamn snitches."

Brenna sniffed. "What do ye expect when you make powerful enemies?" She gestured to them and swept across the room to fumble with a tapestry hanging on the far wall. It was an ugly thing, a depiction of a mythical dragon, and not a very good one, but Susanna had assumed the tapestry hid another crumbling wall. Instead, Brenna revealed a short door cut into the wall, the dark wood standing out against the crumbling plaster.

Brenna tugged on the round handle, but the door didn't budge. "Can you lend some of that brawn, Gid?"

"I should have guessed," he said, yanking on the door and freeing it with a creak. "This lead to one of the tunnels?"

"Aye, and at the end is the basement of a building Des would appreciate you forgot ever seeing."

"I can do that."

"You'd better."

Susanna rose on tiptoes, peering over Gideon's shoulder into the darkness of the passageway revealed by the door. The air that escaped smelled faintly of damp wood, and no light penetrated the darkness.

"I won't forget your help," Gideon told Brenna before grabbing Susanna's hand. Her instinct was to tug away. She did not want to go into that darkness with him.

"We'll see what you say after a few hours. This door is the only way in or out. Ye'd better stay there until Des comes for ye."

With a grim look of resignation, Gideon tugged her forward. Susanna gripped the door's casement. "What about Beauty?"

"The dog?" Brenna asked, with a quick look over her shoulder. "She's a fine specimen. Growled at Mrs. Cummings, so I like her already. Now, you'd better hurry." She pushed the door closed, and Susanna snatched her fingers inside. Darkness enveloped them, cutting off every last sliver of light.

"Don't tell me you're afraid of the dark," Gideon said, and though his words grated, his voice was reassuring. The hand on her wrist slid down her hand, and his fingers twined with hers. "Come on, Strawberry. If we stand too long in one place, the rats will think we're dinner."

"Rats!"

With a laugh, he tugged her forward. "Staircase here. Watch your step."

Reluctantly, she put a hand on the damp wall and guided herself down the creaky slope of stairs. There were about a dozen, and then the ground evened out. The corridor seemed wide enough for the two of them, but she desperately wished for a lamp or candle so they would not be in complete darkness.

She jumped at the sound of scurrying feet nearby, and Gideon squeezed her hand. "It's probably a cat."

"But you said before—"

"I was hoaxing you."

But he hadn't been, and whatever she had heard had not been a cat.

"The rookeries are known for having hundreds of hidden tunnels. Helps when a rook needs to escape one of the thief-takers. They're perfectly safe. I've been in them a hundred times."

He pulled her forward as he spoke, and his voice soothed her frayed nerves. He must have known he had that effect, because he continued to speak at a slow, measured cadence.

"Another set of stairs, Strawberry."

She slid her foot forward, feeling for the first step.

"We'll hide down here for a time, and Des will come for us when it's safe."

Hand on the wall again, she negotiated the steps. "What if he doesn't come?"

"He's got a store of valuables down here. He doesn't want us as permanent guests."

The steps, only four or five this time, ended, and they were once again on flat ground. Gideon paused and released her hand. "I'm right here. Touch my back."

She felt a fool, but she clung to the back of his shirt for comfort. His raised hands felt along a wall of some sort then rattled something made of iron.

"There's the handle," he said. With a shove, he opened a door. She stumbled after him, moving aside so he could close the door again.

When that was done, she stood in complete stillness as Gideon moved about. "Wipes and clothing," he muttered, sorting through various handkerchiefs and shirts. Something rattled. "Sounds like silver." He pressed something cold and solid into her hand. "Glim-stick, Strawberry. Your favorite."

She tried to shove it back at him, but he closed his fingers over hers on the shaft. "Keep it. You might need it."

"That makes me feel so much better."

He laughed then tugged her backward. "Sit." Hands on her shoulders, he pushed her down onto a surprisingly soft surface. She moved back and forth then ran her fingers over the velvet material. It felt very much like a couch or chaise longue. She stretched her fingers but couldn't feel the end of the furnishing.

"How is it a man ends up with clothing and furniture in a room underneath Field Lane?"

"I told you," Gideon said, sitting beside her. "He fences stolen goods."

"Who would steal a chaise longue? How would you even carry it off?"

"You don't really want to know the answer to that, do you?"

"No." She closed her eyes and felt tears sting the lids. With a sharp nip to her lips, she fought them back, but it would take more effort to keep them at bay. Her emotions raged wildly close to the surface. One moment she was running in fear of her life; the next moment her heart was pounding from the thrill of Gideon's touch, and a moment later her legs were wobbling in terror.

She should be begging Gideon to take her back home. She wouldn't put it past him to have engineered some of their close calls to elicit just that response from her.

If she asked, he'd take her home as soon as they were free of this...prison. She hesitated, but that's what it was for the moment. She could be safe in her own home, dressed in clean clothing, comfortable in her own bed.

All she had to do was ask.

She drew a deep breath, but the words wouldn't come. She didn't want to go home. She didn't want her comfortable life back.

She didn't even want to be rid of Gideon. She actually *liked* him. Perhaps that was part of the danger and the thrill. How long until he rid himself of her? How close to the fire did she dare to venture before he burned her?

Susanna wanted to be burned. She wanted him to kiss her again and touch her again and put his hands on her. She shouldn't want that. Ladies didn't have such wanton desires.

Nor did ladies traipse about the rookeries of London with known criminals.

"If my mother could see me now, she would probably need smelling salts to revive."

"And that's to be avoided?"

She laughed. He was always making her laugh, even when she did not want to laugh. "It's never happened before. My mother has an unusually strong constitution."

"Then we shall have to think of even more shocking antics if we want to properly distress her."

Susanna ran her hand along the soft velvet of the chaise. She imagined it a rich eggplant in color, but she supposed it could as easily be an ugly golden yellow.

"It does not take much to distress my mother. I disappoint her daily."

She felt Gideon shift beside her, and his fingers touched hers on the longue. "If that's the case, what does it matter what you do? You disappoint her no matter what."

Susanna opened her mouth to protest and immediately closed it again. "You're right."

"Of course I am."

Susanna ignored him. Something inside her had broken open, and she half expected light to pour from her chest. Her heart was suddenly weightless, her shoulders no longer encumbered by a yoke, her lungs expanded and filled with—

She coughed. The air in the underground room smelled moldy and felt heavy with dust. That wasn't the point. Susanna could breathe. Finally, she could breathe.

She held Gideon's hand in hers and squeezed. "You're right," she said again.

"I know. I'm alw—"

She slapped his hand on the chaise. "I cannot believe I didn't realize this before. Nothing I do will ever make my mother approve of me. I will never please her. Why am I trying so hard?"

"Might you loosen your grip on my hand?"

She released him and stood, too filled with enthusiasm to sit still. "You don't understand. I'm free now. I can do what I want—break all the rules. I'm done trying to be perfect." She bounced on her toes, her feet all but coming out of the too-large boots she wore.

"I do applaud your sentiments, but you might think again before you break *all* the rules. From all appearances, you had a comfortable home with slaveys and plenty to eat. You might not like the way the rest of the city lives."

She sank beside him. "Do you think I care about all of that?"

"Yes."

She tried to elbow him, but he evaded her. "I don't need servants and silk gowns and six courses at dinner."

"You only say that because you've never lived without. If I were you—"

"Which you're not."

"True, but if I were, I'd make amends with your lady mother. I could put up with quite a great deal if it meant I'd end the day with a six-course meal every night."

She laughed. "You're just like Marlowe. All she did was eat when I first met her."

Beside her, his body tensed. She felt as though the room grew darker and uncomfortably warmer.

"I'm nothing like Marlowe," he said. "She always belonged with the swells. She tried to fit in with the rooks, but there was something about her too good for the likes of Satin and the Covent Garden Cubs. She's where she should be now."

She heard the note of longing in his voice and felt the accompanying stab of jealousy in her chest. Foolish to be jealous over his friendship with Marlowe. Marlowe was married to Dane, and blissfully so. Even if Marlowe had been free, it was not as though Susanna had any claim on Gideon or ever could. Their stations in life were too sharply divided.

"Did you love her?" she asked suddenly. The words were out before she even realized she did not want to know the answer.

He snorted. "Half the cubs were in love with her either because she was the best thief among us or because she was the prettiest girl they knew."

She moved to face him, even though she couldn't see his face. "But did *you* love her?"

A scratching in the far corner broke the long silence.

"I shouldn't have asked," Susanna said finally. "It's none of my concern."

Gideon took hold of her arm before she could turn away. "I would have loved her," he said, "if I thought she'd ever love me back."

Now her heart clenched for a very different reason. She heard the pain in his voice, and she wished she could take it away.

"She never knew I was in love with her. She was

always oblivious to the way men looked at her. She didn't think she was pretty, thought her…ah, bosom was an annoyance."

Susanna shrank slightly. Marlowe was generously endowed, much more generously than Susanna herself. If that was the sort of figure Gideon preferred, she could not hope to catch his eye. "You never told her how you felt?"

"And have that between us? No." Silence. "I kissed her."

The knife in Susanna's heart twisted. He had probably kissed dozens of women. He had probably done much more than kiss them, if the skill he'd shown with her in Des's room was any indication. Why should she care if Gideon had kissed Marlowe? She didn't want to care, but she couldn't seem to persuade her emotions to listen to reason.

"I thought maybe if we kissed, she'd feel some of what I felt."

Susanna understood his meaning very well. She knew how she felt when Gideon kissed her. How could Marlowe have failed to fall in love with him? "And?" she asked.

He answered, his voice too low to make out the words. "Pardon?"

He jerked away from her. "I said, she laughed."

Susanna gasped. And then she laughed. "I'm sorry." She covered her mouth to stifle the giggles. "It's not amusing. You poor man."

"I was a boy then and my little heart easily crushed."

"Oh." She reached for his arm, but he shook her off. He didn't want her sympathy, and she did not blame him. "How did you recover?"

"I swived every pretty girl I could find and drank myself into a stupor."

Susanna caught herself before she toppled off the chaise longue. No one had ever said anything so shocking to her before. She'd never even heard the word he'd used, but it did not take much thought to decipher its meaning.

"A-and did that help?"

She could hear him smiling when he spoke.

"It didn't hurt." He sat beside her again. "She didn't feel the spark when I kissed her. I couldn't make her feel it. It's either there or it's not."

A spark. That was an apt description of the way she felt when he kissed her. Her insides lit up, and her body felt as though it were on fire, burning with heat and vitality.

"Do you—" she began then clenched her fists.

"Do I...?" he prompted.

"Oh, it's irrelevant," she said quickly and hopefully lightly. "You were saying about Marlowe? Or should we call her Elizabeth? I never know what to call her."

"Susanna." His voice was low and teasing. "Ask me."

"Ask you what? You mean what you call Marlowe?"

But he wasn't fooled by her too-high pitch or her rapid speech. He'd known or guessed what she was thinking. Ridiculous that her cheeks were hot and probably bright pink, when no one could even see her blush.

Whatever creature shared the space with them continued scratching in the corner, its movements loud in the growing silence as he waited. And waited.

"Fine." She huffed out a breath. "Do you feel any spark when you kiss me? I withdrew the question because it's a foolish one. Let's not discuss it."

"But I want to discuss it."

His thigh pressed into hers as he moved closer, and she felt him twine a long lock of her hair around his finger.

"You do?" There was that breathless quality in her voice again. How did he manage to do that to her every time he touched her? Every time he looked at her—and she couldn't even *see* him looking at her at the moment.

"I feel more than a spark when I kiss you. I feel a hundred tiny sparks, lighting me up, burning out and sparking new fires."

"Yes," she murmured.

"You feel it too?"

"I don't understand how Marlowe couldn't."

He used her hair to tug her closer. "Because Marlowe and I weren't right for each other." His lips brushed her cheek, his warm breath flickering on her skin. She tingled inside, felt tiny explosions building.

"Neither are we," she pointed out. "You're…"

His lips kissed the corner of her mouth.

"And I'm…"

His hand slid into her hair and cupped the back of her head. "You're?"

"Dying for you to kiss me."

"Then I should do so with haste."

His mouth met hers in a hot tangle of lips and tongues and heat. Shimmering sparks flooded her body and tingled through her. Her head swirled, making her dizzy with desire. Clutching his shirt, she hung on for fear she might lose her grip and tumble away.

Dimly, she became aware he'd taken her in his arms and lowered her down on the chaise. His powerful body, all lean, muscled strength, covered hers. She wrapped her arms around his back, dug her fingers into the hard contours of his flesh, and felt him shiver. His lips took hers more roughly, and his kiss turned deeper and more passionate.

He really did want her. He responded to her touch much as she responded to his. The thought sent more flickers of desire into her belly, and she slid her hand down to explore his body. His back was sleek and hard, his waist narrow and trim. His buttocks—

"What are you doing?" he asked, lifting his lips from hers.

"I'm sorry." She pulled her hands away. "I only wanted to touch you."

"Keep touching me like that, and before you blink, I'll have your skirts up to your neck and my cock buried inside you."

She should have been shocked by his words. She should have slapped him for speaking to her that way. Instead, she couldn't resist putting her arms around him and pulling him back to her. This time she kissed him, her mouth taking his, tasting him, exploring the fullness of his lips and the rough stubble on his jaw.

"Do you have any idea how much I want you right now?" His voice was low and thick, and it rumbled through her as she licked a patch of skin on his neck. He tasted like wood and salt and man.

"As much as I want you, I imagine."

He pulled back. "And what exactly is it you want? I don't think you even know what you're saying."

"I do," she protested. "I know what men and women do. I've read books."

"Oh, books!" He shook his head, and she felt his soft hair tickle her forehead. "I've never read a book about…"

"Copulation," she supplied, thinking perhaps he lacked a term that was not cant.

"Right. But I can promise you *copulation* in reality is much different than in books. So I ask again, what is it you think you want?"

She might have answered quickly. She might have said, *You*, and kissed him again. Instead, she considered. In the medical book she'd found in her father's library, it had referred to the man's engorged organ penetrating the woman's body. Was that what she wanted? His organ inside her body?

It seemed a strange thing for two people to do, and yet she could not deny everything she'd done with him so far had been far more pleasurable than strange.

"I want to copulate with you. I know I'll be ruined," she added hastily. "I'll be ruined anyway."

"Give me strength," he murmured and lowered his head to her shoulder.

"I know what copulation entails," she said, in case he still thought her ignorant. "You penetrate my body with your engorged organ."

His body shook, and she realized he was laughing. She smacked him on the back. "What is so amusing, sir? I know I'm correct."

"Sir?" He lifted his head. "After all this, you call me *sir*?"

"Oh, never mind. Get off." She shoved at him, and he caught her hands.

"Not quite yet, Strawberry."

She stilled, held her breath. Her heart hammered as though it desired freedom from the confines of her ribs.

"Then you'll…"

"Copulate you?"

"I think it's more accurately said, *copulate with you*."

"I don't give a…shilling. I won't do it."

Her breath huffed out. Her ears were ringing, and she couldn't have heard him correctly. "Why?" she asked, her voice small and high to her ears. "I thought…you said you felt sparks."

His hands on her wrists relaxed. "Oh, I *want* to copulate you—copulate with—take you. But you deserve better than a tumble on a stolen couch in a dirty, rat-infested tunnel under Field Lane."

"I knew that wasn't a cat." She shoved at him, her cheeks hot with embarrassment. She'd all but thrown herself at him, and he'd rejected her. She would go home a virgin after all.

"Get off," she demanded.

"I don't think so."

She stiffened. His tone had an ominous quality to it, a tone that said I'm-not-done-with-you-yet.

"I can't let you go without teaching you something."

"I read the book."

"This is better than a book."

Thirteen

His MOUTH TOUCHED HER LIPS LIGHTLY WHILE ONE hand slid down her raised arms. His other hand held them above her head as he kissed her. When his fingers reached the bare skin of her neck, she shivered, and his caresses changed to feather-light strokes. He stroked down her sensitive flesh until he reached the edge of her bodice. His mouth trailed after his fingers, branding her where her skin already burned from his touch.

"Gideon."

"You'll like this," he murmured. He yanked her chemise down then tugged on her stays, freeing her breasts. They ached for his touch, and she bucked when his mouth settled on her nipple.

He suckled her with his mouth and fondled her with his hand, the tug of his mouth eliciting an answering pull between her legs. She was warm and heavy at the juncture of her thighs. Pressure built, and she squeezed her legs together in an attempt to alleviate it.

His mouth continued to work her, and the urge to move rose until her legs parted and her hips moved of their own accord. She wanted something, needed it. She was close. If he would only touch her…

She was appalled when she realized where it was she wanted him to touch. She'd been pressing against him, wantonly rubbing her body against his.

"Don't stop now," he murmured against her bare skin. "You must be almost there."

His words were incomprehensible at the moment. "What are you doing to me?"

"Do you want me to stop?"

"I…"

He released her wrists and ran his fingers down her arm, over her bare breast and then across her abdomen. When his fingers slid lower, she could not stop a moan. He moaned in response and reached for her skirts. His hand was warm on her ankle. He slid his fingers up, the calluses rough on her soft skin. When he reached her knee, she slammed her legs together.

"Problem?" he asked, his voice sounding light and affable.

"What are you doing?"

"Showing you something you won't read about in books—at least not the ones you're like to encounter." His fingers slid up her leg, and she had to gulp in a breath.

"Do you want me to stop?" His fingers brushed across the tangle of hair at the junction of her thighs, and she squeaked.

"Tell me if you don't want this, Susanna. I'll stop if you ask."

"I…"

His fingers walked down, and her thighs were moist enough that he slid between them. The shock of pleasure made her cry out.

"Open your legs, Strawberry."

She shook her head. He couldn't have seen the motion, but he must have guessed.

"I can do this with your knees locked, but you'll like it better if I have more room."

"I shouldn't," she whispered.

"Oh, no, you definitely shouldn't. This is the sort of thing you go to hell for."

His fingers wiggled and slid back and forth. Her knees weakened.

"This is the sort of thing you should slap me for even thinking about."

One finger dipped inside her, and her muscles clenched in anticipation. Pleasure and desire mingled until she couldn't help but relax her muscles.

"Open your legs, Susanna."

She gave in to the demands of her body and allowed her knees to fall open. He slid his fingers over her again, over a spot so sensitive she cried out when he stroked it.

"This is where my… What did you call it? Engorged organ? This is where I'd penetrate you." He slid two fingers inside her.

She writhed as he slid in and out. She couldn't hear him any longer. She could only feel.

"And then I'd thrust in and out, like this. And if I do it just right…"

He paused, slowing his movements until she moaned and every muscle in her body tensed.

"…if I slow down. You like it slow, don't you? And rub my thumb right here…"

His thumb circled her, and the sudden explosion took her by surprise. Her entire body shuddered violently, and she saw actual sparks before her eyes. Pleasure like none she'd ever imagined spiraled through her, wracking her body, until she collapsed like little more than a doll.

When she could catch her breath again, she reached out for Gideon. "What just happened?"

"Climax," he said.

From his voice, he was still located near her knees. She'd fallen back onto the longue, her head at an awkward angle at the base of the rising arm. She didn't care. She couldn't conceive of ever moving.

"That was almost too easy," he said.

"The book didn't mention that."

He chuckled. "No. I imagine not. Let me show you something else the book didn't mention."

"Gideon." She tried to sit and wished, for what felt like the tenth time, she had some light. Then she felt his stubble brush her thigh, and she shrieked.

"What are you doing now?"

"Something no proper lady would ever allow a man to do to her."

She reached for his head, attempting to grasp his hair. "Then by all means, cease."

"Are you sure that's what you want?"

He must have turned his head, because she felt the warmth of his breath *there*. *Between her legs*. His day's growth of beard stung the skin of her inner thighs. Susanna tried to summon shock as she realized exactly where his head was located. She tried to tell him to stop.

But her body was already tensed for more of his touch. She wanted what she knew he could give.

"Shall I stop?" he asked again. She clenched her hands at the laughing tone in his voice. She wanted to tell him to stop just to spite him.

"No!" she flung at him.

He pushed her legs open, and she waited for the sweet assault of his fingertips. Instead, something soft and warm slid against her.

His tongue!

"Why are you doing that?"

"I wanted to taste you." He licked her again, his tongue flicking against her until she moaned.

"You taste exactly how I imagined. Sweet and ripe, like a strawberry."

"This is wicked."

He made a sound of assent and licked her again.

She gasped. "This is beyond scandalous."

His tongue worked her, finding a particularly sensitive spot and teasing it until she panted with need.

"This is..." She couldn't think. Susanna tried to tell him to stop, but the words wouldn't come. Instead, she gripped his hair and threw her head back in ecstasy.

"Yes, yes, yes. *Please*."

Her world shattered. Her body exploded into a thousand tiny points of pleasure, each sensation sweeter than the one before it. When she slowly drifted back into herself, she stared blindly at the darkness around her. Thank God for the darkness. She could not bear to look Gideon in the eye after what he'd just done. Susanna feared she'd never cease blushing.

"Move over." He crawled beside her on the narrow chaise longue and gave her a small shove. She didn't move. Her body was far too heavy to lift. Instead, he fit himself behind her, propping her up sideways, one arm draped over her midsection possessively.

She could smell her scent on him, and she could feel his erection pressing into her bottom. Why had he left her a virgin and himself unsatisfied?

"You'll have to speak to me again at some point," he murmured. He sounded completely normal, as though he hadn't just had his mouth…his tongue…

"Too shocked to speak?" He chuckled. "I told you I'd show you a few things not in books. What did you expect, Strawberry, for me to behave as a gentleman?"

She rose to her elbow. "That's rubbish. You're far more of a gentleman than I think you like to admit."

"Do you think so?" His hand moved up to cup her breast. She hadn't bothered to pull her stays up yet, and his rough hand on her bare skin caused her to inhale sharply. "Want me to show you, again, how wicked I can be?"

"No." She removed his hand, placing it back on her abdomen. "I don't think I can survive any more. And," she continued before he attempted to disprove her, "I do not want to test that."

"Too bad."

How she wished she could see his expression. "You almost sound as though you want to…do *that* again."

He nuzzled her neck. "Why wouldn't I? I like the

sounds you make. I like how you taste, how you grab my hair and push my face—"

"Do not say another word!"

He laughed quietly, pressing his lips to the sensitive spot below her ear. "There's nothing to be ashamed of, Strawberry. You're a passionate woman. That's fortunate."

"Fortunate? For whom?"

"Lord Doddering. He'll want a passionate young vixen in his bed."

"There is no Lord Doddering, and I cannot ever do…what we did again."

He rose up, and though she couldn't see him, she imagined he was looking down at her. "That's a shame. I haven't ruined you, you know. You'll go to your marriage bed innocent. No one ever has to know what happens here. If you wanted me to do it again, I'd keep your secret."

He was so very wicked, and not only because of what he was suggesting. The problem was he could read her mind. She did want him to do it again. And heaven help her, when his hand slid up to cup her breast and the other slid between her legs, she let him have his way.

༄

Gideon had never met a woman like Susanna Derring. He barely had to touch her to bring her to climax. She kissed him, moved against him, like she would die if he stopped touching her. She seemed to thrive on his touch.

Her response made him only want to touch her more. He'd finally exhausted her, and she breathed deeply as she slept beside him. He should have been exhausted too, but he had too many erotic thoughts in his mind for sleep. His cock was still hard and none too happy about being ignored.

He could have had her.

She'd offered herself—in awkward, shy phrases. He'd wanted to allow it. Instead, he'd put his mouth on her again and made her scream his name.

He couldn't have said why he wouldn't fuck her. He supposed because, even in the dark, even though she wanted him, he couldn't pretend she was someone other than who she was.

Lady Susanna.

Who was he to take her virginity? He shouldn't even touch her. He was a common thief who'd grown up among the refuse of Seven Dials and shouldn't have dared look at her.

He'd done much more than look.

One day he might deserve more. When he got his necklace back and left Seven Dials and the Covent Garden Cubs far behind. He'd leave Gideon Harrow too. Take on a new name, become a new person. One last act of thievery to make him an honest man. Maybe in a new city or the countryside, he'd find a girl with sweet curves, a pretty smile, and long strawberry-blond hair.

Gideon clenched his fists.

"She's not for you," he muttered to himself. "Do the job and get out before your luck runs out."

Mrs. Cummings had found him. It was only a matter of time until Beezle did. Hell, Beezle might have been sitting in Des's kitchen that very minute. And if he so much as smelled Gideon nearby, he'd slink away and lie in wait like a hungry cat.

He didn't know how long he lay there before he heard footsteps on the stairs. Gideon put a hand over Strawberry's mouth and shook her awake. "It's me. Someone's coming."

She stiffened.

"Do not make a sound."

She nodded, and he released her mouth. He could feel her work to straighten her dress. He felt the floor beside the couch for the wooden handle he'd found. It felt like the handle for a wheelbarrow or plow and would make an adequate weapon.

The glow of light pierced the darkness, sliding under the space below the door. Gideon used the light to creep across the room, avoiding tripping over any articles, and stationed himself beside the door.

He raised the weapon and met Strawberry's gaze. She looked terrified and hauntingly beautiful. In the dim light, her hair made a dusky halo around her pale face. Her eyes were impossibly large and dark, while her lips were swollen and red. She looked like a woman who'd been well and thoroughly pleasured.

Gideon wished he could see her thus all the time.

The latch for the door lifted, and the hinges creaked as it swung open. Gideon raised his handle as the intruder lifted the lamp to reveal the assortment of stolen goods.

"Gid?" Des asked.

"Here." He lowered the handle and blew out a breath.

Des twisted the light to shine on Gideon, and his gaze went immediately to Gideon's hand around the handle. "Going to do me in, were ye?"

"Never know who might come looking for me."

"That's the truth. Mrs. Cummings didn't believe ye weren't 'iding in the house. Brenna finally threatened to set the dog on 'er if she didn't leave."

"Beauty?" Strawberry pushed her hair off her shoulders. "Is she hurt?"

"She's perfectly fine. Chewing a bone at the moment." Des's eyes swept over her then flicked to Gideon. "I suppose I don't have to ask how ye've been passing the time."

Strawberry's cheeks turned as red as the fruit he'd named her for.

"Is it dark yet? I appreciate your hospitality, but I'd like to move on before Beezle comes looking for me."

"I'd like that too. Still an hour or more before nightfall. Days are long in the summer. Are ye 'ungry?"

"No," Susanna said.

Gideon ignored her. "Yes. She's hungry too. I heard her stomach rumble half a dozen times."

"It did not!" She blushed again.

The swells were strange. Why should something like a stomach rumbling embarrass her?

"There's a public house across the street. Food is decent. Better than Brenna makes at any rate."

Gideon patted his pockets. "No blunt."

Des looked at Susanna.

"She doesn't have any either. Guess I'll have to pay you back."

"Sure you will," Des said and gestured for them to follow him back upstairs.

Dusk was falling by the time the five of them entered the public house. Strawberry insisted on bringing Beauty with them, and Gideon didn't have the energy to argue. Besides, the buffer had a way of sensing trouble. If Beezle made an appearance, Beauty would alert them.

Susanna had to be coerced into eating at the public house. Ladies didn't do such things. Gideon had grinned. "This is no time to start acting like a lady."

He'd moved away quickly so she couldn't reach him.

Des and Brenna sat on one side of a long bench, and Gideon and Susanna sat on the other. Beauty lay under Susanna's feet, her head on her paws. Gideon had chosen seats for them at the end of the table, in case he needed to leave quickly. He had a view of the door, but no one he knew had gone in or out. Susanna sipped her ale daintily and claimed she wanted nothing to eat. He ordered her stew and potatoes anyway.

If she wouldn't eat it, he would. Why not? Des was paying.

While they waited for their food, Gideon tapped his foot to the fiddler standing on a table beside them and playing a lively jig.

"Sometimes the fiddler's woman sings," Des said loudly to Gideon.

"Voice like an angel," Brenna added.

"Not that you'd know what that sounds like, considerin' ye're 'eaded for 'ell any day now."

Gideon laughed. "Thought you'd be hoping for my long life and toasting to my health. I can't pay you back if I'm dead."

"You? Pay me back?" Des pointed at him with the mug of ale. "We're even now, is my way of seeing it."

Gideon clinked mugs and drank.

"What debt do you owe him?" Susanna asked. Her

voice sounded all the more refined and elegant with the accents of Field Lane in his ears.

"He didn't tell you?"

She shook her head.

"A few months ago, Gid and I cracked a house."

"We robbed it," Gideon translated. "Des usually sticks to fencing goods, but he lost Beezle's property before he could sell it. Beezle gave him the choice of cracking the house or getting his throat slit."

Susanna gasped.

"I didn't lose the cargo," Des protested. "Bow Street recovered it. Two different things." He looked back at Susanna. "In any case, I like my throat the way it is, so I did the job with Gid. I was the budge, and he were the rum dubber."

When her brow furrowed, Des gave Gideon a look. "Where the hell did you find her?"

Gideon smiled tightly.

Des signaled for more ale. "I was inside the house, throwing the cargo out to Gid. The owners came home and caught me. Gid could have run, saved his bony arse."

"But he didn't," Susanna said.

"He risked his neck to go in after me. Got me out."

"Lost the cargo though," Gideon said. "Had to crack another house. Had better cronies that time."

Susanna set her mug down with an audible thump. "Good Lord, exactly how many houses have you cracked?"

The crowd began to clap and whistle as a woman with black hair so long it was almost to her ankles and dark skin sashayed past the tables, her skirts tinkling.

Gideon spoke in Susanna's ear. "I'd tell you, but I don't think I can count that high."

She gave him a look so full of shocked innocence, he couldn't stop himself from kissing her.

She shoved him back. "Gideon!"

Oh, but he liked shocking her. He was sorely tempted to do it again. Brenna motioned to the table where the fiddler pulled the woman up beside him. "Ye're in for a treat now, lads."

"Is she a Gypsy?" Gideon asked. "She has the look."

"Aye. That's the rumor," Brenna said without taking her gaze from the singer. "Who knows if it's true?"

The fiddler began a slow song, the music haunting and high. The Gypsy singer swayed to it, letting her hips rock from side to side. Then she took a deep breath and began to hum. Her voice was low and melodic. Gideon leaned forward.

> *"Tell me the story of a lass and her love,*
> *Tell me of two hearts broken.*
> *Tell me the story of a lass and her love,*
> *Tell me of passions awoken.*
> *Bonny was she, faithful was he,*
> *Never a day were they parted.*
> *A red coat he donned and marched off to a song,*
> *Leaving her brokenhearted."*

Susanna gripped his wrist, and Gideon pulled his gaze from the singer.

"A sad song," he said, nodding to the Gypsy. "Do you know it?"

She shook her head.

"She'll repeat the first verse, and then in the second verse the soldier is killed in battle. In the third, the lass takes her own life."

"Then the ending is cheerier."

He tapped her on the nose. "No, but the music is." His foot tapped faster as the fiddler found a rhythm and his bow flew across the strings. Des swept Brenna into his arms, and they joined the half-dozen couples skipping about the room.

"Come on," Gideon said, standing and holding his hand out to her. Beauty barked and rose to her feet.

Susanna blinked up at him. "Are you asking me to dance?"

He spread his hands. "Hasn't anyone ever asked before, Strawberry?"

"Yes, of course, but—"

"Then come on!" He pulled her to her feet and spun her around. Her hair flew out, forming a fiery-gold halo about her head and shoulders. He took her waist and pulled her into the fray, swinging her about by the arm, trading her off, and taking her back again.

The wrinkle between her eyes told him she was concentrating far too hard on the steps of the jig instead of enjoying herself. When the Gypsy sang again, he twirled her until she wobbled.

"Stop thinking so hard, Strawberry," he called over the fiddle. "Feel the music."

She stumbled, dizzy, and he caught her in his arms, turned her again. She clung to him, head down, but when she looked up again, her eyes were bright with excitement.

Gideon let out a cheer and danced her around the

room. The dog barked wildly, her tail wagging ener-
getically. By the time they'd made it halfway around,
she was leading him and clapping and stomping with
the most energetic of them. Brenna took her arm,
and the two held hands and spun. When their hold
finally broke, Gideon caught her and swept her off
her feet, twirling her until she tilted her head back
and laughed.

His heart ached at the sight of her, all that wild hair
and her bright cheeks. She was the picture of freedom.
She danced another song, but the food had arrived,
and Gideon sat and ate. He kept an eye on her, but
the men here wanted nothing more than a drink and
a little music. Beauty gave him an imploring look, and
he passed her meat under the table.

Damn dog.

When Susanna finally sat beside him, sides heaving
and hair damp against her forehead, she gulped down
her ale and then took his and swallowed that too.
Gideon grabbed her hand before she could steal Des's.

"Oh no you don't. Eat, or you'll be so drunk I'll
have to carry you to Vauxhall Gardens."

She swatted his arm. "Ladies are never drunk, my
good sir."

"Glad to hear it. Humor me, and eat the stew,
my lady."

She ate, but when he looked again, she had more
ale in her hand. It wasn't long before she pulled him
to his feet and insisted on a dance. Gideon couldn't
refuse her.

He clapped as she raised her hands above her head
and twirled until her skirts flew out around her.

Throwing her head back, she laughed, and he caught her just in time, kissing her playfully.

She turned the kiss into something more. Gideon was half ready to drag her back to Des's when he felt a prickle of unease skitter across his neck. He pulled away, his gaze sweeping the room.

A few men looked familiar, but none of them were Beezle's cubs. None of the men or women who met his gaze were enemies. The door to the public house closed, and Gideon had a moment to wonder who might have left. He almost followed, then Strawberry kissed him again and laughed, and he was swept back into the dance.

Fourteen

"REPORT," BROOK SAID, HIS EYES DARK WITH HIS usual skepticism.

Dorothea shifted her gaze from the disheveled Bow Street Runner who had just entered her drawing room, back to Brook. Her younger son had been born a skeptic. Perhaps that was what made him so good with puzzles.

Dorothea refused to call Brook an investigator. She chose to overlook the fact that her son kept an office in the same building as the Bow Street Runners and was hired to find missing persons and stolen property. The younger son of the Earl of Dane did not have a profession. To her mind, this sort of investigatory work was a hobby.

One at which he excelled.

The Runner glanced at her then clutched his hat against his chest. He wore a shabby coat and a stain on his trousers. His face was unshaven, and she had all but yelped when Crawford had shown him into the drawing room. She thought he'd been a rogue until Brook had greeted him.

"You found her?" Brook asked him, his voice betraying no hint of either annoyance or eagerness. For herself, Dorothea could not resist clasping her hands together. She might have stood, but then Brook would be forced to stand as well.

"I think so, sir," the Runner said, his gaze on Brook. "I found a girl who matches the description."

"Where?"

"A public house in Field Lane."

"What?" Dorothea did rise then. Field Lane? What on earth would her daughter be doing in such a place? "You must be mistaken."

Brook was at her side immediately. "Mother, Mrs. Castle already confirmed seeing her in Seven Dials. Field Lane is not so far. Let's hear what Mr. Sawyer has to say before we make any judgments."

"Of course." Her fingers hurt from being clasped so tightly together.

Brook pressed on her shoulder, and she sat again. Where was Dane? Shouldn't he be there by now? She'd sent for him yesterday, even though Brook had advised against it. Brook didn't see that Dane could aid the investigation, but she wanted her elder son for more selfish reasons. Dane was solid and strong. She could lean on Dane. Brook was never one to tolerate any emotion. Even as a child, he'd refused her hugs and comforting pats when he stubbed a toe or scraped a knee. Susanna had wanted too much coddling, and Brook none. Dane had accepted what she gave, never seeming to want more or desire less.

"Go on," Brook ordered Sawyer.

The disheveled man glanced at her again. "I spotted her at a public house. I'd heard a rumor of a lady and a dog going up against Dagger Dan."

"Who?" Dorothea asked.

Brook waved a hand. "Rumor."

Sawyer nodded. "Must be, but I heard she had strawberry-blond hair, so I stayed put, kept my eyes open. She came into the public house for dinner."

"Alone?" Brook asked.

Sawyer shook his head. "She was with two men and a woman. I don't know the woman, but Des is a fencing cully."

"He has a dolly shop?"

"That one. But she wasn't as friendly with him as she was with the other."

"What exactly do you mean by friendly?" Dorothea asked in a frosty tone.

Brook raised a hand. It was exactly the sort of gesture she detested. How dare he put her question aside?

"Who was he?" Brook asked.

"Don't know him, but he was familiar. Maybe one of Beezle's gang."

Brook's eyebrows rose with interest.

"Who is Beezle?" she asked.

The men ignored her. *Really, the gall!*

"Did she appear to be harmed? Were they holding her against her will?" her son asked.

"No, sir. She was…" Sawyer's gaze darted to her again.

Dorothea glared back at him. "Out with it, young man."

He crumpled the hat. "She was dancing, your ladyship. She danced with Beezle's man, laughed a lot, and from the way she was drinking, probably overindulged in that area too."

"This cannot be Susanna."

Sawyer plucked at his crumpled hat.

Brook pressed his lips together. "I'd better go take a look."

Dorothea pounded her fist on the edge of the couch. "I tell you, it's not her. You are wasting your time searching drinking establishments. She was abducted. She would never go to Field Lane willingly or dance in a public house!"

She rose, and Brook climbed wearily to his feet.

"You are wasting time." She pointed a finger at Brook.

Instead of agreeing with her, Brook clapped Sawyer on the shoulder. "Good work, sir." He steered him to the drawing room doors. Crawford opened them, and Brook said something she could not quite hear.

Then he turned back to her, the look on his face weary and guarded.

"I'm for Field Lane. I doubt she's still in the public house, but it's a start."

Dorothea raised her chin. She could not allow her lips to tremble. "It is not she."

Brook tossed her imperious look right back. She'd taught him that, much as she would have liked to blame his father. "It is Susanna. Sawyer is one of the best Runners I know. He's not mistaken. His information confirms what Mrs. Castle told us. Susanna was in the company of a man." He shoved his hands in his pockets. "I had thought to question her again as to his identity. She knows, but she won't say for some reason."

"I don't understand." Dorothea hated the tinny quality of her voice. She sounded like an old woman.

"Don't you, Mother?" Brook said with uncharacteristic venom. She could feel his gaze burn into her.

"You've kept her under your thumb since the day she was born. She doesn't take a breath without you telling her when to inhale. If she had a more docile spirit—"

"I would not need to keep her in check!" Dorothea realized she was shouting and lowered her voice. "This is precisely the sort of thing I was afraid would happen."

"Why?" Brook asked. "She has always been obedient. There were days I wished she would tell you to go to the devil, but she never did."

"How dare you!" Her voice did waver now.

She did not want to hear this—because he was right. She *was* to blame. She'd held on too tightly and governed Susanna out of fear instead of love.

"What are you not telling me?" Brook asked. Relentless. Her son pushed and prodded until he had the answer he sought.

Dorothea sank onto the couch, and the large furnishing all but swallowed her. "Vauxhall Gardens," she whispered.

Brook folded his arms across his chest. She'd have no sympathy from him. Perhaps that would make it easier to say. She didn't want sympathy, not after all these years.

"She asked to go to Vauxhall Gardens, practically begged me to go. I told her no, but she would not let it go. That was just last night."

"Why didn't you tell me this before? I'd have sent men to watch the entrance and the roads."

Dorothea covered her face with a hand. "Because I didn't want to consider that she might go there. I didn't want her to make the same mistake I did."

"What mistake is that?"

"I fell in love." She looked toward the window, where the still-open draperies revealed the encroaching night. Another night with Susanna not at home. She could speak of this if she did not look at Brook. He resembled his father too closely for her comfort.

"It was before I met your father. I met a man at Vauxhall and fell in love. He was not…acceptable."

It seemed strange to reduce the love of her life to two words: *not acceptable*. He'd been so much more than that—handsome, kind, witty, charming. Oh, she'd fallen for him the first time she'd met him. She'd given him her heart without even being asked, and she'd never been able to retrieve it.

"My parents would never have consented to a marriage between us, but I dreamed of running away to Gretna Green with him."

From the corner of her eye, she saw Brook shift positions slightly. She'd made him uncomfortable, perhaps even surprised him. No one ever thought of her as a woman, least of all her sons. She was the Dowager Countess of Dane, and before that, Lady Dorothea, daughter of the Duke of Monmouth. She was a commodity, not a person.

"Robert—that was his name—Robert Southey would have never eloped. He had too much honor to do such a thing, which is not to say that I didn't beg him to reconsider. Especially after I met your father."

Now she darted a glance at Brook. She'd not known Erasmus Derring when he'd been a young man. He had already been close to fifty when she'd married him. He'd been married once before, and the union had not produced children. The former countess had died of consumption, and Erasmus wanted a young wife and an heir to his title.

Her parents wanted an earl for their daughter. She'd been bought and sold, like a horse or a cow. No one had asked if she wanted to marry Erasmus Derring. No one had cared that her heart belonged to another.

"Your marriage was not a love match."

She smiled slightly. Brook had a way of stating the obvious that always amused her. She straightened her shoulders. "I did my duty. That's something your generation does not understand. Now there's all this talk of marrying for love. Look at your brother!" She stared out the window again. "In my day, we did our duty."

"And you feared Susanna would not?"

"I feared she had too much of my recklessness in her." Brook's brows lifted.

Dorothea pointed a finger at him. "You did not know me in my youth, young man. I could be wild and heedless of consequences. If the woman your Mr. Sawyer saw was Susanna, it appears all my efforts were for naught."

"If it is Susanna, I will bring her home. If she's no longer in Field Lane, then I'll search Vauxhall. When she returns, she will need to marry immediately."

Dorothea nodded absently. She had already begun a list of potential husbands. None of them were exactly what she wanted for Susanna, but they were suitable matches.

"I have one last question," Brook said.

She inclined her head without looking at him. The sky beyond quickly faded from indigo to black. She remembered another sky, all those years ago, ablaze with fireworks.

"A gap of several years exists between Susanna and me, and you lost at least one child between Dane's birth and mine."

Her gaze fastened on his. She should not be surprised he knew such a thing. He always knew more than she realized.

"You had done your duty by providing an heir and a spare. If your marriage was no love match, were you then free to pursue other interests?"

He did not flinch, even when she shot him a look that would have sent Crawford scurrying for cover. "Other interests—an interesting term for adultery. Is that what you are accusing me of, sir?"

He lifted one shoulder in a careless gesture. "I'm merely asking a question, not accusing you of anything."

"I'm still your mother," she said, rising from the sinking cushions of the couch. "And I am still the Countess of Dane. Go ask the rabble in Spitalfields or St. Giles your questions." She swept out of the room and was just outside her private chambers when she collapsed. Edwards was beside her in a moment, of course, but Dorothea did not want her maid's help.

She pushed her off and tottered to her room on her own, shutting the door firmly in Edwards's face. Her maid spoke through it, called to her, inquired if she needed anything, but Dorothea didn't hear a word.

She sank onto the floor, the same floor where she'd sunk all those years ago when Dane had been just learning to walk. She'd been light-headed then from the loss of blood, and she remembered looking down and seeing red streaks on her pale legs. Blood pooled on the rug—a different rug then—creating an irregular circle of red. The loss of another child, a little girl, devastated her. Brook's birth a year later healed some of the pain, but Susanna's birth took the last of it, all but the scars on her heart.

Susanna had been so much more than the daughter she'd lost. She'd been the life Dorothea might have known.

Dorothea's heart ached, thinking of the past. Her confession to Brook brought all the memories back. She had tried so hard to forget him for so many years. Even after all this time, her heart still clenched when she thought of him. Her pulse still quickened.

She still loved him, still could imagine his lips on her neck, her wrist, her mouth.

She still felt like a young woman, although she was almost fifty. When she peered in the glass, she still looked young. No gray streaked her hair; few lines marred her face. But there were days she heard herself speak, and she felt ancient. She sounded so matronly, so serious, so critical. Where was the spirited girl she'd once been? Had she lost that girl when she'd lost the love of her life?

She would always regret walking away from him, but she'd had no other choice. If she'd left, Erasmus would have taken her children.

And now Dorothea wept because she'd had no choice, because her life had been one of sorrow and very little love. And it was her fault. How could she blame Susanna for running away when she herself had done the same thing before coming to her senses?

"Oh, my darling," she sobbed. "Forgive me. I wanted to protect you."

But there was no protection for any of them now.

❧

The world spun in a swirl of color and sound and sweetness. Gideon whirled her, his strong arms always catching her just when she feared she was twirling too fast and would fall. His mouth on hers was sweet, as was the ale in her cup.

She'd drunk too much. He'd warned her against it, but she'd been in no mood for warnings.

The music must have slowed, because her body moved slowly, and she allowed her head to fall on Gideon's shoulder. He had broad shoulders, strong shoulders. She wondered what they would look like if she removed his shirt.

"Not here, Strawberry," he said, pulling her hands away from the collar of his shirt.

"I'm not a strawberry," she said. At least she tried. The word *strawberry* was suddenly quite stuck on her lips.

"You are to me." He lifted her into his arms, and she emitted a little squeal as her feet left the ground and her head spun ever faster. She closed her arms around his neck, afraid she might lose her balance.

He carried her past dancing lights and laughing people and into the cool, dark night. The breeze felt good on her heated skin, even if the angry sound of men's voices made her shiver.

"I have you," he told her. "Back to Des's."

"Beauty?" She almost toppled out of his arms, looking for the dog. Before he righted her, she spotted the small, white face looking up at her. "There you are."

He pushed a door open, and they stumbled into a darkened room. "Where are we?"

"I told you. Des is in the dolly shop. We can stay in the flat until the drink wears off a bit."

His voice was deep and low, and she pressed her lips to his neck, feeling the vibration against her skin when he spoke.

"I want to see Vauxhall," she said. Her mouth moved against his skin, and she tasted him—slightly salty and smelling a bit of smoke from a wood fire.

"Not like this. Give it an hour or so." He sounded different. His voice was tight and strained, and she realized his hand on her back gripped her much tighter than was necessary. Was it possible her lips on his throat affected him?

She tasted him with her tongue, then ran her mouth along the line of his jaw, reveling in the feel of the harsh stubble on her soft lips. When she reached his ear, she nibbled at the lobe. When he did this to her, it drove her to madness.

"Oh no."

Suddenly she was on her feet. Her knees crumpled, but he caught her and pushed her into a hard chair. His hands were on either side of her, his face not far from hers. Dark hair spilled over his forehead.

"None of that."

"Why not?"

"You're floor'd. You don't know what you're doing." He brushed her hair back and secured it behind her ear. The gesture made her want to rub her cheek along his hand, much like a cat asking to be stroked.

"I knew what I was doing. I was testing whether or not I could arouse you. Did I?" She reached for his trousers, and he jumped back.

"This is not a good idea."

He moved away from her, and a moment later a lamp flickered to life. Now she could see his face, his green eyes dark with desire.

"Why not?" The more he protested, the better idea it seemed. "Are you afraid you will lose your control if I touch you? Could I do that to you? Make you forget to act like a gentleman?"

His throat worked, and she knew she had that power. This afternoon he had played her body until she was all but mad with need for him. Now she wanted him to need her.

"I told you," he said, his hands on the table behind him. "I'm no gentleman."

"Prove it." She put her hands on his hips, and stroked them down over his thighs, close to the growing bulge in his trousers.

He clasped her wrists. "Unless you want me to take you on this table, you should stop."

"Will I like it?" she asked, gesturing to the table. "Being taken on a table?"

"You'd like it."

She rose, and he steadied her with the hands that still gripped her wrists. But when she twisted her hands, he released her. She reached for her dress, withdrew one of the pins and then another, until the bodice fell forward.

His gaze was on her chest, and she saw his tongue wet his lips. She couldn't remember where Brenna had secured the other pins and tapes, but the gown was large enough that she could slip it off. She let the garment pool at her feet and stood before him in the thin linen of her chemise with only her petticoat still providing some modesty.

"There's no fire," she said. "I'm cold."

"Then you should stop removing your clothing."

She stepped out of her boots and placed her bare feet on the floor. She'd told Brenna to burn her stockings. They'd been beyond repair. Now she untied her petticoat and stepped out of it.

"Do you want me to stop?" she asked.

"Hell no." His voice was rough and gravelly. She might have been scared if she didn't know him, if she didn't trust him.

"I've been imagining you naked all afternoon."

She tugged on the string of her chemise, loosening it and letting it fall. "I hope I live up to your expectations."

He took an audible breath. When he exhaled, the breath quavered, and he looked at her so intently, her skin was hot from his gaze alone. She knew she should be embarrassed. She would have been if she hadn't

been fortified by drink. As it was, she liked him looking at her. The heavy warmth settled low in her belly,
and she ached for him to touch her.

Even more, she *needed* to touch him. She twisted
her fingers into his shirt and yanked it up and out of his
waistband. Obligingly, he dealt with the fastenings and
lifted his arms so she might remove the garment. His
chest was a marvel to her—lean and golden in the lamplight. She'd always thought men's chests had hair, but
his was smooth, the muscles shifting when he breathed.
He was breathing heavily as he wound a hand around
her bare waist and yanked her against him.

He was so warm and solid. Her hard nipples brushed
against his skin, and she enjoyed the friction so much
she did it again. He blew out a breath and cupped her
bottom, pressing her into his hard member. A slow
gush of pleasure infused her, and she looked into his
beautiful eyes and touched her mouth to his.

She'd wanted to think she'd been in control until
that point, but she realized then she'd never had any
sway. She was completely in his hands and at his
mercy. He took her mouth with a fierceness that
thrilled her, his hands rough on her bottom then sliding up to cup her breasts.

"You are so soft," he said against her mouth. "I
didn't think a woman could be so soft."

"And you are hard." She'd managed to wriggle a
hand between them and brushed it over his erection.

He inhaled sharply, but he didn't stop her. Instead,
he kissed her again, allowed her to loosen the fall on
his trousers. The warm, hard length of his erection
sprang into her hands, and she touched it gingerly. His

tongue stroked hers, and she realized he was kissing her as he wanted to be touched. She ran her hand up and down the length of him, following his guidance.

Suddenly, he lifted her onto the table. The wood was smooth and warm beneath her bottom, and she moaned when he kicked her legs open and pressed himself between them. He was so deliciously hard against her softness. She pressed back, rubbing herself wantonly against him.

"I have never," he gritted out, "wanted a woman"— his breath was labored—"this much."

"I can feel that." She moved her hips, and he groaned. "I want you."

"You want a climax," he said.

She protested, but he pulled back and yanked her thighs forward so she was balanced on the edge of the table. He bent over her, kissing her until she lay back and he could have her as he wanted. His hands were everywhere, on her breasts, her belly, in her hair. And his lips...

"I don't think I can ever get enough of you," he said, his gaze on her face.

She didn't know what to say to that, so she pulled him down for another kiss and tried to wrap her legs around his waist. He pushed her thighs back down, and kissed his way between them.

Yes, this was what she wanted, she thought as he lapped and suckled and made her cry out again and again. This was what she wanted, she thought as her hips pistoned and she shouted with pleasure.

But when it was over, and he moved away to right his clothing, she knew it was not what she wanted at all. She wanted more than his mouth and his hands. She wanted his eyes on hers, his body pressed against hers, his lips calling out her name in ecstasy.

She wanted all of him.

⤳

"We can't stay here," Gideon said after she'd dressed. A pity she had to dress. She had the most beautiful body he'd ever seen. She was long and lean and fit him perfectly. Her pale flesh was perfect, not a single blemish or pockmark to mar it.

He'd never seen a woman so perfect—not that he'd seen that many, but enough.

The hair at the junction of her thighs had been the same red gold as that on her head, and when he'd parted her legs, she'd been red and ripe as a strawberry.

He hadn't taken her.

She thought that was what she wanted, but she would have come to regret losing her virtue to him. She wouldn't regret the pleasure. He knew that much.

She looked at him over her shoulder, arms raised as she attempted to twist all of that thick, long hair into a neat and tidy style. She wouldn't succeed. It was too wild and tangled now, and he wouldn't have had it any other way.

The more wanton she looked, the more beautiful.

"To Vauxhall?" she asked, her lips curling into a smile.

"Yes. We should go tonight. We were seen at the public house."

She lowered her hands, giving up on her hair. "By whom?"

"I don't know. It's a feeling. When you live in

the rookeries long enough, you learn to trust your instincts. We should go."

She checked her dress and glanced at the dog. "I'm ready."

He wished he could say the same. He'd take her to Vauxhall, and then she'd be through with him. He'd have served his purpose.

That was what he wanted, wasn't it? He wanted his necklace and a new life. He wanted to put London behind him, to put Gideon Harrow behind him.

She lifted her glim-stick from the table with a ghost of a smile. He wondered if she was smiling because she would soon be back in the house the glim-stick had come from. She'd soon have her old life back.

"Let's go then. Stay close to me until we're away from Field Lane."

He opened the door, and Stub grinned at him.

"'Ello, Gideon. Remember me?"

Fifteen

GIDEON DIDN'T THINK. HE YANKED THE GLIM-STICK from Susanna's hand and slammed it across Stub's cheek. Stub staggered back. Gideon dropped the weapon and grabbed Susanna's hand. "Run!"

He dragged her through the door and pulled her into the street. A few feet from Des's dolly shop, Racer stepped into his path. The dog barked and growled long enough to distract Racer, and Gideon stuck out a shoulder and sent Racer toppling to his arse. It wouldn't stop him long, and Racer was fast enough to catch them without even winding himself.

Their only chance was to lose the cubs in the narrow, winding streets of the rookery and then head for Vauxhall. But eluding Beezle's gang was no easy task when Racer and Stub knew the area as well as he.

"This way!" He pulled her into a crowded gin house and shoved people aside to wend his way through the room. They stumbled out the rear, and Gideon slammed the door and pressed his back against the building. The yard was strewn with trash and puddles he did not want to examine too closely. Susanna coughed, gagging at the stench.

"Now what?" she asked, her forearm covering her nose.

"There's a loose board in that fence. We make it through before Racer remembers he can cut us off. If we make it to Fleet Street, we might have a chance. They won't expect us to head for the pleasure gardens. They'll think we're hiding underground and double back. Can you run?"

She grinned at him, and he shook his head, wondering if he imagined it. No. She was having a wonderful time. Probably thought this was as diverting as any night at the theater.

Daft mort.

It was better than a night at the theater. How could he not grin back at her?

He took her hand and dashed with her through the yard. Lifting the board, he pushed her through first then ducked and went through himself. She stood rigid on the other side of the fence, and he grabbed her hand. "Come on."

"Gideon," she whispered, fear in her voice.

He dropped her hand.

Beezle had a knife to her throat.

❧

She didn't scream. The point of the knife dug into her neck, and except for the shaking she could not control, she was too terrified to move. She wanted to close her eyes and open them again at home. She wanted to hug her mother one last time, tell her she was sorry for disappointing her.

Across the narrow street, women called down to men below, and the men answered with equally inappropriate responses. No one seemed to notice or care that she was about to die.

She heard footsteps and darted her eyes in their direction.

"Racer." The man holding the knife to her throat acknowledged the newcomer. Now Gideon was outnumbered. In the dim light escaping from the bawdy house, she could read Gideon's expression. His lips pressed tightly together, and his eyes blazed with fury. He stared at the knife's point on her neck.

She closed her eyes. This would be a good time to pray he didn't attempt anything rash.

She heard a distant rumble and realized it was thunder. None of the men so much as glanced at the sky.

"Beezle. Racer." Gideon gave them mock bows. "Lovely night for a stroll."

So this was Beezle. She understood why Gideon didn't like the man. She didn't particularly care for him at the moment either.

"You know I'll kill you," Beezle said. "Give me what I want now, and I'll do it quickly and spare the girl."

"The necklace?" Gideon tapped his chin. "That's a problem. I don't have it with me."

"Fetch it." Beezle jerked the knife in the direction of the street then laid it back against her skin. "We'll wait."

Thunder rumbled again. And again.

No, that last hadn't been thunder.

Her eyes darted down at Beauty, poking her head through the opening in the fence. The dog gingerly stepped through, growling low in her throat.

"Git!" Racer shouted and lunged at Beauty. She bared her teeth and stood her ground, legs splayed wide, head low.

"How rude of me," Gideon said in that easy voice. "Beezle, this is Beauty. She has a fondness for Susanna—that's the woman you're poking with that knife. If you don't release Susanna, Beauty will rip your throat out." He smiled.

"Call off the buffer, Gideon." Beezle gestured with the knife again.

Susanna jerked to the side. Beezle held tight to her waist, but she'd thrown him off balance. They stumbled, and Beauty attacked. Beauty flung herself at Beezle, the weight of her body sending Susanna to the hard street. Gideon yanked her up.

"Run!"

"Beauty!" Susanna screamed.

"Run!" Gideon shoved her.

She ran blindly, knocking into men who'd come to have a look at the commotion. She pressed through them until she reached a *T*. Left or right? Hands on her knees, she heaved in a breath and wiped her tears on her sleeve.

Thunder boomed in the distance.

"Go right!"

She whipped around. Gideon held Beauty under one arm and ran like a man possessed. "Go right!" he yelled again.

She arrowed to the right, Gideon following close behind. He stayed on her heels, even when it meant slowing down to maneuver around a circle of boys throwing dice, or two men arguing over the carcass of a dog killed in a fight. The prostitutes cheered her on when she ran past, obviously thinking she was one of them.

No one offered any assistance—not that she would have taken it. Still, Susanna's faith in humanity was sorely tested.

"Head for Fleet Street," Gideon yelled.

She threw him a bewildered look. For all she could recognize of their surroundings, they might have been in China.

"This way." He led the way, increasing his pace with an ease she envied. The thrill of escape had given her the energy to run this far, but her strength was flagging.

He turned left and then right and then left and left again. She was lost in the maze. "Gideon," she called, slowing to a jog, "I can't."

"Almost there." He slowed, but not as much as she wanted. She trudged forward, tripping on the ill-fitting boots. Her legs were heavy and numb. Finally, Gideon pulled her against the side of a building, and she rested her head on the stone wall.

Thunder boomed again. A light drizzle fell, cooling her heated skin. "What's wrong with Beauty?" she managed between pants.

He looked at the dog, tucked under his arm like a parcel. "Nothing. I had to pull her off Beezle, and I didn't want to lose her when we ran."

He slicked wet hair out of his eyes and set the dog down. "What are you smiling about?"

"You like her." She nodded to Beauty.

He poked his head around a corner and surveyed Fleet Street. The sounds of carriages and people passing—most of them coming from or going to either Fleet or Newgate prisons—made her feel strangely safe. Beezle would not dare attack them in the middle of Fleet Street.

She bent and scratched Beauty's head. "And you like him too, don't you?" she cooed. Beauty pushed her head into Susanna's hand then jumped up and licked her face.

"Disgusting," Gideon remarked. "Dog spit."

She rose. "Don't be jealous. She'll kiss you next time."

His lip curled, and he peeked around the corner again. "Now what?"

"Now we make our way to Vauxhall. I'm about to steal a gig to drive us there." He pointed an accusatory finger. "Don't argue with me."

"Why would I argue?"

"Because you have a misguided sense of morals and principles?"

"There's nothing wrong with my morals. In this case, the threat of murder trumps the sin of stealing. We take the carriage."

He did it so easily and so smoothly, she wasn't ready when he called to her from the seat on the box. She supposed she'd expected a commotion or a protest from the groom. She'd heard nothing.

He helped her up, and she called to Beauty. The dog barked once, then jumped into the seat. With a flick of the reins, the gig jerked into motion.

"Forgive my driving. I haven't done this often."

"I'd take over, but my mother says it's unseemly for ladies to drive."

He curled his lip. "The more I hear of your mother,

the less I like her. Clearly, you should be the one to drive." He offered her the reins.

"I just told you—"

"Susanna, drive."

She changed places with him and gave the horse a bit of slack, which immediately caused the animal to run faster. The quick pace and the traffic on Fleet Street both terrified and exhilarated her. She threw her hair over her shoulder and tested the reins. Her brothers had discussed driving for hours on end, and she knew the basics even if she had never put that knowledge into practice. She guided the horse right and left, steering him around obstacles and in whichever direction Gideon indicated.

Finally, they crossed Waterloo Bridge and left the city behind for open fields and scattered farmhouses. Gradually, that gave way to inns and taverns, a glassworks building, and the larger houses of several wealthy families.

By the time they reached Lambeth, the drizzle had all but stopped, and the thunder moved off into the distance. When she heard the faint notes of the violin and cello, Gideon told her to slow. She stared at a three-story symmetrical house and a group of people entering it, most likely proceeding into the pleasure gardens. Gideon directed her to drive on, and they soon reached Kennington Lane. Grooms walked the horses of those who had come by carriage, and Gideon directed her to pass them and stop under a tree, the darkness providing them cover. Weary but exhilarated, she hopped down into Gideon's arms.

"You're glowing," he said, holding her far longer than was appropriate.

"I could drive all night." She gave the gig a wistful glance. "I do hope the horse finds his owner again."

"So do I." He set her down and lightly slapped the horse's rump. Horse and empty gig clopped off into the night.

Susanna pointed back along the lane. "That's it, isn't it? Vauxhall Gardens?"

"That's it. Now we have one last problem. No blunt for admission."

"How will we gain entrance?"

"I'm glad you asked."

He led her far away from the lights and noise of the arriving carriages, into the shadows and the darkness of the field and the night. The grass here was long and unkempt, and she stumbled over rocks several times. Beauty ran ahead of them, flushing out rabbits and birds. Gideon kept a hand on her elbow, steadying her. He must have had eyes like a cat's to see so well in the dark.

"This is about right," he said and moved closer to the wall of the perimeter. Susanna looked up. She could certainly not climb that high, and if he did, how would he manage to help her climb over? How could they be certain they wouldn't be caught sneaking in? They couldn't see what was on the other side.

"Not up, Strawberry," Gideon said. "Look down."

He crawled along the base of the wall, reaching into the thick foliage growing along the wall. Beauty sniffed the ground alongside him then seemed to form an idea and trotted ahead. A moment later, she began to dig furiously, and Gideon rose and jogged to her.

He knelt, his head disappearing into the bushes. When he backed out, he shook leaves out of his hair. "Dog found it."

"Found what?"

"Our entrance. Follow me, my lady." And he dropped down to his knees.

❧

Brook stood at the Proprietor's House, the entrance of the pleasure gardens, and studied the men and women streaming past. He'd followed one or two for a better look, but none of the women had been Susanna.

The crowds here were better dressed and better smelling than those he'd encountered on Field Lane. They didn't look at him like he smelled of refuse either, the way Des Stewart had when Brook had slammed him into the wall of his own dolly shop.

"I don't know where they are, thief-taker," Des spat, his face turning red from the pressure of Brook's hand on his neck.

"How do you know who I seek?"

"Ye've accosted 'alf the people on the street. Word is out."

Probably true. "The word I have is you were seen with my sister."

"Your sister?" Des's blue eyes bulged. "I never so much as laid eyes on 'er."

With his free hand, Brook produced a miniature from his pocket. He held it in front of Des's eyes. Recognition flickered before Des could hide it.

"Talk." Brook squeezed Des's throat for emphasis.

"I didn't know she were your sister. I swear."

"If you touched her…"

"No! Put me down. I'll talk. I swear. I were only trying to 'elp out a crony."

Brook lowered Des and loosened his grip, but he didn't step back or give the fence any room to run. "What crony?"

"Gideon 'Arrow. 'E's one of the Covent Garden Cubs." He wiped sweat from his brow.

"I know him." And what the hell was a rook like Gideon Harrow doing with Susanna? Gideon knew Marlowe, but as far as Brook knew, she'd never invited any of her former rooks into Derring House.

"Gid needed a place to lay low. 'Alf of London is after 'im. I owed him a favor." His blond hair was damp with sweat now, and Brook could smell the fear on him.

"And my sister?"

"Gid called her *Strawberry*. I never asked her real name. 'E weren't 'olding 'er against 'er will. I don't 'old with that."

"And Miss Brenna O'Shea? Can she vouch for you?"

Des closed his eyes in a wince of pain. "Don't 'arass 'er. She gave the girl tea and something to eat. Brenna's a good girl."

Brook tapped Des's damp shirt. "If anything has happened to my sister, I'll be back. You and Miss Brenna will spend time in Newgate." He strolled away, past a pile of silk handkerchiefs. Half the monograms hadn't even been removed.

"Don't say that, Derring!" Des called after him. "I didn't do nothing!"

Brook had climbed into the Derring coach and instructed the coachman to drive to Vauxhall Gardens.

Brook was not a man given to gambling. He would not have risked money on the chance Susanna had gone to Vauxhall. But it was all he had left. His mother had said she'd mentioned it. Brook didn't know what the devil Susanna had been thinking, what made her want to see Vauxhall, but he did know she could be determined.

Would she run away just to see Vauxhall? He didn't think she was that foolish, but what did he know of women?

And how was Gideon Harrow involved? He'd liked the thief when he'd met him—as much as Brook could like a thief. But if he was with Susanna, Brook would see him locked away on a prison hulk for the rest of his life. Hanging was too good for the bastard.

Two hours in front of the Proprietor's House at Vauxhall had proved fruitless though. Neither Susanna nor Gideon had gone in or out. He'd walked back to his coach, head down, gaze on his boots.

If she wanted to go to Vauxhall, what would stop her?

No carriage.

No coin for the ferry.

No...

Brook stopped, and a man almost ran into him. With a curse, the man pushed past him and Brook turned back.

Of course he hadn't seen Gideon or Susanna walk into Vauxhall. They'd have no blunt. There were other ways of gaining entrance. Brook turned and arrowed for the entrance.

Sixteen

"It's amazing," Susanna said as they strolled along The Great Walk, bordered on all sides by hedges and trees. She sipped Rhenish wine and gazed at the buildings, which she informed Gideon were of Palladian design. The gardens had been laid out in a rectangular fashion, with straight walks lit by lamps and ornamented by arches, giving way to pretty arbors housing small, intimate buildings for a couple or small group to dine. He pointed out the larger buildings to her porticoes, obelisks, an orchestra, and supper boxes.

She hadn't asked where he had acquired the blunt to purchase the refreshments, and he hadn't offered any explanation. The bubble whose pocket he'd picked wouldn't miss a few shillings.

"I had no idea there were places like this in Town," she said. "I can even hear birds singing—nightingales, if I'm not mistaken."

He made a noncommittal sound. He had no idea what nightingales sounded like. It seemed there was music and laughter everywhere, something new every few feet.

"Oh, look! Do you see those hedges? Those are raspberry and gooseberry bushes and"—she inhaled—"smell the bushes. Oh, and I knew I recognized the perfume of jonquils. But oh! Gillyflowers and lilies and"—she clutched his arm—"fruits and vegetables grow here—beans, asparagus... I don't know what that one is. Peas, perhaps. Those are strawberries."

Gideon was sorely tempted to pluck one.

"Oh, but I must say the trees are by far the garden's best feature. They're quite old. That group there must be over a hundred years in age. I've seen better gardens, of course, but these are really very well tended."

"Thank you."

Gideon spun around, his gaze landing on a man kneeling next to a bed of lilies. The white-haired man rose slowly, as though his knees pained him.

"Robert Southey," he said with a bow. "Amateur horticulturist. I am sorry to interrupt your discussion, but I suppose I feel as though the gardens are partly mine. I've traveled the world in search of specimens for this garden and that of my family. I planted many of these myself."

Susanna dropped a curtsy. Gideon shoved a hand in his pocket, jingling the two shillings he had remaining.

"I'm so sorry if I offended you," Susanna said quickly. "If it's any consolation, I was referring to the Duke of Devonshire's gardens at Chatsworth."

"I've seen those myself. Quite impressive. And I don't take any offense. My work here is merely a hobby when I'm in London. My travels keep me away for much of the year. Most people come for the entertainment, not the walks, and those who do come for the walks aren't looking at the flowers."

"Do you always tend gardens at night?" Gideon asked.

Southey glanced at the bed he'd been weeding. "If I have the urge. The best time to see the gardens is in the day. You're right about that."

"Vauxhall isn't open during the day, is it?" Susanna asked.

"No." Southey squinted, and Gideon knew she'd won him over. She won everyone over.

"If you want to come back tomorrow, I'd be happy to show you around."

Susanna practically bounced with pleasure, but she looked to Gideon for an answer.

"Do you give everyone you meet day tours?" Gideon asked.

"Only the rare few," Southey said, smiling at Susanna. She smiled back.

If there was a con in this, Gideon hadn't figured it out yet. That didn't mean he wouldn't keep looking.

"Why are we among the privileged?" Gideon asked.

Susanna gave him a frown.

"You aren't," Southey said with a dismissive glance. "She is. I'd be delighted to see you again, Miss—"

"Mrs. Harrow," Gideon interjected. They'd agreed she wouldn't give her real name in case her brother was looking for her, but they'd never agreed to pose as husband and wife.

Susanna made a credible attempt to hide her surprise at his statement. She schooled her features into another smile. "I'd be delighted to partake of the tour.

If you don't mind, I will bring my husband." She barely stumbled over the word.

"He's welcome if he's with you." The older man reached into his pocket and withdrew a tattered card. "Bring this for admittance."

Susanna took it, handed it to Gideon. "Thank you, sir. Might I ask why you invited me, considering you mentioned you rarely give day tours?"

Southey scratched the white hair above his ear. "I don't know. I suppose…" His dark eyes stared past her and into the shadows of The Dark Walk, just a few feet away. "You remind me of someone I knew a long time ago."

"Oh." She all but cooed.

Gideon took her arm and pulled her toward The Dark Walk. She looked over her shoulder. "We shall come by after breakfast, if that's agreeable."

"Perfectly."

"Until then, Mr. Southey."

Gideon supposed she would have curtsied if he hadn't been dragging her.

"Don't allow that dog to dig in my flower beds," Southey said as they retreated. "Not sure how you even managed to sneak her in. They're not allowed, you know."

"Oh, no!" Susanna shook her head. "She would never dig in the gardens."

The shadows of The Dark Walk closed around them, and Gideon pulled her deep into the deserted path. He well knew it only looked deserted. Off the path, hidden by foliage and muted light, couples strayed from the crowds for a moment of passion. Of course, molls worked here too, taking coin for their favors, but most of them preferred The Great Walk. The Dark Walk was too far out of the way to attract customers.

Gideon nodded to a constable who passed, and moved along the walk at a leisurely pace. The space between lamps lengthened, and the darkness held sway. Gideon paused in a shaded spot, listening closely for sounds of trysting couples. He heard nothing and took Susanna's hand. She didn't protest when he guided her off the path. She trusted him, a fact he did not want to examine too closely at the moment.

The Dark Walk was thus named because the trees were thicker there and provided a canopy that blocked out the light. But he led her to a secluded patch of ground where the soft grass was thick and the branches above opened for a clear view of the sky. Gideon wished he had a coat to lay on the ground. Unfortunately, he'd lost it at some point in the last day. It was probably still on the chair in Des's room. He tugged Susanna down beside him and pointed at the starlit sky. "I have a surprise for you."

"Really?" She might have been a child, with her wide eyes and her excited grin. He loved that look on her face, loved pleasing her.

He lay back on the soft grass and gestured for her to rest her head on his shoulder. She did so without protest, though he knew she probably had no fondness for grass or twigs in her hair. Beauty settled a little ways off, putting her head between her paws and snoring quietly.

"It's a beautiful night," she said quietly.

"With all the lamps on the walks, you wouldn't know it was night. It's darker here. More stars."

"I didn't know one could see the stars in London. I've only seen them in the country."

"There's a lot you haven't seen in London," he said.

She nodded, her head moving slightly on his arm. He turned to look at her, admiring the curve of her nose and the jut of her lips.

"You've shown me so much."

"I could show you more," he said. "I'd like to."

She turned to face him, her lips inches from his. "What are you saying, Gideon?"

What was he saying? He wasn't her husband in truth. He'd never be her husband. They had tonight, perhaps tomorrow afternoon. That was all.

"I'm not here with you solely because of the necklace."

She gave him a wistful smile. "At least you added *solely*."

"I won't lie and say I don't need it back. I do. But I want to be with you almost as much."

"Why?" She closed her eyes. "I should not have said that."

He rose, shifting her head so it rested in the palm of his hand. "Never censor your words with me. You want to know why I want to be with you? The list is too long. To begin, you enjoy every moment. You don't take a single instant for granted. And you're brave. The way you stood up to Dagger Dan, and faced down Corker at Stryker's flash ken. I misjudged you."

She reached up and traced a finger down his cheek. "I misjudged *you*. You're so much more than a thief. You know that, don't you? You're kind and generous. You make me laugh. You make me feel."

She was wrong. He wasn't kind or generous. He was selfish. What could be more selfish than a thief? He watched his back, and the hell with the rest of them.

And now he would prove to her how selfish he could be. He couldn't resist her any longer. He didn't want to.

He kissed her lightly. "What do you feel now?"

"Love," she whispered. "I know I shouldn't, but I've fallen in love with you."

It was as though she'd reached inside his chest and grabbed hold of his heart. He felt a tightness in his chest, and for a moment he couldn't breathe.

"What did you say?" he finally managed on a gasp.

She smiled and cupped his face in her hands, those slim, long-fingered hands. "I said, I love you, Gideon Harrow."

The words were a punch in the face, a knee in the gut, an elbow to his lungs. When had he last heard those words? Age five? Six? He'd been tucked into the pallet that served as a bed, the rough, sheet pulled up to his chin. His mother's rough, red fingers gently smoothed the hair back from his forehead.

"Sleep, Gideon. I love you, sweet boy."

He closed his eyes. He didn't want to remember that time. He didn't want to feel the pain of the loss again.

He didn't want to look at Susanna and know he would lose her too.

He pushed up and back, tilting his head back to stare at the sky. He couldn't breathe; the memory of his mother's hands caressing his forehead was too vivid.

Susanna sat, pulling her legs to her chest and wrapping her arms around her knees. "I said something wrong."

"No."

She rested her cheek on her forearm, turning her face toward him. Waiting. She didn't demand. That wasn't her way. He was coming to see that her demand he take her to Vauxhall was not her usual way. She must have been desperate to resort to such uncharacteristic behavior.

"The last time someone said…that." He swallowed, trying to wet his dry throat. "I was remembering my mother."

"She died when you were very young."

He nodded, stared at the tiny pinpricks of light in the velvet blanket above. Was she up there somewhere, looking down? What would she have thought of Susanna? Gideon snorted. She would have thought the girl was too good for him.

She was.

"Has no one told you they loved you since your mother?"

He expected to hear pity in her voice, but if it was there, he couldn't detect it.

"Who would love me?" he asked. "Beezle? Racer? Marlowe?" He laughed at the last name, because it hurt to say it.

"Marlowe does love you," Susanna said, putting her warm hand on his arm. "Just not in the same way you love her."

His gaze met hers. "I don't love her. I thought I did."

How could he explain that since he'd met Susanna, he'd felt so much more than he knew he could? He'd thought what he felt for Marlowe was love. Now he knew it was nothing more than lust, nothing more than amplified affection.

Did he love Susanna?

How the hell was he supposed to know? How did a man who spent his life preying on others change into a man who cared for someone else?

"What's changed?" Susanna asked.

She knew the answer.

He turned and knelt before her, taking her hands. "I'm flattered you think you love me."

She laughed. That wasn't the reaction he'd expected, and he shut his mouth abruptly.

"You're not flattered. You're terrified. You think I don't know what I'm talking about. That if I knew who you really are, what you really are, I wouldn't love you."

"If you knew half of what I've done, Susanna…"

"I know some of what you've done. I know you helped Marlowe escape that crime lord. I know you helped return a little girl to her mother. I know you carried Beauty under your arm to keep her safe from Beezle."

The dog raised her head, regarded them curiously, and went back to sleep.

"You think those were acts of kindness? They were acts of survival. You wouldn't have walked away from them."

"So why didn't you walk away from me?"

"Greed," he said baldly. "I need that necklace."

"So go fetch it. You could have left me behind at any time and gone back to Derring House to search."

Her words vibrated like the distant strings of the music being performed in the Orchestra. "I don't know where it's hidden."

She took his hand in hers, examined it closely. "A practiced thief like you? How long would it take you to find it? An hour? Two?"

Gideon looked down at the hand she held, dark and large in her small, pale one. His hands were dirty with all manner of wickedness—drink, debauchery, theft…murder.

"I know who you are, Gideon Harrow. I know what you've done." Her dark eyes met his. "I want you anyway. I thought I wanted to come to Vauxhall to discover my mother's secrets. I thought if I saw this place, with its closed walks and secluded arbors, I might see something of the woman she'd been before she turned hard. I might understand why she couldn't love me. But you were right."

"What was that?"

She smiled. "You heard me. You said I began this journey because I needed to escape. I did." She squeezed his hand, brought it to her lips, and kissed his palm. "And because I was supposed to meet you."

"You were never supposed to meet me."

"But I did." She slid his hand around her neck and leaned in to kiss him. "I did meet you, Gideon Harrow," she whispered against his lips. "And I don't regret it. And I won't regret anything between us."

His lips took hers. He couldn't stop himself from tasting her. He lowered her to the soft grass, balanced himself on his forearms, and looked down at her. "You'll regret this. You'll wish it hadn't been me."

He stroked her silky hair, spread it out around her like a halo.

"It has to be you." She tangled her legs with his. "There will only ever be you."

He kissed her again, slowly, knowing they had the rest of the night. The crowds didn't leave Vauxhall until close to dawn most evenings. No need to rush. Plenty of time for her to change her mind.

Though she might think this time they shared would last forever, he knew differently. The future held nothing for them. She was destined for a very different life than he. It did no good to imagine what might have been if they'd been different people. She was the daughter of an earl. He was nothing and no one.

He couldn't marry her. He couldn't even give her food or drink without stealing to obtain the funds.

But he could give her this. He could give her one last night of pleasure.

He slid his hand under her skirts, cupping the soft skin on her calf. She inhaled sharply when he brushed against her scraped shin. "Does it still pain you much?"

She shook her head. "Only when I bump it. It doesn't hurt to walk."

"Just a scratch then." He slid his hand higher, over her knee and then between her thighs. He knew what she looked like without the ill-fitting dress and the layers of petticoats and shift. He'd seen her on the table at Des's, and she'd been magnificent. He thought of her long, lean legs now, ran his fingertips up and down them until she shivered and trembled.

Her hands gripped the base of his shirt, yanking it up and diving beneath to stroke his back. He'd been touched by many women, but never like this. Never with tenderness and reverence. Her lips pressed against his jaw, his neck, and her hands smoothed over his buttocks, squeezing lightly.

He used his mouth to yank her bodice down, to take one firm nipple in his mouth, to work it as his hands inched closer to the burning heat of her. Her legs quaked with need, and he slid over the soft curls, drawing a gasp of pleasure from her.

Her hands slid to his hips and then stroked over his hard cock, while his fingers tangled in her curls, circling and teasing. Her hips rose, and he slid a finger into her sleek folds. She was wet and warm and ready for him.

He tried to forget the hand wrapped around him, tried not to imagine the slim fingers stroking from root to head. He slid two fingers into her, his thumb teasing the small nub that would make her come. He could give her that and leave her virtue untouched.

Her hand stilled, then moved deftly to unfasten the fall of his trousers. Suddenly his cock was free and encased in the warmth of her hand. "Susanna," he said in warning.

"I want this, Gideon."

Her hand moved up and down in long, languid strokes, eliciting a deep groan of pleasure from the back of his throat. His fingers moved faster, and her hand stilled as the muscles around his fingers clenched.

"Take me, Gideon," she murmured.

"I won't be able to stop myself if you keep talking like that."

"Good. I want you. I want… Yes. Oh, *yes*."

His thumb brushed against that pulsing bud again, and she opened to him then closed like a vise. A strangled sound of pleasure escaped into the night, muted by a distant thunder. He looked up and into a burst of light as the first fireworks exploded above them.

"Seems appropriate," he murmured.

"Very." She wrapped her legs around his waist, bringing their bodies together so his cock rubbed the heat of her entrance. She pulled his head down and kissed him as more fireworks burst above them. Slowly, he slid into her, into the tight wetness. She closed around him, and he had the urge to thrust deep, bury himself in that warm, moist place.

"I don't want to hurt you," he said. "I've heard it can hurt the first time."

"You'd never hurt me," she murmured. "You feel so good." Her eyes strayed to the sky above them and then back to his face. "It's beautiful. Perfect."

He slid deeper, and she stiffened slightly when he reached the first resistance. His arms trembled with restraint as he waited for her to relax again. Her eyes locked on his, her gaze intent. Gradually, her muscles slackened, and her eyelids lowered.

He inched inside her, deeper into her tight sheath. She gasped with pain, and he forced himself to stop. He was so close. So close to burying himself in her. "I can stop," he panted. "If you want me to stop, say it now."

"Don't stop." She locked her ankles around his back. "Don't ever stop."

He buried himself to the hilt, eliciting a small cry of pain from her. She was tight and stiff, and he kissed her neck and her shoulder in apology. "I'm sorry. I'm so sorry."

A burst of red from the fireworks above illuminated her face, and she was so beautiful. Everything about her was impossibly beautiful. She smiled up at him, kissed him gently.

"I'm yours now. I'll always be yours."

He moved slowly and gently inside her. He could feel her arms stiffen around his neck, and he whispered, "Relax."

"It feels… It hurts. The pain is not intense, but it's more than discomfort."

He pulled back, almost withdrawing. "It's an invasion," he murmured. "You have to welcome it. You have to take me in." He slid in slowly, filling her completely, inch by inch. "Relax."

"Yes." Her head fell back, and some of the tension left her arms and her legs.

"Let me take you. Give yourself to me."

He slid into her, withdrew, thrust again. She moaned, and he stilled. "Did I hurt you?"

"It doesn't hurt so much anymore," she murmured. "I can see how it might feel good if you weren't so large."

He laughed, resting his forehead on her shoulder.

Orange light burst above them, lighting her hair until it appeared aflame.

"Was that the wrong thing to say?" she asked.

"That was very right."

She shifted, clenched around him, and he felt a jolt of pleasure. "Susanna," he choked out.

"You liked that."

She moved her hips, thrust up, taking him in deeper.

"Sweet Jesus. I don't want to hurt you. Slow down."

She clenched around him again, and his vision went dark. "I. Can't…"

"Then let go."

Green light burst above them, then red and orange and yellow as he drove into her, driving until the pleasure spiraled and coalesced. He withdrew just in time, holding his cock and spilling his seed on the grass beside them, throwing his head back in a vain effort to mute the cries of pleasure.

He collapsed beside her, raised his hand, and saw the blood on his fingers.

What the fuck had he done?

Susanna watched the fireworks for a moment, trying to memorize every sight, every detail—the feel of him inside her, the look on his face when he'd climaxed, the acrid smell of the fireworks mixed with the oil from the nearby lamps, the thud of blood in her ears.

She wasn't a virgin any longer. It felt as though a burden had been lifted. She could never go back to the life she'd had before. She could never go back to the scared, rigid girl cowering before her mother. She'd been irrevocably changed.

And she'd been the one to make the decision.

She turned on her side, curled beside Gideon, and stared up at the bursts of light still filling the sky. A few days before, she would have been appalled at the thought of lying in the grass. The idea of lying in the grass with a man, a half-naked man, would have shocked her. And she hadn't even known about the rest—about the pleasure or the way a man felt when he buried himself inside her.

She'd been that sheltered girl, and she'd been so eager to break free of the constraints. She'd wanted to see the world, to explore outside the borders of her bejeweled cage.

Now she knew.

Was this what her mother had sought to protect her from? Susanna shook her head. No. Not this. Her mother had sought to protect her from what was coming. She'd lose Gideon. She knew that much. He wasn't the sort of man a woman like her could keep. Duty, honor, title—those were the ties that would bind a man to her. And bindings they would be without love.

She'd been a fool to fall in love with him. Her heart was already breaking at the knowledge she'd lose him. All this time she'd hated the way her mother dictated every aspect of her life. Now she saw it in a different light. Perhaps her mother wanted only to shelter her from this pain.

"Are you hurt?" Gideon asked, twining her hair around his fingers absently. She wondered if he knew what those small gestures of affection meant to her.

"No. I'm fine. A little sore, perhaps, but it was worth it."

"Next time will be better." His voice hitched. "Not that I would…"

She rose on her elbow and put a finger on his lips. "Don't turn into a gentleman on me now."

"You're a bad influence on me."

She sighed and lowered her head to his shoulder again. "If only you knew how often I've been told that," she quipped.

She felt his chest rumble with laughter and pressed her cheek hard against him. She would think of this moment, of his strong chest and the way it felt under her cheek, when she was old and dying. She'd remember what it felt like to be young and free. For once in her life, free.

"What now?" he asked after the fireworks' show ended and the orchestra began to play again. He'd dressed again and helped her with her gown. But they hadn't left their secluded spot. She felt as though this was their private world. She wished she would never have to leave.

But that was the question she'd known would come. Everything had to end.

"I should take you directly to Derring House, give you the necklace. You've more than fulfilled your end of our bargain."

He didn't argue. She'd wanted him to argue that it wasn't about the necklace, but of course it was. Had she really thought he'd say, "What necklace? It's you I care about"?

"But if I return home now, I'll never come back here. And how many people get to visit Vauxhall in the daylight?"

He flicked his hand, and Robert Southey's card appeared between his fingers. "We do have an invitation. A first for me."

He probably meant it too. How strange that his admission he'd never before been invited anywhere made her want to embrace him. "But we need somewhere to sleep," she said. "I don't suppose we can stay here."

"No. The constables clear everyone out at closing, but there are lodging houses along the road and in Lambeth."

"And will you lighten someone's pocket so we might stay the night?"

He flicked his fingers, and the card disappeared again. He was capable of picking pockets until they could have afforded a room at the Pultney. She had little doubt of that.

"I have a few shillings. I can bribe a groom to let us sleep in the stables."

He pulled her to her feet, and she winced at the soreness between her legs. She tried to hide her expression, but when she glanced at Gideon, his face was tight. He'd seen, and he was almost certainly angry at himself. Who would have imagined he possessed such morals?

He took her hand and led her along The Dark Walk, turning onto a lit path and passing under one of the arches set at the walks' intersections. The crowds grew thicker here, men and women strolling and talking. In one of the arbors, she heard the clink of glasses as people toasted. In another, a harpist played and a woman sang. In yet another, people cheered for a boy who performed tumbling tricks. Susanna paused to watch him, amazed at how high he flew when he flipped backward.

Gideon finally pulled her away, toward the Grove, where the orchestra played and men and women danced or reclined on benches, holding thin slices of ham and all manner of drink. They paused beside the trunk of a tree to watch the dancing, and when she looked down, she saw his foot tapped in rhythm.

"Do you want to dance?" she asked.

He dug his hands into his pockets. "I don't know the steps."

"I could teach you."

"I don't think you could." He didn't look at her, and she felt her eyes sting with tears. Would he say good-bye to her like this over and over again until they finally parted?

She didn't want to watch the dancers any longer and allowed her gaze to rove over the patrons. It occurred to her she might know some of the revelers. She doubted anyone who did not know her well would recognize her in this disheveled state, but it was certainly a risk.

Perhaps her renewed vigilance was the reason she saw him. Or perhaps it was because he moved with purpose while everyone else around them strolled leisurely.

Her hand tightened on Gideon's arm, and he looked at her, leaning close. "What is it?"

"My brother Brook is here."

Seventeen

SHE DIDN'T MOVE. SHE DIDN'T DARE BREATHE. SHE watched Brook march along the path, his hands in his pockets and his eyes sharp. He hadn't seen her yet. The tree obscured them, but given a few moments' more, he would have a direct line of sight.

"Where?" Gideon's lips barely parted on the word.

"Directly across from us. In the blue coat, hands in his—"

"Damn it. He's looking for you."

"How could he possibly know I was here?"

"How the hell did he know where Marlowe was hiding?"

That was a good point. Brook reminded her of a hunting dog. He sniffed out prey. "We have to leave before he sees us."

"I'm in complete agreement. Unfortunately, he's about to pass in front of the Proprietor's House. That's the way out."

"What if we circle around, follow behind him, and exit when he's past?"

"Good plan, if we can circle around without him seeing."

And if he doesn't circle back the way he came, Susanna thought. Brook could be unpredictable, but now was not the best time to mention that.

Gideon clasped her hand, his arm rigid, indicating she should wait for his signal to move. Brook grew closer to the point at which they'd be visible, and her breath quickened. Her heart hammered, and her mind repeated, *He'll see us; he'll see us.*

At the last moment, Gideon tugged her arm, and she walked away from their hiding place. She didn't dare look at Brook. If he sped up even slightly, he'd have a clear view of them.

"Slow and steady," Gideon cautioned. "Go for a stroll."

She wanted to run. If Gideon's timing was off even slightly, Brook would see them. Gideon's firm hand holding hers kept her in check. When she finally dared look over her shoulder, she didn't see Brook.

"Look ahead," Gideon said pleasantly. "You're not worried about being followed."

They circled the Orchestra, maneuvering around dozens of people and waiters and constables. At any second she was certain Brook would appear in front of them, scream, "Aha!" and grab her. It seemed hours passed before they reached the last stretch of paving before the Proprietor's House.

"There." Gideon nodded to the place they'd stood. Brook studied the tree she'd leaned against, and she dug her nails into Gideon's arm.

"How does he know?"

Gideon tugged her into the house, which was quite large, boasting a ballroom and two parlors that she could see. She looked up at a soaring ceiling, ornamented with paintings, barely visible in the dim light. It was a shock of grandeur and almost imprisoning after the openness of the gardens.

"He's good," Gideon said. "All we need do is keep one step ahead of him."

⁓

The lodging house was called the Three Ducks. It was not the sort of place her mother would have ever allowed her to stay, and she had no more than a peek inside a dark window before Gideon spirited her out to the stables. After a quiet discussion and an exchange of coin with a groom, Gideon settled into an empty loose box with a horse blanket on top of straw.

Susanna sank down into the straw without comment. Gideon wondered if she would have seated herself in the dusty straw so easily a mere two days ago when he met her. He wondered where he would be at the moment if he hadn't. Far away from London, much farther than Lambeth.

And yet, he couldn't wish himself anywhere else at the moment.

He placed a hand on her shoulder. "I'll be right back, just outside. If you need me, call out."

She gave him a tired smile, her eyes warm when they met his. The love he saw felt so close to the surface it made his heart pump faster. He didn't deserve that love.

Perhaps that was why it was such an incredible gift.

He stepped outside, moved away from the door of the stables and out of the lamplight. Full dark surrounded him like a warm blanket. Crickets and other insects chirped, but otherwise the countryside was eerily quiet. So accustomed to the sounds of the city was he, that the silence unnerved him. He loosened the fall of his trousers and peed against a tree, whistling a tune he'd heard at Vauxhall that night.

When he was done, he turned back to the stables and almost smacked into the man standing behind him.

"Harrow."

Gideon balled his fists and pulled his arm back. Sir Brook Derring stepped easily aside, obviously expecting the attack. The absence of a target caused Gideon to stumble, and Brook caught him by the wrist and neatly twisted his arm behind his back. A moment later, the rough bark of the tree dug into the flesh of Gideon's cheek.

"Where is she?"

"Go to hell." Gideon forced the words through compressed lips.

"Is she hurt?"

"I didn't touch her."

"Bollocks." Derring yanked him back and slammed him into the tree again. "You expect me to believe that?"

Black sprinkled with white pinpricks dimmed Gideon's vision for a moment. He shook the pain off. "I didn't do anything she didn't want."

"I should kill you," Derring growled into his ear.

"Go ahead. If you don't, Beezle will."

"You have a knack for making enemies. Too bad. I saw so much potential in you."

Gideon tried to twist his neck to see Derring's face. Potential? What the hell did the man mean by that?

"I also know my sister. She's done larking about. My mother has taken to bed with worry. Bring me to her."

"No." Gideon growled when Derring yanked his arm up painfully. "Break my arm, but I won't tell you."

"Then I'll search the lodging house and the stables, turn it upside down, until I find her."

"No you won't." The air whooshed out of Gideon's lungs as Brook pressed his forearm against the back of Gideon's neck. "*Bluff!*" Gideon wheezed.

"You bloody bastard. I should break your neck."

"Too much honor," Gideon choked out, hoping to God it was true. The pressure on his neck eased. Gideon knew when he had the advantage. "If you kill me, you'll still have to go in and fetch her. Then everyone will know Sir Brook Derring's sister, Lady Susanna, was alone with a cove like me. You might as well announce it onstage at Drury Lane."

If there was one thing Gideon knew about the gentry, it was that they prized their gentry mort's lily-white reputations. Sir Brook wouldn't ruin his sister any more than he'd kick a dog.

Gideon took three breaths in the long silence while Derring considered. Finally, the man shoved him hard and said, "It goes against every fiber of my being, but you've left me no choice except to trust you."

"Careful you don't break your teeth on those words."

"You betray that trust, and you betray not only me but Marlowe. You remember Marlowe?"

The words were like a punch in the balls. Gideon grunted. Derring knew he'd never let Marlowe down.

"Have Lady Susanna back at Derring House by noon tomorrow, or Beezle will be the least of your worries. Marlowe will come for you, and if she doesn't scare you, think about this: every Bow Street Runner in the city will be looking to slit your throat."

"Every Runner?" Gideon snorted. "You think you have that much power?"

Derring released Gideon's arm and swung him around. "I may not be a Runner, but I have their loyalty. They consider me one of their own, and the Runners protect our own. Susanna is my sister, and by extension, the responsibility of every Runner on Bow Street."

"I'll have her back."

Brook gave him a long look, searching for some thing in Gideon's face. Finally, he looked away, lip curled with disgust. "Do you need blunt?"

Gideon snorted. "I don't want your chink."

Derring released him with a shove. Gideon's head hit the tree and bounced back.

"Get out of my sight. I look at you and feel sick. You could have been one of us."

Gideon's ears rang from the impact with the tree. The jolt must have affected his hearing. "One of who?"

Derring leaned close. "A Runner."

Gideon gaped at the man. "Don't make me laugh, thief-taker. I'd never be one of your cronies."

Derring backed away. "No. You wouldn't, would you?"

The darkness closed around Derring, and Gideon leaned against the tree until his vision returned and the hammer in his brain ceased slamming against his skull. Finally, he made his way back to the stable.

Susanna lay with one arm curled under her cheek, her eyes closed, and her breathing regular. He stood above her and watched her sleep until the first rays of light turned the darkness beyond a slate gray. He'd risked everything for her—his future, his life. He wanted to believe it was for the necklace, but it had always been her. The first moment he saw her, he'd lost the battle.

Come what may, he didn't regret it.

A few more hours and he'd return her—back to the life she'd been born to, the life where she belonged. Back to the bosom of her family and all those who loved her.

And he'd go back too—back to life as a rook in Seven Dials, a thief, a faceless cove no one cared about.

❧

She woke wrapped in Gideon's arms. He was so warm, and she felt incredibly protected pressed against his chest. He smelled of hay and horse, the scents reminding her of Northbridge Abbey, her family's country estate. She'd always loved it there. Returning to London for the Season always felt like stepping into a gutter. She smelled the city long before she ever saw it.

She wrapped her arms around Gideon, buried her face in his coarse shirt. With her ear pressed to his chest, she could hear his heart thumping slowly and steadily. She parted the collar of his shirt and pressed her lips to the warm skin of his throat. His heart thumped faster, and his hands closed on her sides, pulling her closer and firmly against his hard member.

Heat rushed to her belly and pooled lower, making her very aware of the ache between her thighs. She rubbed against him, molding her body to his. He moaned and buried his lips in her hair, brushing against her ear. She shivered and slid her body against his.

"Are you attempting to seduce me, Lady Susanna?"

"Yes." She angled her hips. "I think I have succeeded."

His hand cupped her breast, his palm circling the nipple until it grew hard and ached for his touch.

"We're not alone. A groom might come in at any time."

"Then we should be quiet."

He chuckled. "Wanton girl."

He bent his head and took her breast with his mouth. She arched up, biting her lip to keep from crying out. His warm tongue on her skin sent shivers of pleasure through her. She wrapped her legs around him, making no secret of what she wanted from him, where she wanted him to touch her.

His mouth still on her breast, his hand cupped her ankle then slid up to tickle her calf. When his fingers brushed lightly against the back of her knee, she caught her breath and suppressed a moan. Finally, his hand moved deliberately over the sensitive skin of her thigh, skimming over the place where she ached for his touch. She bowed into him, parting her legs when his fingers delved into her slick flesh.

When his fingers entered her, she hissed in a breath of pain.

"I'm sorry." He pulled back, his hands off her in an instant. "I hurt you."

"Shh." She put a finger over his lips and kissed him gently. "I wasn't expecting the soreness. Touch me again."

The wary look in his eyes, the meaning behind it, slayed her. He *did* care about her. He didn't want to hurt her. Did that concern extend only to her body, or did it also encompass her heart?

"I don't want to cause you pain."

"If you do, I'll tell you. You'll stop."

His eyes darkened into that dangerous look that made her forget to breathe. "You think it so easy for me to stop? When I touch you, I don't ever want to stop."

"Then don't." She kissed his cheek, his lips, the scar slicing through his eyebrow, his temple. "Don't ever stop."

His hands were everywhere, his fingers gentle as they teased her body into a feverish state of arousal. When his finger entered her again, she barely noted the soreness, only that the extra sensitivity made her more eager for that hard length of him to slide between her legs.

"You're ready?" he said, sounding surprised. "Let me…" He bent, presumably to take her with his mouth, but she stopped him with a hand on his cheek.

"I want you," she whispered. "I want to join with you, feel you move inside me."

His eyes were the dark green of an ancient forest. "You say it so sweetly, so properly. Somehow you make it more erotic than vulgar speech ever could."

"I don't know the vulgar terms," she said, feeling her cheeks heat, as they always did when he pointed out her näiveté.

"I don't want you ever to learn them." He pushed the hair back from her temple, cradled her face in his hand. "If I hurt you—"

"You won't."

"—I'll try to stop. God help me, I'll find a way."

He slid into her, slowly and with exquisite tenderness. She felt a slight discomfort but no real pain. Her body accommodated him, closed around him, welcomed each careful stroke. He moved deliberately and with great skill. She hadn't known there was skill in this act, but the way Gideon knew exactly when to press forward, when to draw back, when to rock into her was definitely skilled.

His gaze never left hers, and he seemed to read her needs in her eyes. If she felt a flicker of pain, he slowed, and when a frisson of pleasure raced through her, he quickened. The pleasure built and built, coalescing into exquisite torment. She angled her hips up, taking more of him.

"Let go," he murmured. The intensity in his eyes undid her. She flew over the edge, the pleasure knocking her over like the fierce wind of a storm. It lifted her up, spun her around, drained her of all resistance until she couldn't imagine ever feeling anything so wonderful again.

And then Gideon was gone, his withdrawal almost painful. He spilled his seed in the straw beside her, heaving in great gasps. The arm supporting him trembled, and his head hung down, his dark hair a damp tangle on his brow.

"Why do you do that?" she asked quietly when he'd righted his clothing.

He gave her a bewildered look then blew out a breath. "I forget what an innocent you are." He pushed his hair off his forehead. "I don't want to get you with child."

She touched her belly lightly. A child. She had not thought of that. "You're protecting me."

"No." He took her hand and pulled her to her feet. "Don't look at it that way. This doesn't always work. If I really wanted to protect you, I wouldn't touch you."

She wrapped her arms around his neck. "You're not that cruel."

"Your view will likely change."

She drew back, pressing her arms stiffly to her sides. "It won't." She looked away, her gaze fastening on the matted straw where they'd slept twined in each other's arms. She'd known the morning would come, and it would herald a farewell.

"Shall we pay our visit to Mr. Southey? I know you are anxious to claim your payment, but—"

"I'll take you to Vauxhall." He moved quickly away from her, bending to brush straw from his trousers. "I'd like to enter through the Proprietor's House once instead of under the fence. Never had an invitation anywhere before." His words were light and teasing, but his voice held a hint of bitterness.

She'd insulted him, and she'd done it to goad him. She wanted him to tell her he didn't care about the necklace anymore. It was her he wanted, and the necklace be damned.

Unfair, she knew.

Of course the necklace mattered. It was worth more money than he'd probably ever imagined. She hadn't asked his intentions, and she didn't plan to, but she suspected he would sell it and use the money to leave Town. He'd want to start a new life.

She wanted that for him. She wanted him to have a future where he'd be safe.

She had wanted to be part of that future.

It took the better part of the morning to walk back to Vauxhall. The night before, Gideon had concocted a story about his pocket being picked and having no money to take the ferry back across the Thames. They'd secured a ride as far as the lodging house with an older couple whose eyes Susanna could not quite meet. She was certain they didn't believe she was Mrs. Harrow and could somehow see she was no longer a virgin as clearly as if it were written on her face.

When they finally reached the gardens again, Susanna was desperate for a sip of water. Beauty had run through several marshes and was once again a dirty brown. Beauty'd drunk plenty of the water, but Susanna's nose protested the stink. Her throat felt as dry as parchment.

Her hair clung damply to her neck, and her petticoat felt heavy with the last of the morning dew. Gideon rapped loudly on the Proprietor's House, showing Southey's card when the door finally opened. They were admitted, and Susanna studied the paintings they had seen the night before. Hogarth, she decided now that she saw them in the morning light. She breathed deeply of the fresh air in the Grove when they finally stepped outside.

A man carrying a heavy bag of what looked to be potatoes jerked his chin in the direction of the Chinese

Pavilions, and Susanna and Gideon found Southey pruning a rose bush. Bullfinches and wrens sang cheerily in the trees, and Susanna lifted her face to the filtered sunlight streaming through the leaves.

Southey removed his hat and bowed. "Mr. and Mrs. Harrow. I hoped you'd come."

Beauty yipped.

"You too, dog," Southey said and tipped his hat.

"You couldn't keep us away," Susanna said with a smile.

Southey gestured to a nearby arbor furnished with a bench and a table. "Some lemon water to refresh you?"

"Thank you." Susanna took the opportunity to rest on the bench for a few moments and drink while Gideon chatted amiably with Southey. "How long have you tended Vauxhall Gardens?"

"Oh, more than twenty years or so," Southey said, leaning back on his heels. "I'm fortunate to be the second son of a viscount. I might have had to join the clergy or the navy, but when I was about twelve, I discovered a new method for farming that more than tripled the yield on my father's land. A few years later, I wrote a paper about it, and now I travel the world showing gentleman farmers, and those who aren't so much the gentleman, how to better work their land."

"You must love it," Susanna said. "You're obviously very talented. It's even more beautiful in the daylight."

"Tending the land is in my blood." He bent and plucked a weed, turning it between his fingers. "I must say, Mrs. Harrow, you do remind me of a woman I once knew many years ago."

"You said as much last night. You seem to remember her fondly."

He dropped the weed and rubbed his palms on his trousers. "That I do. Come, I'll show you around."

They walked, and he pointed out the Handel Piazza and the Rotunda, listing when each was added and the part he played in the landscaping. As they made their way back to the arbor, Susanna asked again about the lady he'd said she resembled.

"Whatever happened to the lady you mentioned? Was she promised to another?"

Southey's long face lengthened. "She was the daughter of a duke, and I merely the second son of a viscount. Her family didn't approve of the match."

Susanna stilled.

"And this was your secret rendezvous?"

"Dorrie and I would meet here every chance we could. She came every night she could get away. We would talk until the sun rose." He rubbed his hands on his trousers and led them on the path back to the arbor. "The days were interminable."

"But the nights passed all too quickly."

Southey smiled at Gideon. "I see the fellow knows just what I mean. You're lucky to have found a lasting love," he said. "Don't let it go. If I could go back, I would do anything and everything to keep my Dorrie. I'd never let her go."

Susanna wanted desperately to look at Gideon, to see his expression. Instead, she kept her gaze on the gravel path before her. Dorrie, a duke's daughter, Vauxhall Gardens…

Susanna's head was down and her gaze on her worn, ill-fitting boots, so she didn't see Southey abruptly halt in front of her. She was almost on top of him when Gideon grabbed her arm and pulled her back.

"What's the matter?" she asked, looking around at the trees and the path dappled with sunlight.

"Dorrie?" Southey said, his voice hoarse with emotion and disbelief.

Susanna jerked her attention to the arbor they'd occupied earlier. She hadn't realized they were so close, and for a moment she was cheered at the prospect of more lemon water. And then she felt as though she'd been struck in the chest by a low-hanging tree limb.

Her mother stood in the arbor, eyes wide with shock.

Eighteen

DOROTHEA STARED AT HER DAUGHTER AS SHE MOVED past the trees shading the arbor and into view. She could hardly believe the girl coming toward her, a dirty mongrel trailing behind her, was her own daughter. Susanna's hair fell in long, tousled curls down her back and framed her face, softening the angular cheeks and chin. Heavy as it was, her hair shifted as she walked, making her hips seem to sway provocatively. Had her daughter always walked thus? Or was it an illusion of the unbound hair and the ghastly dress she wore?

Her lovely daughter—the child she'd always kept neat and clean—had dirt smudged on one arm and straw in her hair. The skirts of the gown were covered in mud and grass, and her boots!

Dorothea could not bear to look.

She made the mistake of looking past her daughter, to the man at her side. He was a ruffian if she'd ever seen one. He had two days' worth growth of beard and a lean, hungry look. The scar slashing across his temple proved his propensity for mischief.

She opened her mouth—she knew not what she would say—when a voice broke the twitter of bird song.

"Dorrie!"

Dorothea stilled, wondering if her mind played tricks on her. She'd come to the arbor because it was the place they'd always met. She'd wanted to see it again, see if it had changed, if her memories of it were accurate. Brook had wanted to go to The Dark Walk, and she'd assured him she could find her own way. Now she heard the voice she answered to in her dreams.

Her gaze fastened on the older man preceding Susanna. His once-bright red hair had faded and the temples were streaked with white. His beard was still a vibrant red and his eyes bright blue. His skin had been darkened to a rich gold by the sun, and his broad shoulders spoke of long hours of hard labor.

"Don't you know me, Dorrie?" he asked. "I'd know you anywhere."

"Robert." She breathed the name like a prayer. Perhaps it was a prayer. God knew he'd been her salvation all those years ago. And now he stood before her, in the flesh. She would have known that slightly drooped mouth and those bright blue eyes anywhere.

Before she knew what she was about, before she could countermand her baser impulses, her feet moved toward him. She ran, feeling twenty again instead of her five decades, and fell into his arms, laughing with abandon. She buried her face in his coat, inhaling deeply the scents of grass, leaves, and soil. She knew his scent, even after all these years. His smell had not changed. Neither had the feel of

his arms around her, the softness of his lips when he
brushed them across her forehead, her cheek. His
beard tickled her lips, the rough hair brushing across
her sensitive skin.

She met his kisses with her own. Part of her mind
was appalled. She knew she should stop. She knew she
must not behave so.

But propriety and rules be damned!

That was what she should have said all those years
ago. Why had she wasted her life outside the circle of
Robert's arms?

"Mother?"

The shocked voice of her daughter barely penetrated her haze of emotion. She would not have ceased
covering Robert with kisses except that he pulled back
and glanced at Susanna.

"What did you say?" Robert asked Susanna.

"Unhand her." Ever stealthy, Brook entered the
arbor, looking directly at Robert.

Dorothea pressed closer to Robert.

"What is this?" her son asked.

Dorothea couldn't think how to respond. It was
as though two very different worlds collided, and the
impact had rendered her speechless.

"Mama is kissing Mr. Southey," Susanna said to
Brook matter-of-factly.

"This is your mother?" Robert asked, his voice
incredulous. His gaze met Dorothea's, and she nodded.

It would all come out now. There was no hope of
concealing the truth.

"And this is your Dorrie," the ruffian added, glancing at her in Robert's arms.

"That can't be," Susanna whispered, her gaze wide and confused. "I thought... I knew... But he's..."

The ruffian cleared his throat. "If I'm not mistaken, Lady Susanna, he's your father."

⁋

Susanna's hand reached for an object of support. She felt nothing and faltered slightly before Gideon caught her in his arms. Immediately, she was wrenched away to Brook's side.

Beauty jumped and barked, dancing between Gideon and Brook.

"And you, hands off my sister. How dare you insult her so?"

Susanna looked from Brook to Gideon and then back to her mother, who was still clutching Mr. Southey tightly.

Gideon gave his best cocky grin. She had almost forgotten it, forgotten how much she wanted to poke him when he flashed it. "I'm only commenting on what I see." He gestured between Susanna and Southey. "The likeness is uncanny."

Brook stiffened, looking from their mother to Susanna and back again.

"I'm sorry," her mother said, her eyes pleading for understanding. Susanna stared at her, at this woman who had rarely shown any emotion other than pride. Suddenly, she seemed so vulnerable and frightened.

Southey pulled back. He didn't release her mother. He kept hold of her shoulders, but he held her at arm's length and studied her eyes. "Is it true, Dorrie? Is she mine?"

Susanna shook her head, even as her mother's mouth worked to form a response. It couldn't be true. She was the daughter of the Earl and Countess of Dane. She was not the child of a horticulturist.

Her mother looked at her, and Susanna saw tears sparkling in her brown eyes.

"No," Susanna whispered. "I don't believe you."

"I'm so sorry, Susanna. I should have told you. I feared something like this would happen. It's why I kept you away—"

Now Southey did release her, and her mother almost stumbled. To Susanna's shock, Gideon caught her arm. Instead of thanking him, her mother snatched her arm away.

"Allow me to explain." Lady Dane held a hand out to her daughter.

"Oh, I think I understand well enough," Southey— her father—said. "You didn't want me to know. You were embarrassed you'd birthed the child of a lowly second son."

"No!" Susanna's mother turned to him, then back to Susanna. She seemed not to know which foe to take on first. "That wasn't it at all. I didn't want to hurt you." Her gaze was on Susanna, but she glanced at Southey, seeming to encompass him. "She could never acknowledge you. You could never be part of her life."

"That was my decision to make!" Susanna cried out, surprised at her own vehemence. "Mine, Mother!"

Lady Dane's eyes widened, but she clamped her lips shut without objection.

"Susanna." Brook put a restraining hand on her arm.

Susanna rounded on him. "Don't tell me to calm down, or I swear I will punch you."

"I think she'd do it too," Gideon said. He leaned against a tree, arms crossed over his chest, looking very much like he enjoyed the drama unfolding. She nodded at him in silent thanks, then looked back at Brook.

"All my life I wondered why I was different. Why did my father ignore me? Why did Mother watch me like a hawk? I thought it was because I was a girl and you and Dane were boys. But that wasn't it at all." She glanced at her mother. "It's because I wasn't one of you. I'm not a Derring." Her voice rose shrilly. It seemed almost out of her control—along with everything else in her life at the moment.

"I only wanted to protect you." Her mother's voice broke, but she held her head high.

"This changes nothing, Susanna," Brook said. "You're still a Derring. And you will come home with me now."

Lady Dane cleared her throat and straightened her thin shoulders. "That's Susanna's choice, Brook. I'm done protecting her now."

Susanna's jaw dropped. Never once had her mother used the words *Susanna* and *choice* in the same sentence.

"Do what you want with this knowledge, Susanna. I would ask you to think of your family and your future and to act discreetly. I protected you too much. I see that now. It was only one of my many, many mistakes."

Southey put a hand to his heart, as though she'd mortally wounded him. Susanna watched in astonishment as her mother took Southey's hands and pressed them to her heart.

"My mistake was letting you go. I never should have listened to my parents, feared the censure of the *ton*. I'm so sorry, Robert. Can you forgive me?"

He cradled her face in his hands and kissed her lips. "I can forgive you anything."

Susanna wanted to look away, but the sight was too strange. Her mother was kissing a man. Her mother was smiling, crying, acting almost human!

"Please tell me we can start again. Please tell me you still want me after all these years."

Brook made a sound of disgust and pulled Susanna aside. "I don't know what this is all about, but I'm taking you home. I told Harrow if he didn't have you home by noon, I'd come for you."

"Harrow?" She peered back at Gideon, still reclining against the tree as though he didn't have a care in the world. "Gideon? When did you speak to Gideon?"

"Oh, he didn't tell you? I had a conversation with him last night at the Three Ducks. I could have searched the place and ruined you in one fell swoop, but I wanted to give you the chance to return quietly. That looks to be all but impossible now." He spared a glance at their mother, whose head was close to Southey's as they whispered.

Susanna couldn't take her gaze from Gideon. His own eyes met hers, and he raised his brows in question. Susanna swallowed. Her mother had told her to make her own decisions, her own mistakes.

"I don't know if I want to go home with you," she said. "Do I even belong there?"

Brook grabbed her chin, forcing her gaze from Gideon's. "What nonsense is this? Dane is there. He arrived late last night, and he'll tell you what I told you. You're a Derring."

"But I'm not. Not really. I don't know where I belong anymore."

Brook snorted. "Do you think you belong with him? Think of your family and the scandal, Susanna." He jerked a thumb at Gideon. "Do you think he'll marry you? Take care of you? He can't even take care of himself."

Susanna looked at Gideon, searched his face for some indication of his emotions. Dane would help her—help them—if she asked. He'd never allow her to starve, but Gideon had to want her.

Gideon pushed off the tree and sauntered toward them. "Sir Brook is right. You're a Derring, Strawberry," he said. "All I want is what's mine. Then I'll leave you in peace."

"What's *yours*?" Brook's hand rose, but he clenched it before clutching Gideon's throat. "I think you took more than what's yours."

"Stop," Susanna said, as much to herself as the two men. Tears threatened to fall, but she wouldn't allow it. She forced them back, took a deep breath. "He comes with us, Brook. I owe him an item, and then we'll never see him again."

She started away, Beauty at her side. She didn't want to look at Gideon. She wanted to remember the man she'd known last night—the man with the light of exploding fireworks limning his handsome face. She didn't want to see the arrogant man who smiled as though he were the cat who'd run away with the cream.

∽

The carriage ride back was interminable. Brook had forced Gideon to ride with the coachman, while her mother and Mr. Southey—she could not think of him as her father yet—shared one side of the coach, and she and Brook the other. Beauty had ridden in the coachman's seat with Gideon.

Southey asked her dozens of questions. He seemed inordinately pleased to know he had a daughter, which was truly very sweet. He seemed a sweet, kind man. Susanna tried to answer him, but she couldn't think. Her words echoed in her ears, doubling back on themselves until the sound of her voice was magnified a hundredfold.

When she entered Derring House, nothing looked as she remembered it. The chairs, the vases, the paintings were in the same spots, but it didn't seem like home to her anymore. It was the home of the girl she'd been. She'd never be that innocent girl again. She'd never truly belong here again.

Had she ever?

Dane and Marlowe rushed to greet her. Marlowe embraced her, then drew back.

"What is it, Susanna?"

"I…"

"Sit down." Marlowe tried to lead her to a chair in the parlor, concern etched into her pretty features. Susanna still wasn't used to seeing Marlowe dressed in silks and muslins, her hair coiffed high on her head. She wondered—if Gideon had chosen her—whether she'd have become used to seeing him in a cravat and coat.

Brook pulled Dane aside, and Susanna pushed past Marlowe. "I'm fine," she said when Marlowe protested.

"You don't look fine. You look half gone to Peg Trantums."

"I don't know what that means, but I assure you I'm well enough to walk upstairs." Her feet moved until she was in the vestibule at the base of the stairs. "Do you remember our wager, Marlowe?"

Marlowe gave her a puzzled look. "I'm not certain."

"You owed me an adventure."

A smile turned up the corners of Marlowe's lips. "Ah, yes. I should say you've had one."

"More than one." Susanna lifted her skirts and looked up the daunting stairwell.

Marlowe put a hand on the banister. "I'll go with you. You should lie down."

Susanna nodded and started up the stairs. "I will. First I have to fetch something and give it to Gideon."

"Gideon!" Marlowe raced after her, thundering up the stairs in a most unladylike fashion. If her mother had not been so preoccupied with Mr. Southey, she would have chastised Marlowe.

"What are you doing with Gideon? Where is he?"

Susanna turned and stared at the vestibule. Only Crawford peered up at her.

Where *was* her mother and Southey? Oh dear. Did she really want to know the answer to that?

Crawford cleared his throat. "The young man was sent to the servants' entrance. He's waiting for you in the kitchen."

Susanna gave a brittle laugh. "Why would we treat him any differently?"

"I'll see to him," Marlowe said, starting down the stairs. "He won't wait long otherwise."

"He'll wait," Susanna said. "I have the one thing he cares about."

She continued upstairs, opened her bedroom door, and stared at the small, feminine room. It was a child's room, full of frilly pillows and pink upholstery. Her sketchbook and watercolors lay on the desk where she'd left them. She peered at the drawing she'd been working on—a horse with flowers in its mane. A child's drawing.

Her jewelry box sat on her dressing table, untouched. She opened it, lifted the pretty baubles she'd once cherished, and drew out the velvet bag containing the diamond-and-emerald necklace. She could feel it, heavy and thick inside the velvet. She closed her hand around it and started for the kitchens.

"I thought you'd put yourself out of twig, but you look as much a filching cove as always."

Gideon turned from the bread and cheese he'd been stuffing in his mouth and peered up at a beautiful woman standing near the steps to the house—stairs he'd been warned not to even look at. He wasn't worthy. It took a moment before he knew her. In the end, it was her smile that gave her away.

Gideon let out a holler and pulled Marlowe into his arms, twirling her around. She laughed and threw back her head, and for a moment it was like old times.

Beauty raised her head curiously, then went back to the scraps in her bowl on the floor. The cook made a sound of wonder and politely excused herself. Gideon barely noticed. He set Marlowe down and made her twirl.

"Look at you," he said. "You look like a real lady."

"I *am* a real lady," she protested, hands on her hips in a very unladylike stance. "I have the title to prove it."

"You never needed the title," he said. "I always knew you were too good for Satin and his cubs."

She took his hand, led him back to the food. She must have known how hungry he was. "And I always thought the same about you. What are you doing here, Gideon? Why does Lady Susanna look so Friday-faced?"

He stuffed bread into his mouth, telling her the story of Southey and Lady Dane between mouthfuls. She poured him more tea, then leaned a hip on the table and crossed her arms. "Is that the whole reason? It's a shock, but Susanna isn't one to care about titles."

He jerked a shoulder up and gulped the tea, scalding his mouth. "You'll have to ask her."

"I'm asking you."

She leveled her intense blue-eyed gaze on him, and Gideon felt the heat from the too-hot tea rise to his face.

"Gideon Harrow." She grabbed his wrist and slammed the teacup on the table. "What did you do?"

He glared at her. The words *nothing she didn't want* came to mind, but he'd be damned if he said them again.

"It was a mistake," he said instead. "The last few days were a big fucking mistake. I just want what's mine."

Beauty raised her head and woofed. Gideon's gaze jumped to the stairs, and his heart seized in his chest.

No.

Susanna notched her chin high, but not before he saw the flash of raw pain all but crumple her face. She looked like she'd just taken a punch in the breadbasket. Her cheeks colored, and her eyes turned glassy, but she raised her head high as she descended the last steps. She looked like a queen.

"Then take it and go." She held the velvet bag with the necklace toward him.

Marlowe spun around. She glanced between Susanna and him, then backed away. "I'll wait at the top of the steps in case you need me, Susanna."

Susanna gave one regal nod. Marlowe hugged Gideon hard and whispered, "We're birds of a feather. No matter what you've done. But she's my family now. Don't hurt her again."

The dog shouldered her way past Gideon, but for the first time, Susanna ignored the buffer's whines and nuzzles. She shoved the bag at Gideon. "Take it and go."

He stared at the bag. This was what he'd wanted. This was what he'd cared for. In her hands was his freedom.

Why didn't he snatch it away?

Her lips trembled. She tried so hard to be strong, and he was the one who made that a necessity. "Strawberry—"

"Don't call me that. I'm Lady Susanna."

His jaw tightened. "Fine." He snatched the bag, felt the heavy necklace inside. The anticipated relief didn't wash over him.

"You have what you wanted. Go now."

"That's it?" he blurted.

She raised one haughty brow. "Did you expect a good-bye kiss? You have what's yours—what you stole, at any rate. I won't draw out this *mistake* any longer."

"I didn't mean it like that. You weren't a mistake."

"*You* were. I already informed Marlowe our wager was met. She promised me an adventure. I've had one, and you were quite diverting. Thank you, and good-bye."

Gideon's heart pounded, his blood hot with fury. He knew he'd hurt her, but the dismissal hit a raw nerve. That was what she wanted. To hurt him like he'd hurt her.

He hadn't wanted to hurt her.

She pointed to the door. "Have a good life, Mr. Harrow."

He gave her a mock bow, opened the door, and stepped into the bright sunshine. He squinted, surprised it was still day. He felt more like a thief than he ever had in his life. He should be slinking away under cover of darkness.

He pulled the bag open and dumped the necklace into his palm. The stones glittered in the sunlight, but they didn't hold any beauty for him now. Cold, hard diamonds would bring him a cold, hard future.

He set off toward Field Lane and the dolly shops.

⤜⤐

Susanna bit the inside of her cheek. She would not cry. She'd learned composure at all costs from her mother. She must *at all times* exhibit good *ton*.

"Come on, Beauty."

Marlowe wasn't waiting at the top of the stairs, but when Susanna returned to her room, a gold necklace and a note lay on her bed.

You lent me this when I needed a friend. I return it with the same sentiment.

Susanna clutched the necklace in her hand. One necklace in exchange for another.

Beauty trotted to the bedroom door just as someone rapped quietly. Susanna opened it and fell, weeping, into Marlowe's waiting arms.

At some point Marlowe tucked her into bed, closed the drapes, and told her to close her eyes. Susanna obliged, though she didn't think she'd be able to sleep. When she opened her eyes again, her room was dark, and the fire in the hearth burned low.

Something heavy lay across her feet, and she sat just as Beauty rose and licked her face. At least she assumed the hairy animal that smelled of roses was Beauty.

"Did they give you a bath?" she asked, stroking the dog's head. "Brushed you too. Mama will have a fit when she realizes you've been sleeping on my bed."

"Mama knows."

Susanna jumped and whipped toward a cream-colored chair near the side of the bed. Her mother sat in it, her face flickering red in the firelight. Hands folded in her lap and back straight, she looked as stiff and unyielding as any oak tree.

And yet, Susanna had seen her all but melt into a man's arms just that morning. She could hardly reconcile the two women.

Her mother rose, and the bed dipped when she sat on the edge. Susanna stared at her, waited for the lecture.

Instead, her mother smoothed Susanna's hair back from her face.

"I used to watch you sleep when you were a small child," she said finally. "Your little mouth would turn up in a smile, your eyelids would flicker, your hands clench. I always wondered what you could be dreaming about."

Susanna shook her head, words eluding her.

"I made a mistake," her mother said, still stroking Susanna's hair.

"You too?" Susanna muttered. It seemed to be the theme of the day.

"Oh, I've made many," her mother admitted. "I protected you too much. I thought I could keep you safe, keep you from ever being hurt. Instead, I was the one who hurt you." She leaned close, cupping Susanna's face.

Susanna stilled, staring at her mother in shock. Lady Dane had never shown her any tenderness.

"I was afraid you would make the same mistakes I made, but when I saw Robert yesterday, I realized my biggest mistake was in letting him go. I was too hard on you because I was angry at myself. I just loved you so much, Susanna. I knew if I showed it, your father— the earl—would send you away. He always knew you weren't his, but he tolerated you as long as I favored the boys. If I couldn't show you love, I wouldn't show it to anyone. I forgot what it was to feel love. Robert reminded me."

"Why didn't you tell me?" Susanna asked. "After Father—Lord Dane—died."

Her mother sat back. "The earl will always be your father, Susanna. He accepted you. You bear his name. Neither Robert nor I would take that from you. I should have told you. I was scared."

"You?"

"I'm a silly old woman, too worried about what others think of me. No more."

"What does that mean?"

"That means"—she leaned forward and kissed Susanna's cheek—"I plan to be happy. I plan to smile and laugh and sing."

"Sing?" Susanna was appalled. She'd never once heard her mother sing.

"Yes. And I would do something else. I do hope you approve."

Susanna was too afraid to ask. Her mother had never asked for her approval.

"I would marry Robert."

Susanna caught her breath, joy exploding within her. "Oh, yes! Do! You deserve happiness, Mama. I know your marriage was not a love match."

"I want you to know your father, and I want you to be happy, Susanna. I love you, my darling."

Susanna felt as though the words were an ax cleaving her already battered heart open so it was bare and vulnerable. Tears streamed down her face. "I love you too, Mama. I'm so sorry if I made you worry."

Lady Dane hugged her tightly. "I'm happy you are home, safe and unharmed." She pulled back. "You are unharmed?"

Susanna looked down at the white coverlet. "I'm no longer fit for marriage," she whispered. Her mother took a deep breath, and Susanna cringed.

"Did he force you? Hurt you?"

"No." Susanna tried to look up, but her gaze refused to meet her mother's. "He was gentle and...loving."

"Do you regret it?"

"No!" Susanna did raise her eyes. "I love him. I thought he felt the same."

"Perhaps he does."

"Then why did he leave?"

"I would think his leaving an even greater indication that he loves you. What could he offer you by staying? I know a little of him from Marlowe. He has nothing. By leaving, he gives you a chance at a better life. I respect him for that decision."

"You *what*?"

Her mother chuckled. "The lower classes are not completely without their merits."

"Are you sure you are my mother?"

Lady Dane laughed, another sound Susanna could not recall hearing.

"Yes, but listen well, Susanna. This family cannot withstand another mésalliance. Dane's was quite enough. I would not marry Robert if I thought it would hurt the honor of our family, but Robert is the second son of a viscount. I am a widow and do not need to marry for status or money. You, however, are a different matter entirely." She tucked the covers around Susanna. "You had better sleep. Robert will be here in the morning, and I'd like the two of you to spend time together."

She frowned at Beauty, who crawled beside Susanna and laid her head on Susanna's stomach.

"Do you really intend to sleep with this mongrel?"

Susanna patted Beauty. "She's saved me more than once."

Lady Dane sighed. "Very well. I don't like it, but I suppose you are old enough to make your own decisions."

Her bedchamber door opened and closed, and Susanna lay quiet and alone but for Beauty. She thought of Gideon and waking in his arms. Where was he now?

She wiped a tear from her cheek. No more crying. Her mother was right. She had made her decision.

Nineteen

Seeing her mother kiss Robert Southey jarred her. No matter how many times she witnessed the affection between her mother and her father, it still left Susanna feeling slightly shocked and disconcerted.

Her mother giggled. Her mother, the great dowager countess Lady Dane, blushed like a schoolgirl. Susanna had even caught her mother and Southey in a passionate embrace in the dining room. Her mother hadn't even been embarrassed to be caught bent over the sideboard, her hair trailing in the kippers as Southey kissed her neck.

Now the two of them sat across from her in the coach, their hands entwined, their eyes locked. Susanna doubted they even remembered she was present. She didn't know why she'd agreed to go with them to Vauxhall Gardens. But what else did she have to do?

Brook had disappeared again, back to his office on Bow Street or wherever he spent his days and nights.

Dane and Marlowe had returned to the country and Northbridge Abbey. Marlowe had asked

Susanna to come, but she'd wanted to stay in Town and spend time becoming acquainted with her father.

As the coach neared Vauxhall, Susanna began to think this trip had been an error in judgment. The past week, she'd spent every waking moment *not* thinking about Gideon. Concentrating on that task kept her quite occupied. She couldn't control her dreams, and most mornings she woke vaguely aroused and with a sick feeling of loss in her belly.

Her first thought upon waking was always *Gideon*.

Upon seeing the lights of the Proprietor's House at Vauxhall, however, no amount of concentration could shut Gideon out of her mind. They'd walked there together, his hand in hers.

"Are you feeling unwell, dear?" Lady Dane asked.

Susanna jumped. She looked about and realized the carriage had stopped and the footman had opened the door, but she hadn't moved.

"No," she said, smiling tightly. "I was lost in my thoughts."

"Good thoughts, I hope," her father said.

He took her hand and handed her down from the carriage. He smiled kindly, and Susanna felt her heart swell. He was a wonderful man—kind, quiet, cheerful. He was exactly the sort of man her mother needed, and he brought out the best in her. He looked quite handsome in his new clothing. Her mother said he possessed a wardrobe full of stylish clothing, but most days he preferred his gardener's garb. Even though he spent many hours in the small garden behind the town house, Vauxhall and its pleasure gardens was the place he'd wanted to come when her mother had asked if he cared for an evening out.

Susanna reminded herself she did want to see the gardens with Southey and her mother. This, after all, was where they had fallen in love. This was the place her mother had come to heal after the babies she'd lost. And this was the place she'd found Robert again. It seemed fitting the three of them should see it together.

Southey paid for their entrance, and Susanna wandered through the Proprietor's House like the rest of the visitors. She walked slightly ahead of her mother and Southey, giving them privacy. When she emerged from the Proprietor's House into the Grove, she looked up in wonder. It was so lovely, a place anyone might fall in love.

Her gaze darted to the tree where she and Gideon had stood that night, hiding from Brook. There was the path where they'd walked, his arm warm on the small of her back. And if she looked down The Great Walk, lit by hundreds of oil lamps, she imagined she could see the shadier path of The Dark Walk.

She closed her eyes, remembering Gideon's hands on her skin as the fireworks exploded above.

"Susanna, this way," her mother said, linking one arm with her and the other with Robert. "I want to show you my favorite arbor." She tsked at Robert. "Not *that* one!"

The three of them strolled, Lady Dane and Robert laughing and talking. Susanna tried to smile, but everywhere she looked she saw Gideon. Every man with dark hair caught her attention, made her heart pound with anticipation.

Of course, he wasn't here. She would never see him again. When would she stop thinking about him? Pining for him?

Finally, she begged to rest for a few moments in an arbor. Robert and her mother left to fetch a waiter to bring wine and ham. She suspected the errand was nothing more than an excuse for the two of them to steal kisses, but Susanna wanted a few minutes alone. She allowed her shoulders to slump and closed her eyes, the grief washing over her.

Had he ever loved her? Even a little? Was her mother correct? He'd left her because he did love her? And why could she not forget him? They had no future. She'd always known that the daughter of an earl and a thief could never hope to have a life together.

But then again, she'd never thought a widowed countess and a gardener could find happiness.

"'Ello, Lady Susanna."

Susanna gasped and jumped to her feet, whirling around.

A shadow in the darkness moved forward. "That's yer name, right? Ye're one of them Derrings. One of Marlowe's gang."

"Who are you?" she asked. "Don't come any closer, or I shall scream. The constables are everywhere."

"Oh, you don't want to do that. If you scream, you save yerself but damn yer lover."

"What are you talking about?"

She shuddered when the first fireworks popped, illuminating his face. It was Beezle. She should have screamed and run, but she couldn't move, couldn't think. Her lover? Gideon?

"Come with me now, and ye 'ave a chance to save our mutual friend. Scream, and I kill him."

Another firework popped. In the distance, the orchestra played, and someone laughed. The nightingales chirped.

Beezle, the snake in the garden, held out his hand. With a whimper, Susanna took it.

৵৽

Gideon looked about Sir Brook's office on Bow Street and wondered what the devil he was doing there. He wondered what the devil he was doing in London. If he had any sense, he'd be in Yorkshire or Scotland by now. He sure as hell wouldn't be standing in the middle of Bow Street, thief-takers all around him and a stolen necklace in his pocket.

And he sure as hell wouldn't be in the office of the man whose sister he'd defiled just eight nights ago.

But Gideon hadn't been able to leave London. He'd tried. He'd made it as far as Richmond, and then he'd gone back. He'd found himself standing in front of Derring House, staring up at the lighted windows, wondering which one was hers, wondering if she was still in Town.

He was a cod's head.

"What the bloody hell are *you* doing here?"

Gideon turned. "Good to see you too, Derring."

"No it's not. I should kill you."

"But you won't. Besides, I'm here to do a good deed."

Derring stomped across the room and all but threw himself into the chair behind his desk. "You've decided to hang yourself?"

"No. I've decided to give you this." Gideon's hand faltered, and he forced it into his pocket. He grasped the necklace and pressed it tightly against his palm, feeling the edges and points of the diamonds cutting into his flesh.

Do it fast, Gid. That's the only way.

He slammed the necklace down on the desk and stepped away, forcing his gaze to Derring's face and not the sparkle of the jewels.

Derring looked at the necklace and then at Gideon. "What the devil is this?"

"Stolen goods. Thought you could find the owner."

Derring's eyes narrowed. "What's in it for you?"

That was the very question Gideon had been asking himself. Every time he tried to leave London, the pull he felt for Susanna tugged him back. But that wasn't all. Derring's words that night outside the Three Ducks lodging house played over and over in his mind.

You could have been one of us.

The idea was ludicrous. Gideon Harrow, a Bow Street Runner. But the more he'd thought about it, the more the idea had taken root and dug deep.

He'd be a damned fine Runner. He knew all the rookeries, knew every gull and fambler and resurrection man. He knew every flash ken, every rag-and-bones shop, every school of Venus. Who would be a better Runner than he?

It wasn't as though he liked filching. He'd never liked taking what wasn't his. He'd done it to survive and because it kept the Covent Garden Cubs alive. But he didn't belong to Beezle's gang anymore.

He didn't belong anywhere.

He met Derring's gaze. "You said the Runners look after their own. I want that."

Derring's lip curled. "You think you can be a Runner?"

"I could be a hell of a Runner."

Derring lifted the necklace, dangled it in front of him. Gideon's gaze dropped to it and then back to Derring's face.

"And how do I know this isn't a game? Some new con?" Brook asked skeptically.

"Because Beezle wants me dead, and you're holding my ticket out. I'm stone dead if I stay in London, but I'm still here."

Derring didn't say a word, merely fingered the necklace.

Footsteps pounded outside the office, and a sharp rap sounded.

"Come," Derring said without looking away from Gideon.

"Sir." A breathless voice could be heard over the creak of the door opening. "You're needed—"

The Runner broke off, probably catching a look at Gideon.

Derring made a gesture with his finger. "Go on."

"It's your sister, sir."

"What?" Derring had barely begun to rise when Gideon whirled around and grabbed the man by the throat.

"Lady Susanna?"

The man's sharp eyes bulged with fear, and he shook his head.

"Get back." Derring jerked Gideon's shoulder, hauling him off the Runner. "What about my sister, Sawyer?"

"She was abducted, sir. From Vauxhall Gardens."

Gideon's mind raced. Vauxhall? What the hell was she doing at Vauxhall?

"Word came from one of the constables there. She was with your lady mother, and when the countess couldn't find her, they began to search. They're probably still searching. I was about to tell you, when this came." He held out a dirty, torn pamphlet advertising a *ridotto al fresco* at Vauxhall Gardens.

Gideon couldn't breathe as he watched Derring open the paper. It was as though a heavy wooden plank had been laid over his chest and piled high with rocks. The weight suffocated him.

Derring made a sound like a low growl in his throat and handed the pamphlet to Gideon. He didn't read as fast as Derring, but he worked the words out.

"Where is this Rouge Unicorn Cellar?" Derring asked.

"Seven Dials." Gideon threw the pamphlet on Derring's desk. He would kill Beezle. He would strangle the man's last breath from his body.

"We send a half dozen men," Derring said. "I want MacKenzie, Baker, Joy—"

"No." Gideon shoved Derring against the desk. "You read the paper. No one but me can go, or Beezle kills her."

Derring shoved back, his hand circling Gideon's throat and pinning him to the wall. "What the hell kind of new game is this, Harrow? Dipped your toe into abduction now?"

Gideon fought for breath as the words swirled in his mind. "You think I'm in on it?" he rasped.

"Beezle's your arch rogue."

"No!" Gideon kicked out, slamming a toe into Derring's thigh. Derring cursed and released him.

Sawyer took hold of his arms, pinning him before he could strike Derring again.

"This is your fault," Gideon spat. "You call yourself a prime investigator, but you can't even protect your own sister!"

Hunched over, Derring looked up at him through wild hair. "It's you he wants, Harrow. If you want to blame someone, blame yourself."

Gideon would blame himself for the rest of his life. He'd never forgive himself if anything happened to her. The fucking necklace again. He should have given it to Beezle in the beginning. He never would have met Susanna. She'd be safe at home now, doing…whatever the gentry morts did. She'd have been better off never knowing him.

His gaze locked on the necklace, lying forgotten on Derring's desk.

"That's what he wants," he said with a nod, struggling against Sawyer's hold. "He's either gambling I'm still in London, or someone snitched. I'd wager my life on the latter. Too many snitches in the rookeries. They'll sell a cove for a glass of frog's wine."

"Why take Susanna if he wants you?"

Gideon slumped, and Sawyer, feeling no resistance, released him. Gideon slid to his knees on the floor. "Because he knows she means something to me. Half of Field Lane saw us together. He's figured out who she was, and he took her to get the necklace from me."

Derring glanced at the necklace then back at Gideon.

"This is about the necklace?"

"This is about settling old scores. Marlowe is out of his reach, so he found the only other person who matters. I'm going in, Derring, and I'll make sure she walks out. You try to go in, and he'll kill her without blinking."

"How do I know you'll do what you say? I send you, and I may never see her again."

"You'll have to trust me."

Derring barked a derisive laugh. "Try again."

Gideon met Derring's stony gaze without smiling. "I love her, Derring. That isn't something I say lightly, or ever. If I don't send her safely out, you're welcome to kill me."

"Oh, I will. Slowly."

"But you have to give me the chance."

Derring stared at him, his gaze hard and shrewd. Gideon met his gaze with his own unblinking one. He didn't know at what point he'd fallen in love with Susanna. Probably the first time she'd slammed him over the head with that glim-stick. He sure as hell didn't want to be in love with her. He'd cared for Marlowe all these years and where had that gotten him?

What he'd felt for Marlowe couldn't compare to Susanna. He thought he'd been in love, but his heart had never felt like a knife had cut it open when he'd thought he'd lost Marlowe. Now, just the thought of losing Susanna made his life pointless.

"A man like you," Derring said, his mouth curved in a sneer, "you don't know what love is. Susanna was never more than a sword racket to you."

Gideon clenched his fists. "We're wasting time. The note said before dawn, or he moves her and we wait for another message. I don't know about you, but I don't want her near Beezle another minute, much less another day."

"I don't trust you."

"And I don't like you. But I will save your sister."

Derring nodded to Sawyer. "Call for Joyce, Baker, and MacKenzie. Then I'll tell you my plan."

Gideon rose to his feet. "No. Seven Dials is my territory. *I'll* make the plans."

❧

Susanna huddled in the damp cellar, her arms around her knees. A thin, long-legged boy who couldn't have seen twenty yet paced in front of her. He was the one Gideon had called Racer. Upstairs was the other, the one they'd hit with the candlestick. She didn't know his name.

But she knew Beezle.

She was afraid of Beezle, and now she realized her mistake was leaving Vauxhall to go with him. She should have known she was the bait to trap Gideon. Why hadn't she had faith that Gideon never would have allowed Beezle to catch him?

She hadn't been thinking. She'd wanted to see Gideon again. She'd been willing to pay any price. Now she would. Before the night was over, Beezle would probably kill her.

Gideon wasn't coming for her. He wasn't even in Town. She'd tried to tell Beezle that, but he'd told her to shut her potato hole. Was she a fool for hoping that

Gideon might come? That she still had a last chance to see him?

She was a fool.

If Gideon came for her, Beezle would kill them both. She stifled a sob.

Racer turned his head sharply to study her, then went back to his pacing. Susanna shifted positions on the cold, hard floor. She wished she had a chair. More than that, she wished she had a weapon. She felt so helpless sitting here, waiting for Gideon to come.

And what of her mother? Her poor mother. They'd just begun to build a relationship. The past week had been the first in her life that she hadn't stiffened when she heard her mother coming. Lady Dane had been almost a different person. She still occasionally ordered Susanna to sit up straight, but she also embraced her without warning and kissed her on the forehead when Susanna retired for the evening.

She'd never thought she'd want her mother, miss her mother, but she did. Beezle would kill her, and then she'd never see her mother marry Mr. Southey—her father. She'd never embrace her mother again. Or Dane. Or Brook. Or Beauty.

Poor Beauty. Who would scratch her behind the ears, the way she liked?

The cellar door creaked open, and Racer shot to attention. "All's snug?"

"Talked Barbara into two glasses of ale. Beezle just stepped out. If you hurry, you can drink it down."

Racer took the steps two at a time. At the top, he glanced down at her and hesitated. He must have decided she wouldn't try to escape, and he slipped out the door. Susanna lowered her chin to her knees just as a loud scrape sounded behind her. She scrambled to her feet, looking for a weapon. She'd heard rats scurrying about the dark recesses of the cellar, but if that had been a rat, it would be the biggest rat she'd ever laid eyes on.

She heard the scrape again, and this time she could locate it. The crates stacked in one corner moved! As she stared, the crates moved again. Susanna pushed herself against the steps, sliding into the shadows. She'd worn a dark green silk dress to Vauxhall with a matching cape. Thank God she hadn't chosen the cream or pink. She would have been easily visible.

The crates moved again, and the edge of a door appeared in the wall. Finally, a bald head poked in. "'Ello? Lady Susanna?"

"Corker?" she whispered.

His eyes found hers, and he grinned. "It's me." He glanced over his shoulder. "Found her."

At that moment, something thumped in the public house above them, and a man cursed. Glass shattered, and Susanna cringed as the ceiling shook with more thumps.

"Right on time," Corker said with a smile.

"I don't understand. What are you doing here?"

"Rescuing you."

Another thump and a crash. She couldn't have heard him correctly. "I beg your pardon."

"That's Lighter, Jonesy, and Dab upstairs, making mischief to keep yer lookouts busy so we can rescue you."

She didn't understand it. Corker and the other men she'd met at Stryker's ken being here made absolutely no sense. And she didn't care. She pushed away from the staircase, lifting her skirts to hurry across the floor. "If Lighter, Jonesy, and Dab are upstairs, who is with you? Mill?"

"No," said a voice she knew well. Gideon stepped into the cellar. "I am."

Susanna's feet refused to move forward. She could hardly believe he was really here, really standing before her.

He looked beautiful. She didn't know how else to describe him. She supposed some might have seen only the jagged scar across his temple and said he looked dangerous, but to Susanna it was a mark of all he'd endured and survived.

He'd shaved, and though his wavy hair still brushed the collar of his coat, she could see it had been combed. She lifted her hand before she realized she couldn't touch his smooth cheek, couldn't run her fingers through his hair, tousle it the way she liked.

She gripped the fabric of her dress in her hands instead and tried to think what to say, what to do.

"Did he hurt you?" Gideon asked.

She shook her head.

"Will you come with me now? I don't know how much time we have."

Another crash from above and the sounds of shouting from someone who obviously meant to quell the unrest. Gideon looked up then back at Susanna.

"Not much, I wager," Corker commented.

"You came," she whispered, her voice not entirely under her control. "I thought you'd be far away by now."

He nodded, his eyes never leaving hers. "I should

have been. But I couldn't seem to leave London. Not when I knew you were here."

Susanna stepped forward then gasped when Corker grunted and fell to his knees. He pressed a hand to his head, and it came back covered in blood.

Gideon swung around, a knife in his hand, but Beezle was ready for him. He stepped out from behind Corker and slammed the metal bar against Gideon's wrist. With a shout of pain, Gideon dropped the knife. Beezle kicked it across the room, and it clattered against the stairs a few feet from Susanna.

Beezle gestured with the bar for Gideon to move into the cellar. "That's far enough," he said before Gideon could reach her side.

Susanna trembled, tasting blood in her mouth where she'd bitten her lip in fright. They were all dead now. Beezle would kill her and Gideon and maybe Corker too. And it was all her fault.

The cellar door opened, and Racer and the other rushed down the steps, cutting off Susanna and Gideon's exit. Beezle smiled, his teeth yellow and rotten in his thin-lipped mouth. He slapped the metal bar in his hand.

"Gid, you and me have unfinished business."

Twenty

His breath whooshed out of him at the first stroke of the metal bar. Beezle had gone for the breadbasket. It didn't cause much damage, but it hurt like hell. Gideon doubled over then staggered to his feet as Beezle raised the bar again. If the bastard thought he would stand here and take a beating, he'd be unpleasantly surprised.

"Grab him," Beezle ordered Stub.

Gideon rounded on the short, stocky cub. "Touch me, and I'll fucking kill you."

"Watch out!" Susanna screamed.

Gideon lunged to the left, and the bar hit him solidly in the back of the shoulder. Pain, like hot fire, lanced through him. His legs crumpled and he fell, rolling just in time to avoid the smack of the bar on his head as Beezle brought it down. He scurried back, helpless as Beezle approached, bar raised high.

"If you kill me, you'll never have the necklace."

"I'll take it off yer dead body."

Gideon scooted back again, losing sight of Susanna as she shifted to the left. Good. He didn't want her to see his head bashed in.

"You think I'm an idiot? I don't have it on me."

Beezle paused, but only for a moment. "I don't care."

Fuck. Beezle wanted Gideon dead more than he wanted the necklace. It was the betrayal, not the theft, that angered the arch rogue most. When Gideon had gone over the hasty plan with Derring, he'd known Beezle might find him before he could free Susanna. Gideon had counted on the arch rogue wanting the necklace enough not to kill him before Susanna could escape.

He'd guessed wrong.

Beezle raised the bar high. "I've been wanting to do this for a long, long time."

Gideon heard Susanna scream, and the shuffle of feet, but all he could see was the black arc of the metal bar. It swung down and clattered to the floor beside him. Behind Beezle's bent body, Susanna stood with her hands high and her eyes wide.

Beezle rose up and reached for Gideon's knife in his back.

Susanna had grabbed his knife and stabbed Beezle with it. She backed away just as Beezle wrenched the knife free.

"No!" Gideon shouted as Beezle went for Susanna.

Gideon lunged forward, smacking into Stub, who cuffed him hard enough to send him sprawling. The cub pulled him to his feet as Beezle advanced on Susanna.

"You want to play with knives?" Beezle asked, voice thick with pain. "Let's play." He raised the knife, and Gideon closed his eyes.

❧

The blur of white streaked across the dim cellar, rising before her just as Beezle raised the knife. Suddenly dog and man tangled together on the floor.

"Beauty! No!" Susanna leaped forward, halting when she heard the dog's high-pitched squeal of pain.

Beezle shoved the limp animal off him and rose to his feet, the bloody knife still in his hands. She ran to Beauty, knelt down beside the warm animal, saw the blood on her fur.

"Get up," Beezle said, gesturing with the knife.

Susanna stood, glancing at Gideon, now behind her and still wrestling with Beezle's man. She wanted to see his face one last time. When she turned back, Beezle hissed at her. His black eyes reflected pain and fury. She watched in horror as he slid the knife into his boot and pulled a pistol from his coat.

She heard an exclamation of fear from Racer, and Corker lifted his bloody head.

"I'm through playing," Beezle said, cocking the pistol.

He raised it, pointing the weapon at her. Susanna's heart hammered in her chest so loudly it blocked out all sound. Her vision dimmed until all she could see was Beezle's grin.

And then suddenly she slammed into something hard and unyielding. Her head struck a flat, solid surface, and everything spun. She heard the shot of a pistol, felt a slice of pain, and saw nothing but red.

⤜∾⤛

The force from the slug knocked him back on his arse, and Gideon grunted in pain. He could add this injury to his long list of scars and wounds.

If he lived.

The way his breath caught in his chest made that seem unlikely at the moment.

He tried to crane his neck to catch a glimpse of Susanna. He couldn't find her. He tried another angle, wincing at the pain when he moved.

Derring had come at just the right time. He'd burst through the door, shocking Stub enough to distract him. Gideon had broken free of Stub in time to reach Susanna, shove her aside. But she'd gone down hard. Now he couldn't see her. Had he hurt her?

Derring knocked the pistol out of Beezle's hand and instructed one of his men to grab the arch rogue. Beezle yelled something, fought, but Gideon couldn't manage to keep his eyes open to witness the outcome.

"Susanna," he said, his voice hoarse and quieter than he wanted.

But Derring heard him and bent down beside him. "Some rescue this is. You're shot."

"Susanna," Gideon forced out. "Is she hurt?"

"A moment." Derring stepped away. Gideon tried to rise, to see where he went, and the pain sent him spinning into darkness.

❧

"Susanna. Open your eyes, Susanna."

She tried to open them, but she would have much preferred to sleep longer. She was so tired, so weary.

"Young lady, open your eyes this instant or the doctor will give you another of those foul-smelling tonics, and you'll sleep for another three days."

Three days? Doctor?

Gideon.

Her heavy eyes opened, closed, and opened again.

"Mama," she whispered.

"Thank God! For once, you obey me."

Susanna blinked and shifted her gaze. She was in her room, the drapes pulled, but daylight was visible through the thin muslin and lace. She tried to sit, but the room spun, and her mother put a hand on her forehead.

"Slowly, darling."

Darling. Then it hadn't all been a dream—her mother and Mr. Southey, Beezle and Vauxhall Gardens, Gideon.

Where was Gideon?

"I have to see him," she said, trying to rise again. "He was shot."

Her mother frowned at her, concern clouding her gaze, then nodded. "I'll help you sit."

Susanna tried to use her legs to push herself up, even as her mother hooked her under her arms. But her legs were tied down or useless. She couldn't even feel them. "Mama, my legs. I can't move them!"

Instead of looking horrified, her mother pointed a finger at the bed. "Get off, fleabag."

Inhaling sharply, Susanna rose on her elbows as Beauty raised her head then set it down again. The dog had draped herself over Susanna's legs.

"Beauty!" At Susanna's words, the dog's ears pricked up, and she licked Susanna's hand. Susanna dislodged her legs and rose on her elbows. The dog's pink skin showed on both edges of a large, white bandage situated around her middle.

"I had the doctor treat her before she could drip blood all over your room. The dog wouldn't leave your side." Her mother's voice was annoyed, but her eyes were on the dog, and they shone with something like admiration. "She'll heal soon if she'll lie still. She's not supposed to walk up and down stairs, but since she whines and cries incessantly if she's not with you, I've had to assign Jimmy to carry her up and down when she needs to eat or go out. I am sure the man will tender his resignation any day at the indignity. Carrying a dog!" Her mother huffed, but Susanna could see beyond the hard outer shell now. Her mother was beginning to like Beauty. She'd always respected loyalty.

"Thank you, Mama," Susanna said, taking her mother's hand. She squeezed, and Lady Dane looked down at her.

"Why do I have the feeling there's something you're not telling me?" Susanna asked. "Is it Gideon? He's dead, isn't he?"

Blackness hovered at the edge of her sight. She'd seen him fall. She'd heard the pistol discharge. He'd taken the pistol ball for her. He'd died to save her.

"If you're referring to that thief, the answer is no. Probably would have been better for you if he had died—"

"Oh, there I beg to differ." Brook rapped on her door. "I heard voices," he said by way of explanation before he stepped into her room. "If he'd died, the city would have one fewer Runner for the force, and I can always use a good man. If I can convince him to join."

"Runner," her mother scoffed, moving aside so Brook could stand beside the bed. "He's a thief."

"That thief saved your daughter's life." Brook glanced at Susanna. "He was shot, but he's recovering."

"He's alive?"

"At the moment. Do you want to see him?"

Yes. No. She didn't know the answer.

"Does he want to see me?" she asked.

Brook gave her the sort of look he'd given her when they'd been children and she'd asked him to play dolls with her. He took her hand and pulled her out of bed, a bit faster than she might have liked, but she was on her feet. Maggie, her maid, immediately covered her night rail with her wrapper and cinched it tightly closed.

"You are not allowed to become that girl," Brook said, his voice teasing. "I can't tolerate a woman who doesn't think for herself. The question, the only question you need ask is, do *you* want to see him?"

Susanna felt her chest tighten with anticipation, fear, lust, and yes, love. Brook was right—he was always right, annoying man. She couldn't wait for what she wanted any longer. She had to take it with both hands.

She took Brook's hand. "Where is he?"

❧

Gideon's side hurt like the devil had prodded it with his pitchfork. Burning heat shot up his flank, and icy cold slid back down. Gideon forced himself to walk the length of the small, plain room and endure the discomfort. Even though he winced with every step, he couldn't afford to lie still. Beezle, that bastard, had escaped. So much for Derring and the Runners. If Gideon had his way, he'd hang them all.

The door opened, and Derring filled it, face long with disapproval.

"What the fuck do you want?" Gideon ground out. Three more steps until he reached the wall. Two…

"Some men know the benefit of rest after an injury," Derring said.

Gideon snarled. "Those men don't have a price on their head. Beezle will be back, no thanks to you."

Derring's face grew longer and stonier. Unless Gideon missed his guess, Derring was none too happy at the men's failure. One Runner had rushed to Susanna's side when she'd fallen. The other two had gone for Beezle, but he'd managed to escape, wounding both of the men with a knife he'd hidden.

"You're safe here for the moment."

"All the same," Gideon panted, reaching the wall and leaning his shoulder against it for support. "I'm eager to go and give your slaveys the room back."

Derring had put him in the servants' quarters. Gideon didn't know why that should rankle. Derring could have left him for dead. He could be crawling his way across the filthy ground floor of the Rouge Unicorn Cellar instead of this room, which smelled lightly of lemon and wax.

Gideon didn't even deserve the servants' quarters, but he didn't like to be reminded of his station.

Far, far below Susanna.

"How is your sister?" he asked, stalling before he made the trek across the room again.

"Ask her yourself." Derring moved aside.

Gideon's world tilted, and when he righted it, Susanna stood in front of her brother, her face pale and her eyes wide. Seeing her beautiful and whole after the ordeal washed the last vestiges of pain away. He couldn't feel anything but the pounding of his heart when he looked at her.

"You're hurt!" She crossed the room in three strides and put her hands on both his arms. She smelled, as always, of flowers and clean linen. Her unbound hair tumbled in waves down her back, one curl falling over her shoulder and brushing lightly against his hand. A wave of desire slammed into him, and he staggered back against the wall.

"You should lie down. You're not well enough to be up and about."

"I'm fine," he lied. He was desperate to touch her bare skin, kiss those pale pink lips. He flicked a glance at Derring, standing like a sentry. Gideon would never touch Susanna again.

"Another turn about the room, and I'll have my strength back. Then I'll be out of your house." *And your life.*

"No!" She tugged him toward the bed, and he followed without thinking. "You must rest. You cannot possibly think to leave. Brook, tell him."

Gideon raised a brow at Derring. "Yes, Brook, tell me."

"The doctor says you need another two or three days to recover. You are welcome until then."

Susanna pushed at his shoulders, lowering him to the bed. Gideon sat, wiping the sheen of sweat from his upper lip. "Forgive me if I'm eager to take my leave."

Susanna glanced at her brother and then back at him. When her gaze met his, Gideon thought, *Look at me. Only me.*

"A moment," she said to Gideon, holding a finger up.

She spoke to her brother in quiet tones. Derring shook his head, and Susanna's rapid whispers grew more heated. Gideon would have listened, but without Susanna's touch, the pain in his side returned and bloomed, blocking almost everything else out. He'd kill Beezle for shooting him, watch him dance at Beilby's Ball, the noose tight around his scrawny neck.

The door clicked shut, and Susanna leaned against it. With a start, Gideon realized they were alone. "Isn't your brother afraid I'll ravish you if he doesn't stand guard?"

"You're in no position to ravish me at the moment, more's the pity."

Gideon jerked his head back. What the hell did she mean by that?

She pressed her hands against the door and filled her lungs. Her breasts, beneath the thin wrapper she wore, rose and fell, and Gideon realized, quite suddenly, her feet were bare. Her pink toes peeked from beneath the white hem, so clean and pretty.

"I was afraid you were dead," she said.

"Not yet."

"Brook told me you gave him the necklace. You never fenced it. Never left Town."

Gideon didn't speak. Three, four steps at most separated them, but it felt like a thousand. He wanted to hold her, bury his head in her hair, pull her down on the bed beside him and infuse himself with the warmth that would make him feel alive again.

"He wants to make you a Runner."

"God knows he could use a good man."

"Exactly." A smile played on her lips. "So could I, Gideon." She stepped forward, hesitated, took another step. He barely resisted the urge to hold his hands out to her.

"I'm sure the *ton* is teeming with good men."

"I don't want them." She shook her head, knelt before him, and slid her hands into his. "I want you."

"No."

She placed a finger as light as a feather on his lips. "Yes. Marry me, Gideon."

He grasped her wrist, pulled her hand away from his mouth. "What the devil is this? Another of your larks?"

She didn't flinch at his harsh tone, merely brought her other hand up to wrap around the hand holding her wrist. "I love when you touch me," she said. "You can't know how much I've missed it."

He released her as though she had burned him. "You'd better go back to your room."

"Why?" She arched a brow. "If I stay, will you kiss me?"

"I might do a hell of a lot more than that."

Color bloomed in her cheeks. "Good. That's what I want—you, every day and every night. I know it's not right or proper, and I know you don't care about those rules. So I'm asking you to marry me. Please say yes."

"You don't know what you're talking about."

"Yes, I do. I've not been able to stop thinking about you since we parted. I love you, Gideon."

"No, you don't. I'm not the right man for you. I don't deserve you."

"You saved my life, more than once. You risked everything for me. I don't deserve you, but I want you anyway. You must feel something for me."

"That's not it, Susanna." He rose, flinching at the stabbing reminder of his wound. "The things I've done… I'm not worthy to marry you. Or anyone."

"What have you done?" She looked up at him from her knees. "Took the pistol ball Beezle meant for me? Saved me from Dagger Dan? Found me food, clothing, a place to rest after I'd all but forced you to accompany me?"

"You didn't force me. I wanted to go with you."

Hope flashed across her face. "Why?"

He closed his eyes. "Do you want to know how I got this scar?" He brushed his hand over it, feeling the smooth, raised skin under the pads of his fingers.

"You told me. You fought a boy from a rival gang."

"I was twelve, and the other boy a few years older. Satin caught him in our territory and brought him back to the flash ken. Told me to fight him."

"And he had a knife?"

Gideon nodded. He could see the dark flash ken in his mind, smell the stench of it, hear the *drip, drip* of water from one of the corners. "Satin had either let him keep it or given it to him. Made the fight that much more interesting."

"I don't need to hear this."

Gideon hauled her to her feet, held her wrists. "Yes, you do. This is who I am. I fought him, and when I stumbled, he held me down and cut me."

Her face contorted with pain, almost as though she felt the agony of the knife slicing her own skin.

"Everyone cheered him on. There's nothing quite like watching blood spilled. Watching a fight to the death. That's what it was. He'd kill me, or Satin would kill him."

A tear ran down her cheek, and her eyes filled with pity.

"I don't want that." He nodded at her face. "I don't want pity. I don't deserve it. You think I had pity for him? I pushed him off me, and the knife hit the floor." He could still hear the thud when it landed on the packed earth. "I reached it first, and when he came for me, I plowed it into his chest."

Gideon swallowed the bile that rose when he remembered the soft yield of flesh as the knife slid in, the warm gush of blood over his fingers, the tangy smell of it.

Another tear slid down her cheek.

"I drove the knife in and up, and when he went limp, I kicked him to the ground. That's the man I am, Susanna. You don't want me." He released her and stepped away, the pain of memories and fresh wounds almost felling him.

❧

Her heart broke for him, for the boy he'd been, for the innocence lost. She needed to wrap her arms around him, hold him, whisper words of love to him. That

would come later—she hoped. He'd allow it in time.
He'd forgive himself in time.

"You're wrong," she said.

His gaze jerked to hers, and she read surprise
and confusion.

"I do want you. I want all of you, Gideon. The
good and the bad. I don't care what you've done. All
of that's in the past. I know who you are now. I know
who you can be."

He stared at her as though she were half-mad.

"Don't say no. Don't say you won't have me."
She took a chance and threw herself into his arms.
He caught her, pulled her hard against him. Pleasure
exploded like a firework in her heart. He *did* want her.
He must.

"How can I resist you?" he murmured into her
hair. "You break down my defenses."

"You don't need them with me." She clutched him
tightly, the pure joy of being in his arms again making
everything else in the room, in the world, fade away.

"I'm not free to marry you. Beezle escaped, and
he'll come for me."

She pulled back and met his gaze, her own expression concerned.

"Let me catch him. Let me prove to you I'm
worthy by—"

She silenced him with a kiss. She'd intended it to be
a quick kiss, but when she might have moved back, his
immobile lips softened. Heat coiled through her when
he parted her lips, dipped his tongue inside.

Breathless, she clung to him when they separated.
"Don't ever say that," she managed through gasps of

air. "You have nothing to prove to me. I love you for who you are."

"I want to be better."

"I spent my whole life trying to be someone my mother wanted me to be and failing miserably. I would never place that burden on anyone else. I want you. *You*, Gideon, as you are. I ask you again, take me as I am, marr—"

"No."

Cold seeped into her, weakened her legs until she needed his arms to hold her. She tried. She didn't know what else to say. She would lose him.

"You're wrong about me."

Tears blurred her vision. She should walk away now, escape before he saw her cry, before she began to weep.

"I do care about rules, and I won't have you propose marriage to me."

He released her shoulders and knelt, still holding one hand. Susanna swiped a hand across her face, unsure whether her eyes deceived her.

"What are you doing?"

"I love you, Susanna. Despite our differences, despite your fondness for mongrels and glim-sticks, despite the fact that you've made an honest—well, mostly honest—man of me."

She laughed. She couldn't help it. The joy spilled out of her.

"Lady Susanna, will you marry me?"

"Yes." She fell on the floor, all but knocking him over with her embrace. "*Yes.*"

He kissed her, his lips soft and tender on hers, his hands circling her waist and moving up her back possessively. *Yes*. She wanted to belong to him, only him, now and forever.

A sound broke through the haze of passion, and she jolted when her mother appeared in the open doorway. Susanna sucked in a breath. "Mama."

"I see I am interrupting."

Gideon pulled Susanna to her feet. "Lady Dane, a pleasure to meet you again."

"Is it, now?" She raised a brow. "Might I ask exactly what you were doing to my daughter?"

Susanna tried to speak, to save Gideon, but he silenced her with a wave of his hand. "I kissed her in celebration. She has just agreed to be my wife."

Her mother's expression didn't change. Her thin lips remained pressed together, her eyes suspicious. "I do not think Susanna has the power to grant that request."

Susanna bit her lip. She'd thought her mother understood, thought things had changed between them. Now she would have to marry without the countess's blessing. She was not yet twenty-one, not of an age to marry without parental consent. How would they obtain the funds to elope to Scotland?

"You will have to speak to her father," Lady Dane said.

Susanna jerked with surprise.

"Her father?" Gideon asked. "Mr. Southey?"

"Yes. Tell him you already have my approval. Tell him you wish to marry with all possible haste."

Susanna ran to her mother, who opened her arms and hugged her tightly.

"This is not what I wanted for you, but I can admit now that I was wrong before, and I may be wrong now. And so I wish you every happiness, darling," her mother whispered. "I hope you find as much as I have."

"Thank you," Susanna said with another hard squeeze.

"No, thank you. Because of you, I found love again." Her mother kissed her cheek. "I couldn't be more pleased, more proud of you, Susanna. Be happy and marry with my blessing."

Twenty-one

HE HADN'T LIVED TO SEE THEIR WEDDING DAY. GIDEON Harrow had to die—rumor had it he'd been killed by a slug ball from Beezle's snapper—in order for Dudley Dorrington to be born. Dudley Dorrington was a distant cousin of the Derring family from somewhere in Lincolnshire.

Or perhaps Nottinghamshire.

Dudley had cropped hair, a clean-shaven face, and a wardrobe full of fine coats, trousers, breeches, and blasted—no, *bloody,* because he spoke like the swells—cravats.

Dudley was an inspector for private hire by the very wealthy and very discreet. He also worked closely with the Bow Street Runners, often using Sir Brook's office. So far he'd proven himself one hell of an inspector. Though he'd never been in London before, he had the uncanny knack for finding men and cargo in the rookeries. He might have looked familiar, but no one could quite place him.

Lady Susanna Derring had fallen in love with her distant third—or was it fourth?—cousin at first sight.

They'd married as soon as the banns were called. And now, today, Dudley Dorrington was the husband of Lady Susanna.

Of the options offered by Sir Brook, Gideon had chosen the name *Dudley* because every time they were in public and Susanna was forced to call him Dudley, it made him smile. Who the hell named a brat Dudley? Gideon almost felt sorry for those coves.

And he didn't mind at all that Susanna still called him Gideon in private. They would have ample time for her to use his real name now that they had wed.

Susanna said the wedding was lovely. Gideon didn't know what the hell it was. He hadn't even looked around the church. Easier to avoid the Earl of Dane's and Sir Brook's scowling mugs that way. Easier not to spot Corker and Dab loitering in the back of the sanctuary, or Des and Brenna sitting in the front. He didn't know how the hell they'd heard about the wedding, and he didn't want to know. He wanted only to survive this wedding breakfast and corner Susanna alone.

She'd looked stunning in her pale pink gown, the sunlight streaming through the windows behind her and lighting her hair until it seemed to shimmer with pale fire. Her large eyes had never left his face as her father, now Lady Dane's husband, had placed her hand in his. He'd looked down at the white-gloved hand resting in his own gloved one. He'd thought about how he'd never owned gloves before. He'd thought about how none of that mattered to anyone anymore. She was his, and she didn't care about gloves or titles or wealth.

Gideon supposed that was for the best. He would never be a wealthy man on an inspector's salary. At least not what she considered wealthy, but Susanna said she was content to live modestly. Until he had saved enough to rent a flat of their own, they resided at Derring House. Gideon planned to earn the blunt he needed quickly—anything to escape the dour-faced Crawford and the gong summoning all to dinner.

After today, he'd sleep in Susanna's room. Derring had him moved to a guest chamber after the betrothal had been announced, but Gideon found he felt more comfortable in the servants' quarters.

He suspected he'd be most comfortable in Susanna's bed—if the wedding breakfast ever ended.

"Not long now," Marlowe whispered, pausing at his side.

Gideon gave her an innocent look, and she laughed. "I know you too well, Gid—sorry, I mean, *Dudley*. I can read your thoughts. You can't wait to tumble her."

"Why, Countess, I don't know what you mean."

Her blue eyes danced with merriment. "You always were good at aping your betters. The way I see it, she loves you exactly as you are."

"Foolish mort."

She smacked his arm. "Not at all. Now, off with you. Keep an eye on Des before he makes off with the silver."

Gideon's gaze cut to his friend across the room. Des was indeed eyeing a silver serving spoon with interest.

"Did you ever think you'd see Des Stewart and the Earl of Dane in the same room with a half-dozen thief-takers, and Gap and Tiny?"

"Can't say I did. Can't say I think any of them will ever be invited back again either."

Des slipped the spoon into his coat, and Gap shoved Tiny back, sending him sliding into a footman whose tray of champagne toppled over.

"Susanna does try," Marlowe said with a sigh. She put a hand on his chest to indicate he stay where he was. "I'll take care of it. You go upstairs and find Susanna."

"Upstairs?"

She winked at him. "Oh, didn't you know? She's in her room waiting for you."

"And you waited this long to tell me?" he called after her. He all but sprinted from the room, not caring how eager that made him appear, not caring that the entire room probably knew exactly where he was going and what he would do. He cared only for Susanna.

Gideon knew which door was hers. He'd seen her maid come out of her room and scuttle down this hallway.

Gideon went straight to her door, knocked softly, and heard her call, "Who is it?"

"Me." He looked nervously down at his shoes. "Gideon. Your husband." He said the last loudly, in case one of the brothers was nearby. Brothers could be notoriously overprotective of their sisters. Best to remind them of his new status.

"Come in."

Gideon pushed the door open and halted. He'd cracked houses smaller than the bedchamber. White and pink surrounded him—pale pink walls, white curtains edged with lace, dainty furniture adorned with small vases filled with flowers.

And the bed.

Gideon closed the door and locked it.

A snowy-white counterpane covered the large bed behind filmy, thin drapes that would hide nothing. White, frilly pillows formed a small mountain at the head of the bed. Gideon had never owned one pillow, much less fifteen.

"I know it needs renovating," said a voice. Gideon pinpointed it behind a large rectangular screen decorated with flowers. "We can decide on colors and fabrics together," she said.

"Right." The last thing he would do was spend time staring at paint colors. They wouldn't live here long enough to necessitate renovation. Besides, he rather liked the pink and white. He felt clean surrounded by white, probably because he *was* clean. The damned valet Derring had assigned to him had all but drowned him in the bath.

"Take off your coat," she said, still behind the screen.

What was she doing back there?

"This is your room now too."

He shrugged, slipped off his coat, and dropped it on the floor. Yanking off his boots and stockings, Gideon stepped onto the thick white rug. His toes burrowed into the softness. Who needed a bed when the floor was so soft?

He wiggled his toes and clawed at the cravat the valet had given him to wear. When that was beside the coat on the floor, he shed his waistcoat and stretched. He felt almost normal again, except for his cushioned toes. He enjoyed peeking his toes in and out of the rug until he caught a movement and looked up.

All of the blood rushed from his head, and though he tried to speak, he barely managed a grunt.

Susanna leaned negligently against the screen, her hands at her sides, her long strawberry-blond hair down about her waist in shining waves. Her large eyes fixed on his face, and as he stared at her, the color rose prettily in her cheeks. At her neck sparkled diamonds and emeralds from a familiar necklace.

"What do you think?" she asked.

"I think I must be dreaming." Gideon was proud he managed that much. Susanna wore nothing but the necklace.

He'd seen every part of her unclothed, but never like this. Never with the white sunlight filtering through the curtains and dancing on all that pale porcelain skin.

"Brook said he hasn't located the necklace's owner yet." She ran a hand up the curve of her hip, past her small, round breasts, to the sparkling jewels at her throat. "I asked if I might borrow it."

"You put it to shame."

She smiled and started across the room, her long legs slim and shapely. "When you say such things, you make me feel bold." She stopped before him, the rosy tips of her nipples brushing against his shirt. His hands encircled her small waist, his skin instantly warmed by her flesh.

"I'll say more then. I like you bold."

She undid the buttons of his shirt and slid it up, trailing her fingers along his abdomen as she raised the material. "I like being bold." She dropped his shirt on the floor. "I am tired of waiting for permission, of waiting for my life to begin. I didn't wait for you to ask to marry me." She reached for the fall of his trousers. "And I won't wait for you to take me to bed." She loosened the trousers and shoved them over his hips. "I'll take you."

"If this is marriage, I believe I will like it," he murmured.

"I like you, Husband"—she smiled at him—"though I am still not used to seeing you with your hair shorn."

"I look respectable."

"Not quite."

Her bare breasts pressed against his chest, their softness distracting him from her hands working his trousers down until she cupped his bare buttocks. His cock was hard and more than ready. Even though she'd always been extremely responsive to his touch, he didn't want to rush her. He wanted this first time to last. He wanted to remember it as the beginning of his life with her, his life after the Covent Garden Cubs.

"You'll be the death of me," he murmured in her ear. He pushed his cock against her belly. "Feel that? I want you."

"Then let me take you to bed." She took his hand, and he stepped out of his trousers and followed her. She pulled him onto the bed until he knelt in the middle with her. With both of them naked, he forgot the social classes between them. Nothing but the two of them mattered.

He took her mouth, cupping the back of her head and sinking his hands into all of that soft hair. She opened for him, stroking his tongue with hers and pressing her body wantonly against his. Her hands roamed his flesh, her hands fisting in his hair, her nails scraping his back, her fingertips on his belly, then wrapping around his cock. She slid her hand up and down until he had to dig his blunt fingernails into his palms to keep from ravishing her.

Gideon lowered his mouth to her breasts, to the pale pink nipples standing so erect and so ready to be tasted and pleasured. He sucked lightly, his hands sliding down her stomach to her pelvis and her thighs. She gasped with pleasure when he used his tongue to lave the straining bud then blew cool air on the wet flesh. Her skin flushed dark pink, and he went to work on the other breast.

"I could do this all night," he said, circling her flesh with his tongue while she arched and her head lolled back. "I could pleasure you like this for hours."

"Touch me," she demanded, and though he was already touching her, he knew what she wanted. His fingers moved in slow, expanding circles toward the junction of her thighs. The hair, slightly darker than that on her head, brushed against his fingers, and he delved inside. He was not surprised to find her wet for him. He was surprised when he parted her lips and ran a finger over the sensitive bud between them. With a gasp, she shuddered and cried out.

He pressed against her, watching her hips move to the rhythm of the pleasure, and when she finally met his gaze, her dark eyes were bright with desire.

"Do you know how rare that is?" he asked. "That you find pleasure so easily?"

"How could I not?" She planted her hands on his shoulders and pushed him back. "When you touch me, I come alive."

The pillows cushioned his head and left him at the perfect angle to watch as she kissed his chest and his belly. She wasn't quite brave enough to kiss his cock, but he could see her thinking about it.

"Next time," he said, tilting her chin up and bringing her mouth to his. The curtain of her hair shrouded them both in a soft, dark cocoon. He guided her body until she straddled him, positioning her until the soft wetness of her core hovered just above his aching cock.

"What now?" she asked, levering herself up. Her breasts tilted upward, the peaks like cherries on a snowy hill. The new position also brought skin to skin, and her mouth opened into an *O*. Her eyes grew large and dark. "Oh, I see."

"You wanted to take me." He arched his hips. "Take me."

"Yes."

She slid over him, sheathing him in liquid warmth. She faltered at first, and he showed her how to move, how to find friction and ride it to climax.

She had stamina and enthusiasm. Finally he felt her tense, and in a single movement, he rolled her under him.

"What are you doing?" she panted, probably angrier to have her climax postponed than at the change of positions.

"I want to see your face," he said, linking his fingers with hers on the bed. He moved inside her, and she clenched her fingers tightly.

"Please don't stop."

"No." He slid out, then very slowly back in until he was buried deep and thick.

"Oh, yes." Her hips arched as she sought more friction. "Hard, Gideon. Fast."

"So demanding."

He plunged in hard and fast, and he watched her control waver. His was breaking too.

"Susanna."

Her hazy gaze met his, and her lips curved into a smile.

"I love you," he said, grasping her hands tightly.

"And I love you."

Hands and bodies linked by love, they tumbled into forever.

Acknowledgments

Thank you to my fabulous agents, Joanna MacKenzie and Danielle Egan-Miller, for their constant, unwavering support. I am thankful every day you chose to work with me.

Thanks to my lovely friend and assistant, Gayle Cochrane, for the myriad things you do for me and for just being there. Thanks also to the Shananigans: Kristy, Connie, Lisa, Nicole, Barbara, Patti, Ruth, Misty, Flora, Susan, Sue, and Sarah!

Thanks to the Brainstorm Troopers, especially Margo Maguire, who sparked the idea for this series.

Thank you to my editor, Deb Werksman; my publicists, Amelia Narigon and Morgan Doremus; and all the wonderful professionals I'm privileged to work with at Sourcebooks.

Thank you to my friends, Amy and Emily, to whom this book is dedicated. You motivate me to get up in the morning and work hard.

Most importantly, thank you to my husband and my daughter for all your patience and support. Thanks to Princess Galen, in particular, who happily (most of the time) shares her Flynn Rider doll and her *Tangled* DVD with me.

About the Author

Shana Galen is the bestselling author of passionate Regency romps, including the *RT* Reviewers' Choice *The Making of a Gentleman*. *RT Book Reviews* calls her books "lighthearted yet poignant, humorous yet touching." She taught English at the middle- and high-school level off and on for eleven years. Most of those years were spent working in Houston's inner city. Now she writes full time. She's happily married and has a daughter who is most definitely a romance heroine in the making. Shana loves to hear from readers, so send her an email or see what she's up to daily on Facebook and Twitter. Stop by her website at shanagalen.com.